SOPHIA
PRINCESS AMONG
BEASTS

For a preview of upcoming books and information about the author, visit JamesPatterson.com, or find him on Facebook, Twitter, or Instagram.

SOPHIA
PRINCESS AMONG
BEASTS

JAMES
PATTERSON
with EMILY RAYMOND

LITTLE, BROWN AND COMPANY
New York Boston London

JIMMY Patterson Books / Little, Brown and Company
Hachette Book Group
1290 Avenue of the Americas, New York, NY 10104
JimmyPatterson.org

Paperback Edition: April 2021
First Hardcover Edition: July 2019

JIMMY Patterson Books is an imprint of Little, Brown and Company, a division of Hachette Book Group, Inc. The Little, Brown name and logo are trademarks of Hachette Book Group, Inc. The JIMMY Patterson Books® name and logo are trademarks of JBP Business, LLC.

The publisher is not responsible for websites (or their content) that are not owned by the publisher.

The Hachette Speakers Bureau provides a wide range of authors for speaking events. To find out more, go to hachettespeakersbureau.com or call (866) 376-6591.

ISBN 978-0-316-41747-1 (hc) / 978-0-316-41996-3 (large print) / 978-0-316-54022-3 (tbp)

Library of Congress Cataloging-in-Publication Data
Names: Patterson, James, 1947– author. | Raymond, Emily, 1972– author.
Title: Sophia, princess among beasts / James Patterson and Emily Raymond.
Description: First edition. | New York: Little, Brown and Company, 2019. |
Summary: In a kingdom besieged by hunger, sickness, and war, Princess Sophia must do whatever it takes to protect the people she loves, even if it means she has to confront the beasts she thought only lived in her books.
Identifiers: LCCN 2019015798 | ISBN 978-0-316-41747-1 (alk. paper)
Subjects: | CYAC: Princesses—Fiction. | Monsters—Fiction. | Death—Fiction. | Adventure and adventurers—Fiction. | Fantasy.
Classification: LCC PZ7.P27653 So 2019 | DDC [Fic]—dc23
LC record available at https://lccn.loc.gov/2019015798

Printing 1, 2021

LSC-C

Printed in the United States of America

PROLOGUE

Sometimes the end is only the beginning. And sometimes what's real is not the same as what is *true*. And the impossible? My friends, there is no such thing.

But perhaps you wish for proof.

Seventeen years ago, almost to the day, I died delivering my child, a beautiful baby girl whom her father and I were going to name Sophia. She was a tiny, fierce, and squalling thing, with coal-black hair and eyes the color of the ocean. When they placed her on my chest, her hands, which had been balled into tiny fists, unfurled like flowers, and my heart broke open with love. *Sophia*.

When she pushed her face against my chest, her cries quieted. I wanted to hold her like that forever, safe in the circle of my arms. But I could feel my strength fading. The room had grown dim, and the rush-covered floor, with its sweet-scented strewn herbs of sage and tansy, was dark with blood. It looked as if a great battle had taken place.

My husband, banished to the hall by the midwives, now burst through the door and flung himself to his knees at my bedside. He lay his great strong hand on my cheek. "My love," he whispered. "Stay. Don't leave us."

If only I could. But I felt death's hands gripping my heart.

Oh, how I would have loved that darling little girl, and how I miss her still. You can imagine that, can't you?

I want you to hear Sophia's voice — her story. Its events have never happened before, and yet it is a tale as old as time, and as ancient as love.

It's a story about the wonder of life, the unexpected power of our dreams and our nightmares, and the secret dominions of ghosts.

Whatever your beliefs, this is a story about our lives and our afterlives. It takes place on both sides of the curtain that some call death, but which I have come to know as life after life.

Or, simply: the Beyond.

My name is Olivia. I died but an hour after my daughter was born. What I suffered is best not to say, and it was a long time ago. Pain fades quickly in memory, but love remains forever, like a flower preserved in amber.

Take my hand. Listen to Sophia's story. It's frightening sometimes, but it's also beautiful and full of hope.

Sometimes the end is only the beginning.

Listen.

PART ONE

CHAPTER 1

Jeanette, my lady in waiting, woke me by tickling my cheek
with the feather end of my quill pen.

"Up late writing again, Princess?" she asked. "And what
was it this time? A song? A poem? Another appeal to the King
about how you should be taught to joust?"

I could tell this last idea amused her; it was another of my
unladylike notions. But I didn't answer. Instead I burrowed
deeper into my feather bolster, pulling the ermine coverlet over
my head entirely. I'd give my father's crown for a few more minutes of sleep. I'd been dreaming something wonderful, full of
longing, and already I couldn't recall any of it.

"Sophia," Jeanette said, her voice still gentle but firmer now.
"It's time to dress. Your father is in the Great Hall, and he expects
you to join him. You know he does not like to be kept waiting."

And so I emerged reluctantly from my bed and dug my bare
toes into the sheepskin rug. It was a damp, chill October morning,

and I shivered as a chambermaid poked the fire into roaring life. My attendants fluttered around the room, silent as moths. One brought fresh linens, and two others were dispatched to retrieve my gown and mantle. Jeanette herself would unlock the lacquer box to inspect the mound of glittering jewels, choosing which ones should encircle my neck or dangle from my ears. Today, as every day, I was to be scrubbed and dressed and pampered and styled.

"You'd think I lacked the arms to do this myself," I muttered as Adelie, the youngest attendant, moved to take off my nightdress.

She suppressed a giggle. These indulgences were my royal right and my royal duty, and we both knew it. My father, the king, insisted on every possible luxury for me—except, of course, that of sleeping in.

I made my way toward the great wooden tub of steaming water, scented with verbena, sweet woodruff, and rosemary. The last rose petals of the season dotted the water's surface, and sinking into the bath was like sliding back into summer's heat.

I almost could have drifted back to sleep (as Jeanette suspected, I *had* stayed up half the night). But I had barely closed my eyes when the door to my chamber flung open, and a scullery maid stood gasping on the threshold, her face as white as milk.

"What are you doing here, Margery?" Jeanette demanded. "This is not your place."

"He's coming," the girl whispered. "What they said—it's true. His army—"

But Jeanette didn't let her finish. She unceremoniously shoved the girl back into the hall and quickly shut the door. Then she turned back to the room and stared at all of us, and finally me, her expression now dark with worry. My attendants stood frozen, some with their hands to their mouths, and all with terror in their eyes. My heart began to pound in my chest.

Ares was advancing upon our realm.

For weeks there had been rumors: from the bitter north would come an army of ruthless knights, laying waste to all that they saw. No village was safe, and no force could turn them back. Ares's men were giants, the people said, and Ares himself could not be slain.

Though I did not believe the fevered whispers of frightened villagers, the threat of any attack unsettled me.

"Back to work," Jeanette said sharply. "It's only kitchen gossip."

Was it obvious to everyone that she was lying? It was to me.

Still, they obeyed her. Adelie, visibly trembling, began to pour a thin stream of sweet almond oil into the bath. When she splashed some onto the floor, I reached out and touched her rough hand. "You have nothing to fear from Ares's army," I said.

All movement in the room stopped again. Adelie's older sister, Elodie, stared at me with huge, anxious eyes. Faye, the chambermaid who'd been stoking the fire, began to wail. Her cry was as sharp as a wounded animal's. "Oh, Princess," she sobbed, "they say Ares's men are monsters. I don't want to die!"

Her panic was contagious. Elodie and Adelie, too, began to weep. But ancient Ana, who had been making my bed, hauled the sobbing Faye upright, slapped a hand over her mouth, and hurried her out of the room. Then she poked her head back through the doorway and threatened everyone else with the switch if they didn't calm themselves immediately.

I looked then at wise, sturdy Jeanette. I had known her my

whole life, and she was the closest thing I had to a mother. I wanted desperately for her to reassure us. But that wasn't her task. It was mine.

I drew myself up from the bath. Adelie, remembering her place, hurried to wrap my shoulders in a soft cloth. "There's no such thing as monsters," I said. "Our enemy may be preparing his attack, but our armies will meet in the field. You are safe inside the castle, which is an unassailable weapon in itself."

"Go on," Jeanette urged. "Tell them."

I made sure my voice didn't betray my own fear. "The moat that surrounds Bandon Castle is our first defense," I explained. "Men cannot swim with swords and shields, and any of Ares's soldiers who attempt to cross the bridge will be shot by our marksmen."

"Suppose some arrows miss?" Adelie whispered.

"Then the enemy comes to the gatehouse's iron-plated door. Should they get through this—which they won't—they find themselves in a narrow, winding passageway, where they will be pierced by arrows shot through slits in the walls." I gave each of my attendants what I hoped was a comforting look. "And don't forget the murder holes," I added, "which allow our guards to pour torrents of boiling water down from the ceiling!"

"Excuse me, Your Highness," Jeanette said, "perhaps before you go on..." She held out a chemise of white linen, so fine-spun it was almost transparent.

I looked down at my body: my breasts goose-fleshed, my legs slender and dripping wet. I had been giving a speech standing half naked in a tub!

I flushed. Propriety had never come naturally to me. "Forgive me," I said, and were it not for Ares, I would have laughed outright. As it was, I stepped from the bath, holding up my arms so Jeanette could slip the chemise over my head.

"Now that you're properly covered," she said quietly, "you can continue to soothe their fears."

"Suppose they survive the gatehouse's murder holes," I went on, as two attendants brought forth a high-waisted gown with trailing sleeves, cut from blue silk shot through with silver thread, and edged with lace as pale and delicate as spiderwebs. "They come to the outer castle wall, where more marksmen wait on the battlements above."

The rustling silk pulled tighter against my ribs as Jeanette set to work on the buttons. It felt wrong to dress so exquisitely on a day such as this, but I knew my father's rules. It didn't matter what forces might be amassing against us; my duty was to look as pleasing as a painting.

Adelie brought me burgundy slippers embroidered with violets, and her sister waited with a velvet surcoat in a rich midnight blue—the shade my father liked for me to wear. Then Jeanette led me to little stool before a tall mirror. I sat down carefully, readying myself for what came next: five hundred strokes of a boar's bristle brush through my long, dark hair. After that, Jeanette would arrange the shining waves into artful clusters, coils, and ringlets. I will admit, I did always like this part.

Elodie seemed to have gained some of her color back, thanks to my reassurances.

Adelie, on the other hand, said, "But what if—"

Jeanette glanced up from her brushing to silence her with a look.

"There's another thick wall beyond that," I reminded them. I gestured to the ancient, leather-bound tome I kept on my bedside table, *Myths: Demons and Monsters.* "You are no more in danger from Ares than you are from the imaginary monsters in this book. You have my word."

Elodie, smiling shyly now, came forward with an ornately etched tray of glittering bottles, each filled with the distilled essence of a flower. I pointed to the eau de rose in its ruby glass vial. I shivered as she touched the dropper to my neck, and the scent of roses—my mother's favorite flower—filled the room.

As Jeanette finished plaiting my hair and fastened a necklace of pearls and sapphires around my throat, I thought of what lay inside that second wall, should it be breached: the broad castle yard, the gardens, the Great Hall.

Us.

But I did not mention this to the women and girls in my bedchamber.

I stood regal in my gown, armored by the splendor of silk and jewel. "Ares's men are soldiers like ours," I said. "They do not have the strength to breach Bandon's walls, and they will not mount a siege with winter fast approaching. They will soon seek easier conquest elsewhere. We should not look upon the coming days as different from any other."

Only Jeanette still looked uncomforted. She bowed her head. "May what you say be true, Princess," she said quietly.

CHAPTER 2

Unescorted, I made my way to the Great Hall, through castle passageways that were empty and strangely quiet. Unless I counted the ancestral figures woven into the richly colored tapestries decorating the walls—my great-grandfather, King Martinus, leading his knights into battle, and his wife, Queen Rosalia, kneeling in a forest, flanked by tame foxes—I passed no one at all.

Usually the long hallways rang with the footsteps of my father's knights or bustled with the busy labors of pages and servants. But not today. I couldn't explain the absence of washerwomen and valets, but the knights, I now knew, had gathered in the armory to polish their swords and sharpen their daggers.

"We will be safe," I said out loud to myself, and the hall's stony emptiness amplified the sound and sent it echoing back to me. *Safe, safe, safe.*

Somehow this served to reassure me—it was as if the castle

itself had a voice—and I began to sing part of the song I'd stayed up so late writing.

> *A lovely girl, so young, so bright*
> *That death sought her for his own*
> *He made her his queen on a winter's night*
> *In a dress of ice and a crown of bone . . .*

In the Great Hall, my father, a huge, gray-bearded man with powerfully muscled shoulders, was hunched in his gilded chair like a boulder. I approached, taking small, graceful steps so that he wouldn't reprimand me, as he sometimes did, for "indelicate behavior." He raised his big, grizzled head and smiled gently at me. But his calmness was deceptive—he could strike quicker than a snake.

If Bandon Castle was our first weapon, my father, King Leonidus, was our second. Our kingdom had tripled in size since he'd ascended the throne after the early death of his own father. His skill with a sword was unmatched, and he could kill with a single blow from his fist. He'd spent more than half his life on the battlefield.

Until last year, that is.

When I turned sixteen, my father—full of wine, and flush with victory in battle—told me to name my birthday gift. *Ask,* he'd said, *and it shall be yours.*

I knew that I could have any treasure from the castle's vaults. If I wanted a carriage of mother-of-pearl and six fire-eyed horses to pull it, I would have it. Had I said that I wished for a dress of ice, my father would have found a way to make one. Gold or silk or fur or diamond—anything I sought would be mine.

But I asked this instead: No more war raids. No more conquests.

How many times had he marched upon some other king's lands, seeking to take what he did not truly need? How many men died for our claim to a forest, for the right to call a mountain ours? Shouldn't we take better care of what we already had?

Our kingdom was large enough, I told him. It was time to stop fighting. Time to protect instead of attack.

Let us not cause any more suffering: that was my argument. What I didn't admit to him, though, was my fear. How when he was gone, the castle felt haunted, and I couldn't sleep from worry. First, of course, was the worry that I would lose my father, having already lost my mother. And if I were left alone, what then? I'd be expected to rule a kingdom by myself—I, who had never even been permitted to dress myself.

Please, I'd said. *Enough.*

My father's face grew ashen as he listened. His hand tightened on the hilt of his sword. But he was a man of his word, and he had promised me anything I wanted. And so Great Leonidus the Warrior King set aside his weapons and shield to honor his only daughter's wish.

Now I bent and kissed my father on the cheek. Sunlight spilled in dusty rays through the high windows, but still the room was dim. As big as it was, it felt cozy to me.

Safe, safe, safe.

"Ah, you are brighter than the sun this morning, my little songbird," he said, as a manservant in blue livery came bearing a platter of bread and meat and a pitcher of small ale for my father, and a bowl of fruit for me. "Tell me, how does this day find you?"

How could I answer his question truthfully? My father was unable to bear the thought of anything troubling me, so I dared not admit my fear of the coming battle.

"I'm well enough," I said, sitting down next to him.

"You look a bit tired," he said.

I lowered my eyes and said nothing. I picked up a slice of apple and then put it back down again.

"You were writing songs all night long again, weren't you?" he asked. I heard a low chuckle. "If only you'd been practicing the harp instead of singing—I know your teacher begs you to."

"And I endlessly disappoint her," I said, offering him a smile. I had neither talent nor affection for the instrument, and we both knew it.

At my father's elbow, the servant poured small ale into his goblet. When he finished, he bowed solemnly and then stood up, his gaze meeting my father's. "To the defeat of Ares's army," he said, as if he were a lord giving a toast.

I turned to him in surprise—he must have been new and untrained to dare to speak in front of the king unprompted.

My father's jaw clenched as he rose from his chair. I put my hand on his to calm him, because I knew his temper. But he roughly shook me off. His lips curled in a snarl, and then he struck the man across the face with the back of his hand.

The blow rang through the hall.

"Father!" I gasped, as the servant crumpled to the ground with a cry of agony.

The guards, too, seemed stunned. Though the king was known for his fury, never had he struck a servant with his own hand. No one moved except the man on the floor, who clutched his cheek and moaned.

Then my father snapped his fingers, and the guards stationed at the door rushed forward and pulled the servant roughly from the floor. The man looked at me dazedly, pleadingly, as they dragged him away by the hair. A dark rivulet of blood trickled down his cheek.

"You know where to take him," my father said to his men, and then he turned back to his breakfast.

"You mustn't let them hurt him more," I pleaded. "It was a misunderstanding—"

He grunted. "You have only me in this world, Sophia, and it is my duty to protect you. I do not care that he forgot his place and believed he had the right to speak. But I will not let you be disturbed by any talk of strife," he said.

"So am I to pretend that Ares will simply pass us by?" I asked quietly.

My father's dark eyes flashed with warning. "Do not speak of such things. Listen to me, Sophia. That man shall be taken to the dungeon, where he will be whipped until he screams. And he deserves every burning lash."

I stiffened at his words. This was a side of my father I hated to see. But had I truly expected him to change after only a year of peace? If so, I'd been wrong. I loved him—of course I did, he was all I had in the world—but I couldn't call him kind. Couldn't argue that he was merciful. And I knew that if I said anything else right now, his wrath might turn against me.

He stabbed his knife into the charred meat on his plate. "I know what is best, daughter," he said.

I nodded. I knew it was best to keep quiet. Though I was his flesh and blood, I, too, was the King's subject. And though Ares's approach troubled us all, we would not speak of such things.

CHAPTER 3

My father sucked the marrow from the center of a pheasant bone and then threw it to Dogo, the snarling hound that kept him faithful company. I could see by his appetite — voracious, as usual — that he had already put our moment of discord out of his mind.

I, however, could not stop thinking about the servant's beseeching eyes. I knew too well what would happen next. He'd be stripped shirtless, his wrists tied to a whipping post. Two men would take turns flogging him until the skin on his back hung down in bloody shreds. And when they'd tired of whipping him, they'd salt his wounds and throw his unconscious body into a prison cell, where he'd wake — if he woke at all — to darkness and agony. All this, the price of a single, well-meaning sentence.

Order must be kept, my father would say, *at any cost.*

Was there anything I could have said that would have spared the man?

I pushed away my golden bowl. I had lost what little appetite I'd had. I decided I would ask Jeanette to tend to the servant, if he was indeed alive, to see that he was given a sip of ale and a crust of bread. Without risking my father's wrath again, there was nothing else I could do.

A princess has no true power, and her crown is but a decoration, if she even bothers to wear one.

A new manservant came into the room to refill our glasses, and he did it so silently he might have been a ghost. My father took a big draught of his ale and wiped his greasy mouth on his sleeve — a sleeve that I myself had embroidered with the blue gentian flowers from our family crest. Well, to be fair, it was not my best work.

"And what will my princess do today?" he asked.

"I'm going to the village," I said. "As I always do on Fridays."

His brow furrowed. I knew he didn't want me to make the journey, though it was my favorite part of the week. He objected to my walking among our subjects as if I were not their superior, just as he objected to my sparring with his loyal knight Odo as if I were not a girl. But he himself had given me my silver sword, and he had never forbidden me to go down to the village. He knew that if he kept me in the castle, occupied only with needlework and plucking at harp strings, I would be a far less pleasant meal companion.

But had he understood how lonely I was, he might have encouraged me to visit the village more often.

"Today of all days, you must be quick," he said.

I couldn't help what I said next. "But isn't Ares's army still days out?"

My father's face immediately darkened. "Have I not made myself clear? I will not have *you* talk of strife, either," he warned.

"I'm sorry," I said quickly. "But don't worry, Father, I'm not afraid of Ares. You'll protect me."

"That I will," he said, nodding his great shaggy head. "I always have."

"And in my own way, I protect the villagers."

My father looked somewhat skeptical. "You're but a child," he said—though not unkindly.

"I am not a child, I'm seventeen. And the villagers welcome me. They rely on me. They need the food I bring."

"Last year was a hard winter," he acknowledged.

"Then came the long spring and summer rains," I reminded him, "and many of the crops fell to rot before they were ever ripe."

I hoped that he'd somehow hear the question I didn't dare to ask: where were the villagers to turn if not to us? We, who had lush gardens, fat livestock, full cellars, and a forest full of pheasant, deer, and elk. If I had my way, we'd share everything we owned. But that wasn't how my father saw it. As far as he was concerned, our family was better than everyone else. Our birthright was luxury, whereas theirs was labor. Our blood was royal; theirs might as well have been mud.

He'd raised me to believe that, anyway, but it was a lesson I hoped I'd failed to absorb.

He drained the last of his small ale and set the goblet on the table with a bang. "We have a duty to our subjects in the village, but always remember one thing, Sophia. They are, for want of a better word, beasts. Never, ever forget that."

I ducked my head humbly. I didn't dare contradict him.

My father put his rough hand on my cheek. "You are so dear to me. Be careful today."

I forced a smile onto my face. "You always act as if I'll never come back." I placed my fingers around his wrist and squeezed it. "And yet I always do."

"There is no honor among beasts, my daughter," he said. "Remember that."

"I am always safe," I assured him.

"Always safe," he repeated.

And it was with those words, I believe, that we tempted Fate, who is more powerful than any king.

CHAPTER 4

After breakfast I went to visit my mother, as I did every morning.

"Good morning, Mama," I whispered, as I sat down on the tufted stool I kept beneath the portrait of her that hung in the hall. Quickly I looked around to see if anyone had noticed that I was talking to a painting. It was a habit I'd been scolded for more than once. A princess should not talk to the dead, they said. It was unbecoming. Strange. *Morbid*.

I would point out that I had no siblings, no friends. Who else was I supposed to talk to? Also, no one dared call my father strange or morbid, though he'd commissioned dozens of portraits of her. He kept at least twenty of them in a single hall near his privy chamber, and I'd certainly heard him bid her likeness goodnight.

To sit before my mother's picture every day soothed my loneliness a little somehow, and perhaps it was the same for my father when he paced that long corridor, the one the servants secretly called the Hall of the Flat Queens.

Here, in her cloth-of-gold gown, with its exquisitely embroidered partlet and heavy, jeweled neckline, my mother looked impossibly beautiful. Impossibly regal. Her skin was opal, luminescent. She had smooth cheeks and wide green eyes under arching, dramatic brows. Her thick braids coiled around her head like a crown. In this painting—my favorite of them all—she wore jewels in her plaits: diamonds that winked like stars in the dark night of her hair.

"I'm taking food to the village today," I whispered. "I don't know what they'll do when Ares comes. We'll have to let them seek refuge in the castle, won't we? It's the only way they'll be safe. Father will want to refuse, but I'll—" I heard footsteps ringing on the stone floor, so I shut my mouth and bent my head as if in prayer. No one would dare reprimand a princess for praying for the soul of her poor dead mother.

But instead of praying, my lips moved with the words of a song I'd written for her a long time ago.

> Once you ruled over forest and fen, reigned over
> > river and sea.
> Now you sit on eternity's throne, watching over me.
> My place is here within the world; I cannot join you
> > yet.
> Though I was too young to remember you, I also
> > never forget.

Jeanette came up behind me and placed her hands on my shoulders. "She married your father when she was just sixteen," she said wistfully. "Oh, if you could have seen her on her wedding day! Her gown was ivory silk, embroidered in gold, and when she came into the chapel she was more beautiful than the sun."

"I can't imagine being married so young," I admitted.

Jeanette turned my face toward her own. "She was engaged to your father by her tenth birthday, you know. And it's high time you were betrothed, Princess. Come the spring, the King will have to reckon with the matter. A kingdom can grow in other ways besides war and conquest, and he'd do well to remember that. A wise marriage means a strong alliance." She smiled gently. "Of course, he doesn't want to part with you. You are all he has! When you leave us, Sophia, we'll both be lost."

"I'm not going anywhere," I said firmly.

"I'm sure your mother told her lady in waiting the exact same thing before she journeyed to marry your father."

I touched the ruby ring that circled my finger. It was meant for her—a birthday gift from my father—but she died before she got to wear it.

"I miss her," I whispered.

"I know you do."

"But how can I miss what I've never even known? Dogo doesn't miss flying. A bird doesn't miss swimming."

"And I myself don't miss being king," Jeanette agreed. "But a girl longs for her mother, no matter what, and that is the sorrow you must carry. It is heavy, I know, and I can only hope it makes you stronger."

I reached out to touch the painting's gilded frame, and my fingers came away dusty. My mother had died when she was nineteen—just two years older than I was now. "Sometimes I feel like she's watching me. Like she's not truly gone," I said.

Then I shook my head. "But I know that's impossible. It's only what I *wish* were true."

Jeanette smiled gently. "There have been times when I sensed her, too. Perhaps she really does visit us. Or maybe we long for it so much that we trick ourselves. Maybe I'm just a foolish old woman, and you are a lonely young girl."

"You're not foolish *or* old," I said. But I did not deny my own loneliness. She saw it trail me like a shadow every day.

"I wish you could have known her." Jeanette sighed. "She was lovely and full of grace, and she sang and played the harp like an angel." She patted my hand. "And on one of your good days, Your Highness, you're almost exactly like her. Beautiful and poised—although your harp skills, Princess, are nearly nonexistent."

It should have pleased me to hear Jeanette's praise, but instead it made me feel a sudden shiver of dread. I didn't want to be just like my mother. I didn't yearn to be sent to marry a stranger in a far-off realm, only to hope I'd grow to love him.

Though I knew it was a futile wish, I wanted to find love for myself.

And most importantly, I didn't want to die before I'd really had the chance to live.

CHAPTER 5

In the stable yard, twelve mounted guards waited to accompany me to the village. This seemed excessive, even for my overprotective father. Each one sat on a pawing charger, and each carried a sword, a parrying dagger, and a billhook. Their shields bore our family crest: a raven with a cluster of blue gentians in its talons.

Red-bearded Odo, who led the men, bowed as I approached.

"I hardly think I need all of you this morning," I said lightly.

"It's a fine day for a ride, Princess," he answered. "My men and their mounts were eager for exercise."

"Liar," I muttered as I patted his horse's sleek dark neck.

Odo's mouth curved up in the faintest shadow of a smile. "Did you say something, Your Highness?"

I looked at him innocently. "Oh, no, Sir Odo."

Though Odo often indulged my whims—giving me my sparring lessons, accompanying me on gallops through Elk

Forest—his first loyalty was to my father. This meant that he couldn't "cause me strife" by admitting that an army of blood-thirsty enemies approached.

And I, in turn, could not point out that I could see the castle preparing for war, because I needed his company too much to vex him. Though age and rank separated us—and though I could never say it—I loved Odo like an uncle. It was because of him that I could swing a sword and fling my roundel dagger into the heart of a target at a hundred paces. He could perform this feat blindfolded, and he'd promised to teach me how someday.

"Are we ready to go, then?" he asked as his charger shook his black mane.

"One more moment," I said. Before I climbed inside the gilt-and-ebony carriage, I peered into our supply cart, which Pieter the groom had hitched to two sad-eyed mules.

I saw vegetables, barley, bread, and smoked venison: everything I'd asked for. But it was so much less than I'd been expecting!

"Why is the cart only half full?" I asked.

Odo's fingers tightened on the reins. "We cannot take more today," he said.

"Why not?"

He looked away from me, too faithful to my father to tell me the truth.

"Your silence is answer enough," I said. "I know the reason. If Ares's men lay siege, we'll need all the food we can get. Bandon Castle will become our cage."

He bowed almost imperceptibly: I was right.

"Except there won't be a siege," I said firmly, "because look at all of you. My father's men are so fierce that just the twelve of you could defeat Ares's whole army."

"I believe we are well prepared for battle, Your Highness," Odo allowed. "*Should* a battle be imminent, which is not to suggest that it is."

I tried not to roll my eyes at him. How ridiculous that my father would not let anyone speak to me of Ares's advance when its signs were everywhere. In the courtyard, great fires had been stoked to boil cauldrons of water for the murder holes. Laborers assembled wooden hoardings high up on the ramparts to protect our marksmen from enemy arrows.

Of course, Ares's army was never supposed to get close to Bandon Castle in the first place. Our knights would cut them down like stalks of wheat on the great field of war, just as they had done with every other foe.

A footman opened the door to my carriage, and, giving the paltry offerings one last dissatisfied glance, I lifted my skirts and climbed in.

I loved this weekly trip into the village. The hours I spent on my errands of mercy were the only hours I was sovereign to myself. Alone in the carriage, with no one to scold me, I was free to sing loudly (and possibly out of tune). Free to pull my hair from its coils, let it fall around my shoulders and blow against my face as the wind rushed through the carriage window. Free to delight in everything around me—at the vast grasslands, the steely curve of the River Lathe, and the snow-tipped mountains in the distance.

In these moments, I didn't have to hold my head as if a queen's crown were upon it already. I could simply be a girl like any other. A girl with no responsibility to rule a kingdom alone—at least, not yet.

The golden, late-autumn sun had come out, and with it my

mood had brightened. It was impossible to imagine anything bad ever happening to us.

"Don't lean your head out the window like a hound," Odo said, trotting next to me.

I laughed and kept doing it just to spite him.

We were but a mile from the village. Already we'd come to their fields, barren now at the end of harvest season. Nothing was left of the oats and barley but broken stubble. The beans had all been picked, and the land lay naked.

The breeze carried the smell of something burning.

I squinted. In the distance, I could see black roils of smoke above the cottages. "Odo, what's happening?" I asked. "What is that burning?"

But he didn't answer, and this time I knew that it wasn't a matter of loyalty to my father: he didn't know, either. Odo's brow darkened, and he spurred his horse ahead to the village.

CHAPTER 6

When my carriage rolled to a stop at the village gate, the horses wouldn't settle. They shook and stamped their feet in their rattling harnesses. I could hear the driver speaking soothingly to them, but they whinnied and tossed their heads. It was as if they, too, knew that something was terribly wrong here.

Acrid smoke hung heavy in the air, and a putrid smell, like that of a bloated carcass left to rot in the sun, assailed my nose. I pressed the sable edge of my cloak to my face and tried not to gag.

What in the world was going on?

From the little thatched huts, the children came running, their legs dirty and their feet bare.

"Princess," they called, and then they dropped to their knees beside the carriage.

I'd never wanted the villagers to fling themselves into the mud to show obeisance, but it was a habit I could not change;

they'd been doing it for generations. I quickly motioned for the children to stand again, and they did, not bothering to brush the dirt from their clothing.

"Fina, what's wrong?" I asked a little girl with dark copper hair and a smattering of freckles across the bridge of her nose. She and her younger sister, redheaded Rosa, were always the first to reach my carriage, the first to touch a grubby finger to its ornate, gilded curves, their eyes wide with awe. In the summertime, they brought me wildflowers from the meadow and pale green eggs from their beloved chickens.

"It's the sickness," Fina whispered, curtsying. She wiped a grimy cheek with the tattered corner of her dress.

"You're crying," I exclaimed.

She shook her head. "Mama said I'm not to cry in front of the princess."

"Don't worry about that, child. But what do you mean, the sickness?"

As if in answer to my question, a young boy began to sing.

Blood and blister, fever and sore—
Death is knocking at your door.
Bodies fill all graves with gore,
But still the dirt cries out for more.

Then Abra, who was second in command to Odo, urged his mount close to my carriage window. "You must return to the castle, Princess." His sword glinted in the sunlight, and his horse's nostrils blew grassy, humid air into my face.

I gestured to the children with their thin arms, their hollow eyes of hunger. It was my responsibility to give them what I could, no matter the smoke and the stench. No matter the sickness, whatever it was.

"After I distribute the food," I said.

"You must go now," he said.

Immediately I stiffened. "Who are you to tell me—"

"They are just beasts!" Abra interrupted. "Not worth dying for."

I leaned out the window. "Beasts, you say? Yes, perhaps they are lower born than you. Does it mean we should ignore their suffering? Does it mean they do not need food?" His gaze flickered. "Do you not give your horse oats when it is hungry? Or are these people's lives worth less than an animal's?"

Silent, Abra turned away from me, and the boy's voice rang out again.

> *Young man, your bride is dying,*
> *Though she be young and fair—*
> *Now Death will be her husband,*
> *No jewels but worms she'll wear.*

What was that awful song?

I knew that I couldn't leave, but nor did I want to linger. The smell turned my stomach, and the smoke seared my throat raw. I turned to my protector and friend. "Odo," I called, "give out what we brought. And please hurry."

The knight dismounted and began to toss out bags of food, one for each household. No one was too proud to hold out a hand, and no one complained that it was less than they might have wished for. Mutely they pushed their way forward, bowing their thanks.

When Odo gave a sack to a toothless old woman, she held it for only a moment before it slipped from her grasp and spilled into the mud. He tried to hand it back to her, but she brushed it away as if it were trash. "Luca is gone," she cried, pointing at Odo as if it were his fault.

Odo shot me a worried look. *Go,* he seemed to be saying, *go.*

The singing urchin had now been joined by others, including a girl who banged a stick on a plate like a crude drum as they intoned:

Maid, your betrothed forgets you
As he shivers and cries in dread.
He'll marry a grave instead of a girl,
With a coffin for his wedding bed.

"Tell me what is going on," I called out to the crowd.

"It's the Seep, my lady," someone said.

I turned to see who was speaking. "The Seep — what is that?"

A haggard, hunch-shouldered man pushed his way through the villagers toward me. "I can tell you everything, Your Highness," he said.

"You will spare her," Abra commanded. "She doesn't need to know."

"Should she be ignorant of this the way she is ignorant of our other miseries?" the man asked. He turned to me. "I'll tell you, Princess, with your leave."

His words stung, but they were true. I came to the village only weekly — I didn't know what it was like to live here in poverty. I didn't know how it felt to be hungry and cold and sick. Loneliness was my only burden.

"Please tell me," I urged the man.

He removed his hat and clutched it in a grimy fist. "The sickness comes on quick in the night. First you shiver so badly it feels like a devil's shaking you," he said, "and a great pain comes into your head. Next, Your Highness, it's like a fire is burning your guts. You want to tear out your insides with your own hands, that's how bad the fever burns. As you lie there, shook by devils

33

and pains, the sores start to come. Tiny blisters pop out all over your body, and they ooze liquid clear as water. And then...then you'd better call a man to dig you a hole in the ground, for that's where you're going next." He bowed and put his cap back on. "That is what we call the Seep, Princess."

"Is there a cure?" I asked, horrified.

The man wiped his sweating brow, and I wondered if he, too, felt the heat of fever. "We know of none yet," he said. "And even strong men die screaming."

Whatever he said next was drowned out by another verse of that grisly song.

> *Mothers, don't cry for your children,*
> *The babes that were taken from you.*
> *You'll see them again before the dawn*
> *For the Seep is your destiny, too.*

With sudden alarm, I searched for Fina in the crowd. "Fina," I called, "where is your sister, Rosa?"

Fina tugged at one of her coppery braids. "In our bed," she answered.

"She's sleeping, though, right? Not sick?"

Before Fina could answer, the chiming of great bells split the air. Their somber notes clanged seven times before stopping, and then only their echoes were left, hovering above us like the terrible black smoke itself. Hearing them, Fina paled.

"What are those?" I asked Odo, as they did not ring the correct hour. "What are they for?"

His hands twisted in his horse's dark mane. "They are the Passing Bells," he said softly.

"He means the Bells of Death," Abra said, his voice much harsher. "They ring when a soul has departed this world."

I turned back to Fina. "Your sister—tell me she's all right!"

For a moment, the girl seemed unable to answer. Then she gathered herself up and spoke steadily as tears streamed down her freckled cheeks. "I do not suppose she is all right now," she said.

"Blood and blister, fever and sore," the little boy sang on.

"Stop it!" I cried, leaning out the window. "Have you no respect?" I struck the side of the carriage in anger. But even sharper was my grief. Poor, sweet Rosa, dead of a plague at six years old. How could this be?

Then nearby I saw a dark-skinned boy—my age, or a season older—turn toward my voice. I saw him raise his arm. And something came spinning through the air, straight at me.

CHAPTER 7

A clump of thick, dark mud, flung from the boy's clenched fist, exploded wetly against my cheek. Some of it dropped down to my chest, smearing into the blue silk. Most of it hurtled into my open, shocked mouth.

I choked and gagged, and by some awful reflex swallowed some of the mud down. The taste was warm, earthy, fecal—

No! Suddenly I couldn't catch my breath. I leaned out of the carriage, retching. My hair, already loosed from its intricate coils, hung like ropes before my face as I coughed and gasped, my lungs heaving, my stomach twisting into knots.

That wretched boy had flung *manure* at me!

My tongue felt coated with it as I spit again and again into the dirt. When I looked up through streaming eyes, he was still standing there, as motionless as a post. His defiant gaze never left my face, even as my father's guards rushed toward him, their billhooks raised.

Abra reached him first and grabbed him by the throat. He drew his sword from his belt and lifted it high above his head.

In another instant, he'd split the boy in half, right down to his groin.

"Stop!" I yelled. "Do not harm him!"

Wiping my tear-streaked face, I tried to sit up straight. Tried to summon the imperious attitude I'd been trained to exhibit, regardless of circumstances. I had been humiliated, and rage flooded through me. But my anger was accompanied by something else. As the boy stared at me so boldly, I felt a flicker of... *admiration*.

Because, obviously, he feared nothing.

"Princess," Odo said, handing me a cloth.

As I wiped myself clean as best I could, I kept my eyes locked on the boy's. His face was fierce, darkly handsome, and in its own way, almost regal. He didn't struggle in Abra's grip; he merely waited, watching me. I could tell that he knew the punishment for what he'd done. Were my father here, he'd already be dead.

But my father wasn't here.

Abra's sword hung in the air. His arm trembled, so badly did he want to bring the blade down and cleave the boy in two.

"Lower your weapon, Abra," I commanded.

Abra's face grew sullen. He hesitated, but he did as I told him to do. He released the boy's throat, and I could see the bruises blossoming already.

"What is your name, stupid boy?" I shouted.

He flung back his shoulders and raised his strong chin. "I am Raphael and proud of it!"

"Why have you done this to me, you insolent beast?" I heard

my father's harsh words echo in mine and, chagrined, I lowered my voice. "Defend yourself, villager," I muttered.

"It is a lesson," Raphael answered boldly. "In subjects your tutors will never teach you about—suffering and degradation. You live in comfort and luxury in your castle on a hill, and you have no idea what it's like to be down here in the village. Here we live in hunger and squalor and shit." Then he smiled. "You've never known hunger or squalor, I'm sure, but now I expect you understand the *shit* part."

His defiance shook me. No one had ever spoken to me like that—not least a subject I could have skinned alive if I chose. "I don't need any lessons from the likes of you," I hissed.

Though he was now held captive between two men who'd rather kill him than watch him draw one more breath, Raphael managed to stagger a few steps toward me as he spoke. "I not-so-humbly beg to differ," he said. "Everyone must learn suffering, Princess, even you. Those mighty Bandon walls can't keep it out forever. I hope Ares and his knights destroy your towering castle. I pray for the quick—no, make that the slow—demise of your father, the so-called Warrior King." Then he spat upon the ground.

That was all it took. Abra's sword had been sheathed, but there was no stopping his fists. He cut the boy a vicious blow across the cheek, nearly spinning him around like a top. Stunned, the boy wobbled and reached out, grabbing onto Abra's arm so he didn't crumple to the ground.

He would have been wiser to fall.

Abra struck him again, and more guards rushed to surround them. The villagers surged forward, and I could no longer see Raphael at all.

"Odo, don't let them kill him," I cried.

Grimly, Odo spurred his horse into the melee, shouting something I couldn't make out. The villagers fell back, and the guards stepped away. I saw the boy's crumpled form lying half buried in the mud. One of his boots was missing, and his bare foot looked impossibly small and fragile.

After another word from Odo, the guards began to drag him away. I could not make out his face, but I could tell there was no life in his limbs. Had they killed him already?

Odo rode back to the carriage and answered the question I hadn't even asked out loud. "The villager lives," he said. "For the time being, anyway."

A guard slung Raphael onto the back of a horse like a sack of grain, and then they galloped away. What he'd said and done was treasonous and an outrage, yes. But he didn't deserve to die by our hands. There were enough ways for him to perish without us being involved: in a battle with Ares's men, or by the fever of the Seep. The threat of death hung in the air, as thick as the curling black smoke.

"Your Highness," Odo said. "We must leave now."

But instead I flung open the carriage door, and I hesitated only an instant before jumping out.

Among the beasts.

CHAPTER 8

My slippers sunk into the cold mud of the lane as I stood face-to-face with the hungry, sick villagers.

Startled, Odo's horse stomped its hoof, further splattering my ruined gown. "Princess Sophia!" Odo said. "Do not—"

I held up my hand, and the ruby ring that had been my mother's shone like blood. "You will not stop me, Odo."

His face twisted in dismay. "I beg of you, do not touch them," he said.

"Are you afraid of us, Princess?" asked the crone who'd dropped her bag of food. "We have no gold, no crowns, it's true—but we are flesh and blood like you."

"I am not afraid," I said. But in truth I could hardly breathe from fear. I knew the villagers would never harm me, but a deadly plague walked among them.

Just as I was doing now.

The villagers stretched out their hands to me beseechingly, as if a caress of my silk sleeve would bring them luck. How carefully my father and I had protected ourselves from them—and yet how fervently they still showed their loyalty. Even now, when their very survival was threatened, they bowed to me, and tried to kiss the hem of my dress.

How could Leonidus ever call them beasts?

As I walked onward, a man stepped out of his cottage, wrapped in a threadbare blanket and nearly too weak to stand. "I've buried my wife and five of my children, Princess," he said. His legs faltered, and he sank to the ground. "Who will be left to bury me?"

A woman in a ragged dress pulled at my cloak. "Our children cry themselves to sleep at night," she said. "Is it better to wake hungry and afraid, or better to go to sleep forever?"

These cruel questions I could answer in only one way. "Follow me to the castle," I said. "My father will give you food and medicine—I will demand it."

But the woman who held my cloak shook her head. "Any one of us might carry the Seep. We cannot risk bringing it into the castle."

Any one of us.

I felt myself begin to shiver as I looked at the anguished, poverty-stricken crowd. What if this woman clutching my cloak had the Seep? What if Fina did? I tried to breathe calmly. I didn't want them to see my fear—only my strength, that they might draw hope from it. If I didn't touch anyone directly, I would be safe. That's what I told myself.

Fina's mother came into the lane then. She walked slowly, carrying in her arms a small, lifeless form. Her ravaged eyes met mine, and then she turned, bearing away her dead child.

I stifled a sob when I caught sight of Rosa's pale, blistered hand dangling above the mud. That sweet girl had once shyly whispered to me that she wanted to be a princess, too. "W-where is she taking her?" I asked the gaunt woman at my elbow.

"To the mass grave," she said. "The child will burn with all the others."

Grief and helplessness nearly overwhelmed me, and tears coursed down my cheeks as I walked among my subjects. "I will bring more food," I promised them. "I will help. You are not alone."

Though my cloak dragged in the mud, and the wind smelled like snow and death, I held my head high, encircled with its invisible crown.

"We must go now, Princess," Odo said. His voice was sharp, and this time I listened to him. I bowed to my subjects, and then I pulled up the dirty folds of my gown and climbed back into the carriage.

I thought again of the boy, Raphael. He had risked his life to display his anger at the horrible state of his village. And as I watched the cottages grow smaller behind me, I understood one thing: there had already been so much dying—and, on the horizon, there was more death to come.

CHAPTER 9

As we approached the castle, the great gatehouse door rolled open to admit us, and the soldiers arming our trebuchets called out in greeting. The carriage driver touched the horses' flanks with his whip, and we clattered through two more heavy iron gates before we came to a rough halt in the courtyard.

As he helped me out of the carriage, Odo glanced pointedly at the smears of mud on my ruined dress.

"I won't let the King see me like this," I said. "Please, just don't tell him what I did."

Odo gave me the most minuscule of bows: he would keep the secret of how I walked among the beasts.

"But you must tell him of the plague," I said. "Tell him about the Bells. Tell him that they need us."

At this, Odo stiffened and looked away.

"What?" I asked. "Will you not speak of it?"

"The king has greater concerns," Odo said. "Ares and his—"

"Surely he cares that the villagers are dying! And we may grow sick, too, Odo! I doubt rank or stature matters to the Seep—do you? All our castle's defenses may not keep it outside."

Odo's face was grim. He inhaled slowly. "I will speak to him, Your Highness." And then he stalked away.

I hurried, unseen, to my bedchamber, where I bathed quickly and then dressed myself—when did that ever happen?—in an old, blue satin gown. I didn't bother to brush my hair or pin a brooch to my breast. Instead, I hurried to where I knew Raphael would be, if he was even still alive.

I had asked Jeanette to look in on the manservant from this morning—but I would tend to the brave, stupid village boy myself.

Beneath the scullery, a set of steep, curving stairs wound down into darkness, and a thick oaken door marked the entrance to the dungeon. This was forbidden territory for a princess, a dank world of vermin, human and otherwise. And yet here I was, pounding to be let in. My candle flickered and guttered in the chill air.

Eventually the door creaked open, and a grotesque, misshapen man peered out. This was Gattis, the keeper of the dungeon, who'd not seen the light of day for decades. His bloodshot eyes, straining out of waxy, cadaverous sockets, looked as though they were trying to crawl out of his skull.

"What brings a pretty flower like you underground to the worms?" he rasped. A gnarled, creeping finger approached my cheek but stopped an inch away. His smile was ghastly.

I did not flinch. "Let me in," I said.

He backed away, bowing mockingly. "Welcome to my kingdom."

I stepped past him into the dungeon and immediately clapped my hand over my mouth and nose. The village had smelled like death, but the dungeon smelled like shit and despair.

"Where is the boy who was brought in this afternoon?" I demanded. My eyes had begun to water, and Gattis, noticing this, cackled drunkenly.

"Below, your Majesty." Then he pointed not to one of the dank, rat-infested cells, but to an iron grille covering a small opening in the floor.

I crouched down and put my face to the bars. Raphael was barely visible in the stinking darkness. His face was bruised, and one eye was swollen shut. Was it blood or filth on his arms? I couldn't tell. The cell was so small that he could hardly even lie down.

"Raphael," I called. "Can you hear me?"

He moaned and tried to turn over. He seemed only half conscious.

I stood up, my head spinning from the horror of it. "Release him," I said.

Gattis laughed as if I'd made a joke. "No, Princess, not even for you."

"I command it!"

But he just blinked his bulging eyes at me. "His life is not yours to save."

"My father—"

"When your father orders me directly, I'll obey him," Gattis said. "And until then, I'll keep the little rotter comfortable here, for I am the king of rats and robbers, and the sovereign of mice and murderers." He raised a hogskin of wine and took a long gulp from it. Then he threw it to the ground and wiped his cankered lips. "To your health, Your Highness," he sang, and then belched loudly. "Remember, everyone gets what they deserve."

I should have known it would be impossible to reason with a torturer. Saying nothing more, I left Gattis in his stinking subterranean kingdom and went to find my father.

He was pacing the Hall of the Flat Queens, and I could tell by the set of his shoulders that his mood was grim, and his thoughts preoccupied with the coming battle. Ares had never before concerned himself with our southern lands, but he had grown restless, pushing across the Dorel Mountains as summer waned, seeking conquest in realms close to ours. If the whispers were true, he had plundered the city of Cedd—but a week's ride away—and slaughtered all its inhabitants—man, woman, and child. As his army pulled out, already fixated on its next battle, the last line of soldiers had set the city's ruins on fire.

But with my father, Ares would finally meet his match.

"Father," I said, touching his arm, "I must ask you for something."

He turned around. He saw my old dress and my loose hair, and his nose wrinkled ever so slightly. No doubt he could smell the rank dungeon on me. "Sophia," he said, "why do—"

"Father, please, I know you have much on your mind, but you must release that villager," I interrupted. "The boy named Raphael."

He let out a bark of surprise. "I will not. The beast committed treason."

"He spoke in justified anger—"

"I don't care. He struck you, and that is unpardonable. He'll rot underground like the corpse he should be."

"But I was the one hit, and I forgive him. He had a *point,* Father. We don't understand what it's like to be poor and hungry."

"Nor should we," he said angrily. "We are not beasts."

"I want him set free."

My father's eyes went cold, and when he spoke, his voice held the whisper of a threat. "Ask it for your next *birthday,*" he said. And then he turned his back to me.

So he blamed me for my last wish—well, so did I. When our knights put away their swords, the word had spread that King Leonidus had become weak, his soldiers fat and lazy. His castle and lands were ripe for plunder.

And now I knew what I did not understand then: that when my father gave me what I asked for, our fate was sealed. Ares's impending attack was entirely my fault.

The knowledge of my mistake nearly crushed me. But even if I could not prevent the impending battle, I could stop this one cruelty tonight. I could save this poor boy from Gattis's hell.

"Father, I beg—"

"No more talk!" he shouted. "Your king commands it."

I honestly thought he might strike me. But I stood my ground. There was more that I had to say. "Did Odo tell you of the Seep?" I asked. "Did he tell you that we have more than Ares to fear? You must send medicine to the village, and food. The villagers are dying, Father. They need our help."

My father said nothing. His face was like stone. He pushed me away down the corridor. "Go," he said. "Leave me alone."

For another second, I stood there, bereft, as my father waited for me to obey him the way I always had. It seemed, somehow, like we were already under siege.

"Go!" he shouted again.

And so, with the painted eyes of my mother gazing placidly down on us both, I did as he commanded.

CHAPTER 10

For the first time since I was old enough to leave the nursery, I didn't dine in the Great Hall. I knew my father wouldn't want to see me, and I didn't trust myself not to enrage him still further.

I told Jeanette that my head hurt and I didn't feel well, and a page was dispatched to bring dinner to my chambers.

Jeanette put her gentle hand on my forehead, and then, after holding it there for a moment, smiled in relief. "You're not feverish," she said.

I sighed. "That's because I'm not actually sick," I said. "I just want to be alone."

But she made no move to leave.

"*Really* alone," I said.

Jeanette stood up reluctantly. "Are you sure you don't want me to stay with you?"

The page entered with a bow, bringing a tray of pheasant,

roasted fennel, and honey wine, which he set on a carved table near the flickering fire.

"I'm sure," I said.

Jeanette ducked her head. "I understand, Princess. I'll look in on you later," she said. She motioned to the page, and then the door closed softly behind them.

Ignoring the dinner, I sat on the sheepskin in front of the fireplace with my legs crisscrossed as if I were a little girl. I opened my book of demons and monsters, admiring for the ten-thousandth time the richly detailed illustrations of the mythical beings that had thrilled and terrified me since I was old enough to turn the pages.

Behold the terrors of dream and darkness, these ancient creatures of depthless night...

I knew every beast by heart. Here was Balor, demigod of drought and blight, whose single giant eye could burn everything around it to dust. On the next page was the imposing centaur, with the head and torso of a man and the body of a stallion, whose arms could crush men's bones like twigs.

The book's margins featured smaller imaginary creatures: the gwyllgi, a black-faced dog whose howls foretold the death of whomever heard them, and the birds of Riannon, whose song woke the dead.

If the birds of Riannon truly existed, would I be brave enough to summon one? Would I wake my poor mother from her sleep of seventeen years?

I would if I could—without a moment's hesitation. The guilt of her death had weighed on me my whole life. If it weren't for me, she'd still be alive.

Maybe this was another reason I'd asked my father to stop his war raids: one killer in the family was enough.

But now our enemies approached us. Was I to be responsible for the deaths of our knights next? What of our servants, should the castle be breached? What of the villagers, dying of the Seep? And, not least of all, there was the poor, wretched boy who lay bloody and beaten in a cell a hundred feet below me—his fate was my fault, too.

I put my face in my hands. I hadn't exactly lied to Jeanette at first: I *didn't* feel well. But it was my heart, not my head, that ached.

Then I looked up at the rich dinner that had been prepared for me. It could have fed six villagers. It was probably more food than Fina's family ate in a week. In what world was that fair?

I'd read about monks of old, fasting in penance, and I decided that I would fast tonight, too. For my mother. For Raphael. For the villagers and the soldiers and everyone else who had ever suffered.

For Rosa.

I sent for the page and bid him take the food away. I only hoped he would get some of it.

Then I turned my attention back to the book, which had been a comfort to me more times than I could count. This was ironic, of course, because its characters were the creatures of nightmares. If they'd ever existed, they would not be my confidants and friends.

But comfort me they did somehow. I turned from the real horror of Ares—of sickness and war and dungeons—to the imaginary horror of these mythical creatures.

Here was the tatzelwurm, whose green-eyed, cat-like face used to haunt my dreams. Its long, slithering body was scaled as a snake's, and venom dripped from its fangs. Even stranger were the Blemmye, headless men with eyes on their shoulders and hideous mouths on their broad, bare chests. And finally, there was Reiper the Destroyer, who left his throne of skulls to walk among the human world. A demon with a prince's face, he killed for profit and pleasure alike, and death followed him wherever he went, obedient as a dog.

These were terrible creatures indeed, but they were not real. Whereas I—a pretty princess, perfumed and bedecked in jewels— had been a true force of destruction.

It was ironic indeed.

CHAPTER 11

I woke with a start on the sheepskin rug, my book of monsters and myths lying open, with the cold eyes of Seth, the jackal god, staring up at the ceiling. The fire had nearly burned out, and the room was dark and cold. Shivering, I pulled my mantle closer around my shoulders.

Goosebumps prickled up my arms. The castle was quiet, but somehow the silence felt wrong. Not peaceful.

Ominous.

"Jeanette?" I called. "Where are you?"

There was no answer. My breathing grew quick and shallow — she always came when I called. As I roused myself to go look for her, the stillness was shattered by a thunderous crash. I shot up to my feet, my heart pounding so hard it felt like a fist punching my ribs from the inside. Then I heard a scream — a piercing, awful cry, splitting the air like it was made of glass. It was the sound of mortal terror.

I ran to the door and wrenched it open. The guards stationed outside my room whirled toward me, their weapons drawn. "Your Highness," cried the tall one, "go back inside."

I heard the scream again, but fainter now. "Who is that?" I demanded. "What's happening?"

The guards didn't answer; instead, they tried to force me back into my room. "For your own safety, Princess," the smaller one grunted, even as I jabbed him with an elbow and spun away from his grasp. The tall one held out his sheathed sword to block my way, but I ducked beneath it and rushed into the corridor.

"Jeanette?" I called again. "Jeanette!" I told myself that if I could just get to her room, then everything would be all right.

"Let her go," I heard one of the guards mutter. "Let her fend for herself."

I had no lamp, and the tallow candles that always flickered in the halls had gone out. Darkness pressed against me from all sides. I crept forward, trailing my hand along the stone wall to guide my way.

I heard heavy footsteps behind me, and then I felt the rush of air as a group of my father's soldiers ran past. "What's happening?" I called after them. "Has Ares come already?"

No one answered. But then one soldier, who came limping behind the rest, staggered toward me. I grabbed his elbow as he tried to pass. "What is it?" My fingers gripped into his flesh. "Tell me what's going on!"

"Someone's in the castle," he gasped. "He killed six guards before he got to me. Princess, you must hide. Lock yourself in your chambers!"

"Who is he? Where is he now?" I demanded.

But the soldier only gave a gasp and fell to the ground at my feet. Quickly I knelt and put my hand on his chest. He was breathing faintly, and my fingers came away wet with warm, sticky blood. My stomach clenched. "Guards, help this man!" I cried, though I worried he was beyond helping.

Wiping my hands on my dress, I stood. I had to find Jeanette. Blindly I inched down the hall, nearly delirious with fear. Somewhere in the castle was a man who'd breached all our defenses. Who'd killed six—perhaps seven—men with ruthless ease.

Was it Ares himself?

Scritch, scritch . . . I whirled around, my eyes desperately, vainly scanning the darkness.

There it was again: a tiny sound, the faintest whisper of movement. I froze. Willed my own heart to stop beating so I could listen, straining to hear that slight break in the silence. Something was moving, creeping—something familiar with darkness, and trying not to be heard. When the sound came again, closer to me now, I recognized it through my terror: the claws of a mouse, scrabbling along the flagstones in the night, looking for its dinner.

My breath came out in a rush. *Look at you, Sophia,* I thought, *afraid of a little mouse!*

I began to creep my way down the dark hall again. The rustle of fabric was just my gown—the eerie whine nothing but the wind. I had to find Jeanette.

Then something caught me by the wrist! Yanked suddenly backward, I was too shocked to cry out. I stumbled, and my head collided against something hard. Stars seemed to burst in my eyes as an arm closed tight across my shoulders, crushing me against what I now realized was a man's chest.

I screamed—earsplitting, bloodcurdling. I screamed until

my lungs gave out and then I breathed and screamed again. Then I felt the prick of a knife blade at my throat, and I stopped.

Silence descended.

I could hear only my panicked breath, quick and shallow. And then his breath, slow and rank. I felt the knife bite deeper into my flesh. A drop of blood slid down between my breasts. I closed my eyes. *Father, save me,* I thought wildly. *Father—*

A mouth moved close to my ear, and hot foul air came from it. "I've caught a treasure. Lucky, lucky me."

"Oh, please," I whispered. "Please don't."

"Please don't what?"

"Please don't kill me."

The wind howled through the loopholes in the walls. Where was Odo? Where were the knights? Where was the King?

"You're much too beautiful to kill, Princess," the voice hissed. *"I think I'm in love."*

The knife pressed into a vein pulsing at my throat, and I could not move for fear. Far away I heard the sound of footsteps and I prayed they were coming toward me. He squeezed me so tightly against him that I had to fight to breathe. But I felt him pause, waiting. Listening.

And then—so suddenly—he let me go. "I'll come back for you," he whispered as I collapsed to the floor.

"Odo!" I screamed as his footsteps raced away. "Father! The killer's right here!"

But, of course, he was not right here anymore. It was only me in the hall now, trembling, my life inexplicably given back to me.

I got up and ran.

CHAPTER 12

There was a terrible commotion near my father's chambers. Men shouted, servants dashed in and out of the room, and knights streamed down the hall in panicked lines, as my mother's calm, painted face looked blankly on. No one bowed to me, or even seemed to see me at all.

I pushed my way inside. The fireplace blazed, and in contrast to the dark corridors, the whole room seemed ignited in its blinding yellow light. I saw my father lying gray-faced on his royal bed, its four giant posters wrought from gnarled, ancient trees. Antony, his favorite manservant, was on his knees. He was praying.

I rushed to my father's bedside. "What's wrong? Antony—"

Then I saw the bandages soaked in blood, and a black trail of it on the floor. Sacheverell, the ancient court doctor, pulled back the coverlet to place a new dressing on my father's stomach. My father's eyelids fluttered but didn't open. He moaned—a hollow, aching sound.

"What's wrong with him?" I took up his limp hand and squeezed it. "Father! Father, can you hear me?"

He didn't answer, and the doctor grimly went about his work. Sacheverell was battle-seasoned: a man who'd pulled arrows from soldiers' eye sockets and axes from their skulls. He could stitch any slash, mend any wound.

I grabbed at his arm. "Tell me you can heal him," I said.

Sacheverell turned to me, his shirtfront dark with gore, his expression distraught. "I have never seen a wound like this," he said.

"What do you mean? Have you forgotten your skills?"

"Princess, this is not a sword scrape. This is—"

"His room is supposed to be guarded! Where were the men stationed outside his door?"

I felt a hand on my shoulder, and I looked up to see Odo, his face stricken. "He was not in his room, Princess," he said.

"Where was he? Was he in conference with his knights? Was he preparing for battle?"

Odo shook his head. "The king was alone, Princess. I cannot understand it, but he went to the dungeon unaccompanied. He was..."—Odo could hardly bear to say it—"attacked upon his return."

My legs gave out, and I sank down onto the bed. "Oh, Father, what were you thinking?" Because I knew exactly what he had done. Though he had refused to release Raphael, he'd gone to visit him. He'd descended into that dank hell to make sure that the traitorous beast—as he would have called Raphael—was still alive, and that he was not being tortured further by Gattis or his henchmen.

His mercy was repaid in blood.

This was all my fault, too. First my mother, and now my father.

I pressed my palm against his forehead. It was damp and as cold as stone. "Father," I whispered. "I'm so sorry. Father, I'm here."

His skin was ashen and his breathing shallow. The new bandage covering his wound was already turning dark and wet.

"You must save him," I begged the old doctor.

"I have applied a balm of egg whites and rose water to the wound," Sacheverell said. "And spiderwebs to help stop the bleeding—"

"Which is obviously not working!"

"We have given him henbane as well, Princess," he said.

"Does it stop the bleeding?" I asked. My hope was small and desperate. "Does it close a hole in a man's stomach?"

The doctor looked away from me then. "It eases pain," he said quietly. He paused, and then added, "It calms the dying."

The *dying*? Surely he was wrong—my father was a warrior! "But I've seen you wrest a wounded soldier away from the grip of Death himself!"

"I am sorry, Princess. This is beyond my powers."

"Please," I said, "you must keep trying!"

But Sacheverell only stood where he was, grave and still, as I lay my head on my father's strong barrel chest and felt its shallow rise and fall. "You're going to be fine," I whispered. "Don't listen to Sacheverell. I will take care of you."

My father took in a ragged, harrowing breath. "Sophia," he whispered. "My sweet songbird."

I sat up, clutching at his shirt. "I'm here, Father. Everything is all right. You just need to rest," I gabbled helplessly.

His lips widened—a smile or a grimace of pain, I couldn't tell. "I'm sorry, my daughter," he said.

"Sorry for what?" I asked. I was crying now, and my tears fell onto my hands, his chest.

"I am afraid that I am about to cause you strife."

"Father, please—" *You can't die. I forbid it.*

"A crown is heavier than it looks. I only wanted to protect you, my child. And now who will?" He struggled to open his eyes. "Is Odo here? I can't see."

"I'm here, Your Highness," his knight said.

"I'm not ready to depart this life," my father gasped. "Who will protect my Sophia?"

In a choked voice, I told him that I loved him. I told him not to worry, that he would heal in no time. He squeezed my hand.

"Perhaps I will see your mother," he said, a ghost of a smile flitting across his lips. His breath was coming quicker now.

"You can't leave, Father," I begged. "I need you. The kingdom needs you."

"I'll tell her how lovely you are," he whispered. "How kind and good you've grown to be. How much..."

I heard the shuddering of his heart as I pressed my face against his chest. Its beat was fast, faint. With my whole soul I wished for it to surge on, keeping him alive, keeping him with me. But a few moments later, it stopped altogether.

I sat up, sobbing, and pounded my fists on his chest. He didn't move. He was gone.

My father—the great Warrior King—was dead.

I no longer had a mother or a father.

And it was all my doing.

For a moment, grief blinded me. The world went utterly dark, and everything around me was a swirling storm of sadness and horror.

Then I felt hands lifting me from the bed. Pulling me up to standing. I opened my eyes and saw every man in the room sink to his knees.

"What are you doing?" I asked, bewildered.

"Your Highness," spoke Odo, his head bowed low. "The king is dead. Long live the queen." Then he looked up, and his fierce, kind eyes met mine. "You," he whispered.

CHAPTER 13

D awn broke pale and cold. I turned in my bed and rubbed my eyes. I felt dizzy, my head full of scenes from the night's terrible dreams. I saw blood pooling on stones, servants wailing, and my father's face gone slack in death. But I was awake now, and I knew the sun would banish the nightmares.

I started to sit up but then fell back against my pillow. It was as if a giant hand had pressed me down flat, and I could not lift myself again. I began to pant and struggle.

Was this another terrible dream? My hands were limp, and my head felt heavy and hot. "Jeanette," I called weakly. "I need you."

In a moment she was by my bed, her normally ruddy face white with worry. "Oh, my darling Sophia," she whispered. "Your father loved you so." Tears slid down her face, and she didn't bother to wipe them away. Instead, her hand cupped my cheek. "You poor, orphaned queen."

Queen.

I gripped the bed as the room spun around me. It had not been a dream! My father was dead, cruelly stabbed in a midnight hallway by an unknown enemy. The kingdom was now mine, and Ares, the greatest threat Bandon had ever faced, advanced against us.

I knew nothing about warfare.

I knew that I should find Odo and learn our plans for counterattack, but in this moment, the grief was too much to bear. I began to shiver, and I pulled the ermine coverlet to my chin with shaking fingers.

"Come bathe and dress," Jeanette urged. "Let me comb your hair. It will make you feel better. Sophia, we must be strong."

I shook my head as I lay quaking beneath the covers. "I can't get up, Jeanette."

"Sophia, you are our ruler now," she said gently. "You must show your people that you deserve their love and loyalty. You are a *queen,* child. You must contain your sadness."

I could hardly take in her words. And I could barely lift my hand to touch her arm. "Jeanette, I feel so weak. It's freezing in this room. Are all the windows open? Has winter come already?"

Her brow furrowed as my legs, against my will, began to seize under the covers. "Sophia," she cried. "What's wrong?"

"You must get Odo," I said to her. "Ares approaches. Odo knows what to do. He will command—" But my teeth chattered so much it was hard to speak.

Jeanette rose from the bed and backed away from me, fear in her eyes. "No, I must get Sacheverell," she said.

I tried to clench my clacking jaws together even as I spoke. "Nothing is wrong with me at all except that my father is dead, and I don't know how to lead an army! Do not bring me that useless old doctor! Bring me Odo!"

Without another word, she ran from the room. Though I tried to keep my legs from spasming, it felt like I was being rattled by an invisible force, as if some unseen hand held me in its grip and shook me to and fro. I gritted my teeth so as not to cry out.

Jeanette was gone a long time, but no maid came in to stoke the fire. Adelie and Elodie never appeared, either. I had often been alone in my life, but on this frigid, awful morning, I was more alone than ever before.

My shaking kicked the covers from the bed and flung the pillows to the floor. But then, just when it seemed like the teeth would be jolted from my head, the convulsing suddenly stopped. I breathed in a deep, grateful breath. Perhaps the tremors had passed and my strength would return. I tried to sit up, but an explosion of pain burst in my head. I cried out, clawing at my temples just as Jeanette, Sacheverell, and a handful of his pupils returned to my room.

They pulled my hands from my head, and Sacheverell took only one glance at me before his face went even paler than usual.

"My Queen," he said, "you are gravely ill."

"What do you know?" I rasped angrily. "You who could not save my father! What good are you to me?"

He bowed his head. "I did my best for my beloved king; his wound was too deep. But truthfully, Your Highness, I am no good for you, either."

"You've lost your skill! Well, no matter—I am not sick." Once again I tried to sit up but could not, and I lay gasping on my pillow. "I have just bid farewell to my father forever, and what you see is my grief. I will be better momentarily."

"I am afraid that is not true," he said. "Your situation is no less dire than the king's."

I turned to Jeanette. "Why does he say that?" But then I cried out in pain again, and I couldn't hear her answer. The invisible force that had shaken me was now driving an axe into my skull.

Jeanette pressed her hand over my mouth as gently as she could. "Forgive me, Sophia, but you must hear this."

Sacheverell, still white as a ghost, spoke softly now. "You have the Seep, my Queen. I am sorry. But you will not last the night."

CHAPTER 14

That wild, keening sound—was it coming from my own throat? The bed seemed to fall away beneath me, and I spun down into darkness. *You will not last the night. You will not last—*

Sacheverell was lying. How could it be that in a matter of hours, life would be taken from me? The doctor was wrong, he had to be. I was barely out of childhood!

The pain in my head grew worse and my limbs spasmed. Then through my sobs I heard a familiar voice.

"My beloved Queen," Odo said softly.

I opened my eyes to see my father's best knight—my own old friend—standing over my bed. His kind face calmed me instantly, though still I shook. I reached for his hand. "Oh, Odo, he's telling me I will not spar with you again," I said.

Odo reached under my pillow and pulled out the parrying dagger he knew I kept there. Its blade flashed in the weak sunlight. "You'll nick me with this soon enough," he said firmly. "Sophia, you will survive."

But even as he said it, I understood that Sacheverell was right, and we all knew it. Poor Odo! Even with my father gone, he still believed that he could not cause me strife! But I let him have his kind lie.

I willed my body to stop shuddering. "There is a favor I must ask of you," I said.

"Anything, my Queen."

"That boy in the dungeon. I want you to take me to him." Somehow I managed to sit up this time. To then wrap myself in a blanket and stagger to a nearby chair took all my remaining strength. "To carry me, hold only to the chair," I said. "Don't touch me, Odo. Don't risk the Seep."

But Odo laughed. "If you die, none whom I have served will be left in this world," he said. "What would life matter to me then? I will take you there in my own arms."

And so he picked me up the way he used to do when I was very small, and he carried me shivering the long way to the dungeon.

Gattis, opening the heavy door, greeted us with a snarl. He was not used to having his domain disturbed so often. "You again," he said to me, his eyes bulging like boiled eggs. "And looking worse than some of my captives, I'd add."

"Do not speak to your queen that way," I snapped.

"The king?" he said, stepping back. *"Gone?"*

I nodded, and his eyes widened even more. But Gattis did not seem aggrieved by the knowledge — only surprised.

"I will see the prisoner," I said coldly.

Already he had recovered enough to sneer at us. "Which one?" he asked.

I would not miss this wretch if death took me! "You know which one," I said through clenched teeth.

Grumbling, Gattis produced a key and led us down a crumbling passage to a dark, dank cell. "The King bade me move him to our most luxurious quarters," he said, and gave a ghastly laugh.

In the corner of the cell lay a crumpled pile of rags.

"Raphael," I called. Even my voice seemed to shiver. "Is that you?"

The pile of rags moved, and a dark head lifted itself up. In the torchlight I saw the glint of his eyes. His gaze was as unflinching as ever.

"Good day, Princess—or is it evening? It's impossible to tell." He gestured weakly to the room. "I regret that I have no manure to throw at you. While there's plenty of rat dung, it's really too small to be truly effective."

"I think you made your point well enough the first time," I said. Gently, Odo set me down, and I used the bars of Raphael's cell to hold myself up.

"So have you come to laugh at my fate?"

"I've come to pardon you."

Raphael blinked at me. "The King changed his mind?" he asked.

"The King is dead."

A shadow seemed to cross over his face—maybe Raphael had not really wished for the death of my father. But he wiped his brow with his filthy hand and said nothing.

"I forgive you for what you did," I said.

Raphael laughed weakly. "That's very noble of you. But I don't need your forgiveness." He turned away from me, and as he did so his ragged shirt slipped over his shoulder.

I gasped when I saw his skin, dotted with dozens of tiny welts. It was just as the villager had warned me. *Tiny blisters pop out all over your body, and they ooze liquid clear as water. Then you'd better call a man to dig you a hole in the ground . . .*

"You're sick," I whispered.

"So now you understand," he said. "Whether you pardon me or not, I will die in this cell."

I did not know what to say to him. I had been born to riches and power, and he had been born to poverty and filth. And yet here we were, in the exact same circumstances: in a dungeon. Dying.

"I am sick, too," I said quietly. *Are you glad?* I wanted to ask.

Raphael said nothing. But then he smiled at me—a beautiful, sad, surprising smile. "The Seep pays no mind to rank or royal blood, does it? Well, maybe we will meet again someday, Your Highness," he said. "Somewhere else. In another life and a better world." He coughed. "Certainly it's difficult to imagine a worse one."

"I'm so sorry," I said. "For everything."

Raphael gazed at me thoughtfully. "Perhaps I misjudged you," he said. "But it's rather too late now, isn't it?"

Odo put his hand on my shoulder. "It's not good for you to be down here any longer."

I knew he was right, but still I hesitated.

Raphael patted the ground next to him. "If you are truly sick, come and sit beside me here," he said. "I'd much rather look at you than at Gattis, even in your state. We can keep each other company while we wait for death. Who will feel his scythe blade first, the lowly beast or the lovely princess? We can make a wager. Doesn't that sound like fun?"

I smiled sadly at him. "No, not exactly."

Gattis pushed past me, shoved a key into the lock, and hauled open the cell door. "Out with you, vermin, if you want," he said.

Raphael shook his head. "I'm not strong enough to move," he said. "And I certainly don't want you to carry me." He turned to me. "Well, if you will not join me here . . . then goodnight, Princess."

"Queen," I reminded him.

He smiled again, and then Odo lifted me up and carried me away.

CHAPTER 15

Ares's soldiers advanced, their looming shadows tall as trees. Bandon's knights, their ranks broken, yelled in panicked confusion. I saw the gleam of gory swords, horses with their bellies slit open, and men writhing on the ground in agony.

My eyes flew open, and relief flooded me. I was in my own bed, not on a battlefield. But the sheets were drenched and my body was wracked with pain. *A fever dream,* I thought, struggling to sit up. *Not the truth.*

Or at least — not the truth *yet*.

The first pale rays of the sun slanted through the room. So I *had* lasted the night, I thought, Sacheverell be damned. But I was so sick that I could barely move. My skin felt searingly hot. Weakly I called for Jeanette, for Odo. Yet it was Abra who burst into the room first.

His shield was streaked with blood, and he didn't bow or wait for permission to speak. "Ares's army is less than a mile away," he said, "and they cannot be stopped. They fight like men possessed. We will make our stand here, at Bandon Castle."

My throat clenched; I could barely whisper my assent. "Do what you will," I said. "Whatever you do, remember…" I stopped as red-hot pain exploded in my head. "Our lives are in your hands."

Odo came in from the hall and hurried to my side. "Your knights will protect you," he assured me. "And I will not leave you."

Faithful Odo. I knew he would guard me from Ares's soldiers. If only he could save me from the Seep.

Abra wordlessly turned to go. He had never much cared for me, I knew that. But this might be the last time I'd ever see him. "Abra," I said. "Thank you. May my father's strength be yours."

His brooding gaze wavered—I was sure I saw a glimmer of sympathy in his eyes—and then he took his leave. The room fell silent except for the sound of Odo's restless pacing, and that of my own labored breath.

The battle for our kingdom was soon to be fought. And there was hope for us, I was sure of it. But not so much for myself.

It was happening just as the villager had said—the burning, the pain—but my mind still struggled to comprehend the horror of it. The kingdom needed me, and I was abandoning it. I didn't want to go.

Jeanette brought a cool cloth and wiped my forehead and cheeks.

"Did you do this for my mother, too?" I whispered. "When she was dying?"

She looked away, not answering; of course she had. My

fingers clenched the sheets and my heart twisted in fear. *I don't want to die,* I silently screamed. *I've hardly lived!*

Then I took a deep breath, trying to find a place of stillness. Hadn't I been trained to behave with grace and composure, no matter the circumstances?

Yes — but I'd never been very good at it.

Sacheverell, whose face was like a death's mask, kept trying to bring in his apprentice healers, but I sent them all away. A fire had begun to burn inside me, and my skin was slick with sweat. Sometimes I could lie still, but more often I shuddered and thrashed, again seized by shivering though I felt as hot as the sun.

Was this what my mother had felt on the day of my birth? Knowing she would die before her daughter learned to walk? Now I would die before I saw my kingdom destroyed — was I fortunate not to witness our downfall?

Jeanette sat by my side and held my hand. It was she who noticed the first blister, like a tiny pearl on the tip of my finger. I wept to see it.

"Death has stalked our family, one by one," I told her. "First my mother. Then my father. And soon — me."

"Hush, child, everything will be fine," Jeanette said.

I was queen for but a day, and my life would be even shorter than my mother's. If I could have one last wish, it would be to see her.

Please, Mother. I'm frightened. Please, come hold my hand as I die.

PART TWO

Chapter 16

I awoke to a terrible, spasmodic shaking. But it wasn't coming from within me now. And somehow—though I couldn't understand this at all—I wasn't in my bedroom anymore. All around me was darkness, cold, a sense of hurtling movement. And what was that *noise*?

Disoriented, I pushed myself up to sitting, and I realized that what I heard was the pounding of hooves, the chuffing exhale of straining horses. I was in a carriage!

But the last thing I remember—

Wasn't it... *dying*?

A particularly rough jolt flung me off the cushioned bench and slammed me against the carriage door.

"Pieter!" I called to the driver. "Where are you taking me? Slow down!"

But either he ignored me, or he couldn't hear my words over the rattling din. The carriage careened on its way, each rut in

the road jarring me out of my seat and punctuating my unspo-
ken questions. Why was he whipping the horses like this? How
long had we been traveling? Where were we going in such a
hurry—to another doctor who might cure me of the Seep?

I pushed back the curtain and a blast of wind rushed in.
Another terrible jolt launched me into the air. When I landed
back on the bench, I bit my tongue, and warm, metallic blood
filled my mouth.

I spat it onto the carriage floor, and still the horses galloped
on. The carriage shook so wildly I feared the whole thing might
fly apart. We took a sharp curve to the right and then a whip-
pingly fast turn to the left.

There was nothing I could do but hold on and try not to
scream.

Then, over the din of pounding hooves, came the low, ominous notes I'd heard just once before. They rolled through the
night like thunder, clanging on and on until I felt them echoing
in my very bones.

The Bells of Death.

My breath caught—I clutched my heart. I knew exactly what
was happening. Those hateful bells were tolling for me.

I knew without question that I was dead, and that my body
was being raced to its grave. Whatever this moment of con-
sciousness was—this last spark of life before eternal oblivion—I
understood that it was both mysterious and brief. And when it
was over, all would be nothingness forever.

The thought overwhelmed me, and I began to weep. How
could I leave the world behind? How could my story end so
soon? I was granted a life of wealth and privilege, but I'd done
nothing of consequence in my seventeen years. In fact, innocents—

and my own father—had died because of my foolishness. And now I'd never have the chance to redeem myself.

Again I was flung from side to side as the carriage continued its berserk journey. I dug my nails into the cushions, but I couldn't hold on tight enough as we swerved back and forth. I braved the wind that wailed like a voice and peered out the open window. I could see a narrow, unfamiliar road, twisting forward into darkness. To the left, cliffs rose toward the sky, and to the right, the ground fell away into a deep crevasse.

Ahead of us, the road veered sharply. I knew we were going too fast—there was no way we could make that turn. I found my voice and I yelled again for Pieter to slow down.

And by some miracle, we did. The drumbeat of hooves grew quieter and the carriage steadied. I was trembling, head to toe. But before I could even catch my breath, the horses surged forward again. We bore down on the curve at a full gallop. We were going to go over the edge!

It was too late. Panic seized my heart, and I closed my eyes and prayed. I felt the final lurch as the carriage left the road and took to the air. So this was how it all would end!

But instead of a plunge to the ground, there was . . . *nothing*.

CHAPTER 17

I opened my eyes. The carriage hung in the air—*weightless.*
All around me, stars glittered like diamond dust spilled across
the bowl of the sky. Comets flashed across constellations. The
moon glowed silver and pulsed as rhythmically as a heart. Somehow, we were not falling. Instead, we were floating! Overcome,
I began to cry out.

"It's beautiful! Why was I afraid of death? There's nothing to
fear! It's so beautiful to die—"

But then came the horrific plummet and I swallowed my
next words whole. My stomach flew up into my throat and my
vision went dark with fear. As we spun dizzyingly downward, I
screamed and screamed until—*impact.* A bone-cracking, earsplitting crash. Dust and rocks exploded into the air as the carriage wheels struck ground and I was flung from my seat. I
crashed into the front wall and it slammed my cheek; tiny stars
burst in my vision.

But somehow the carriage had not shattered, and somehow I was not crushed to pieces. And even more stupefying was this: the horses had landed on their feet, and they were still running!

I clawed my way back up to the bench and leaned out the window again. The sky was black and starless now, and we were on a thin dirt road, with ancient trees growing so close on either side that I could have touched them. My hair whipped around my face, and a branch lashed my cheek. Dust covered my face, my throat, the bodice of my old satin dress. I had never been so disheveled, so shocked, so...free. If this was death, why did I feel so alive?

As we raced through the darkness, I realized in wonder that all weakness had left me. I no longer shook. No fever burned my limbs with its flames. The finger on which the blister had appeared was dirty but utterly smooth.

Was this real?

I leaned farther out the window, and the rushing wind seared my eyes. "Pieter," I called, but still there was no answer.

Wedging my foot into the corner of the seat to balance myself, I pushed myself out farther so that I hung nearly halfway out of the window.

And finally I saw who was taking me on this incomprehensible journey. It was not Pieter at all, but two unknown coachmen. One held the reins while the other stood, hanging on to the carriage with one hand while holding a great torch aloft with the other.

Their shoulders were hunched, their backs broad and misshapen. They had tiny, bat-like ears, and their bald heads were a brackish blue-green in the torchlight. Open sores on their flesh oozed a gleaming slime. I could smell them now—the stench of refuse, of death, of bodies rotting from the inside out.

I gasped in horror, and the thing with the torch turned around. Its pupil-less eye narrowed at me as it curled its purple lips in an animal's snarl. "What are you doing, fool?" it rasped. "Get back inside, you idiot girl!"

My mouth fell open. That was no way to speak to a queen! Alive or dead, I would not be insulted by a putrid blue flesh bag like this one. "Don't you dare—"

The driver cracked his whip across the horses' flanks, and they shot forth in a demonic burst of speed. I lost my balance and lurched—halfway out the window! To keep from slipping even farther out, I dug my nails into the ornate wooden scrollwork, hanging on for my life.

"Stop! I command it!"

The driver only cackled and cracked his whip again. My forehead slammed against the outside wall of the carriage.

I let out a high, piercing cry of pain and fear as over and over, branches lashed my cheeks. I was losing my grip—in another moment I'd fall and be crushed under the carriage wheels. The beastly drivers paid me no heed.

And then, up ahead, I saw something blocking the road.

CHAPTER 18

A sudden sideways lurch of the carriage flung me back inside. My head struck wood and for a moment, the world went pitch-black. As soon as I regained my senses, I scrambled to the window again.

The hideous driver goaded on the horses as his companion swung his torch around like a warrior's flail. I squinted but couldn't make out the pale, narrow shape in the road. As we hurtled closer, I saw that it was a human—a woman. Utterly still, she stood in our way as if frozen. She was tall, wearing a long, white cloak, and her hair was dark and loose about her shoulders.

We bore down on her.

If she didn't move, we were going to run her right over.

I knew that yelling at the beasts wouldn't make a bit of a difference, but I did it anyway. "Stop! By Queen's command, you must stop this instant!"

We were close enough that I could see her face—how beautiful it was, and how serene, like that of a marble angel. She was not at all concerned that a pair of horses and a carriage were about to crush her.

Then slowly she lifted one hand and held it up, palm facing out.

The hideous driver yanked back on the reins, and the horses slowed. Tossing their heads, they came to a halt a mere inch from where the woman stood. Their chests heaved and their hides were flecked with foam. The woman in white, who had not even flinched, reached out to cup their velvet muzzles.

I pushed my tangled hair from my eyes. Nothing in my short life had ever prepared me for such a shock.

It couldn't be—and yet it was.

I threw open the carriage door, flung myself to the road, and ran.

CHAPTER 19

In a night of wonders, this was the greatest of them all: I stood in the middle of an unknown forest, wrapped in my mother's arms.

How could I even fathom it? I couldn't—and yet here she was, warm and solid and real. She was an inch taller than me, and as youthful as a sister. She looked exactly like her portrait, except even more beautiful. Her skin seemed to glow in the faint moonlight, and her heavy eyelashes sparkled with tears.

"Oh, my child," she cried, "is it really you?"

She stepped back, contemplated me at arm's length, and then quickly pulled me against her again. I could feel her tears falling onto my hair.

"I'm afraid to believe it. You have no idea how I've longed for this moment. Every single second, I've prayed for this," she whispered.

I didn't understand what was happening, or where we were,

or how any of this was possible. But I was afraid to ask questions. What if this moment wasn't real? What if none of this night was real? I didn't want to break the spell. She smelled like wood smoke, like roses. Like *home*.

"Oh, Sophia," my mother said, "I would have given anything to stay with you—my riches, my crown, my whole kingdom. And here you are, so beautiful the stars are envious." Her palm cupped my cheek. "My child, I've waited for this moment—not for seventeen years, but for an eternity." Then a quick, bright smile flashed across her lovely face. "You are filthy, though, my dear. The journey must have been a long one."

I turned back toward the carriage and its stamping horses, its otherworldly coachmen. But the road was empty: they had vanished into the night.

My mother slipped her hand through mine. "Come with me now," she said.

I was so happy I thought my heart would shatter. I had no idea that a dream like this could come true.

CHAPTER 20

She led me off the road, turning down a narrow track through the trees. Dry leaves whispered under our feet; otherwise, all was silent.

My mother walked gracefully down the twisting path, her bearing more regal than mine had ever been. Unlike me, she had played the harp beautifully, and no doubt she'd never been scolded for entering the Great Hall with unladylike speed. Had she been happy at Bandon? Had she worn her crown lightly? Did she love my father as much as he revered her? Was Odo her friend, too? I wanted to know everything about her, but my heart was so full I couldn't yet speak.

The path ended in a moonlit clearing, at the center of which sat a small, thatch-roofed cottage. My mother turned around and held out her arms. "Welcome, Sophia," she said. "Welcome home."

It was warm inside the humble room. Rushlights flickered

along the walls, and a fire burned brightly in the fireplace. Bouquets of dried wildflowers hung from the ceiling, filling the room with their sweet scent. There was a bed, a table, two chairs, an ornately carved trunk, and very little else. I had never seen a room so...tiny. So plain. Even Bandon's scullery maids had larger quarters. My mother saw the surprised expression on my face and laughed.

"Oh, my beloved girl," she said. "You must have so many questions! Ask and I will try to answer them."

But my mouth opened and shut again helplessly. Every single moment since I had awoken in the carriage was simply beyond my understanding.

"All right, my darling, sit," my mother urged. "You must be hungry and thirsty. You can eat, and then we can talk."

I nodded, watching as she put herbs and spices into a kettle in the fire. As she did so, she began to sing.

I made a wish, and I asked for you
A black-haired girl with eyes of blue.

Her voice, so high and clear, seemed to shimmer in the air. "That's a pretty song," I whispered. There, I'd finally spoken.

"I wrote it about you," she said. "I used to sing it to you before you were born."

A child of wit and strength and grace
With a warrior's heart and a flower's face...

But then she stopped and gave a small shrug. "That's all I remember. When I left you—when I died, I mean—it was too painful to sing it anymore."

"It's beautiful."

The fragrance of some warm, exotic spice filled the air, and my stomach rumbled. "What is that smell?" I asked. Then I shook my head. "Wait! I don't care about that. There are far too many other things to ask—"

My mother smiled at me.

My mother smiled at me: I never, ever believed I would be able to say such a thing! Until now, all I had had of her were paintings, and Jeanette's stories, and jewels she once might have worn.

"You can ask all the questions you want," she said gently. "I'll set no limit to them. And since you asked, the smell is a warming tea of galangal, clove, and costus root."

And then the questions rushed out, my words tumbling over one another. "How did I get here? How did you get here? Am I dead? I must be dead—I had the Seep, and Sacheverell said I would die, and I was so afraid. I heard the Bells of Death, and they must have been for me. Am I a ghost? Are we both ghosts? Can the living see us? Is this a different world? Is this heaven?" I glanced around the little room again. "I'd always imagined heaven somewhat *fancier*."

Then I looked at her sheepishly. Had I just insulted the eternal home of my long-lost mother? What a rude girl I was!

But my mother didn't take offense. She set a cup of tea on the table, and beside it a small loaf of bread. I broke off a small piece and put it in my mouth. It was warm and soft and chewy, and once I'd swallowed it, my hunger woke with a vengeance. I lost all my manners—I picked up the whole loaf and bit into it like an animal.

"Save room for the soup," she said. Then she laughed a bright bell of a laugh. "Listen to me! I sound like a real mother."

Then she sat down across from me and gazed into my eyes. "You are not dead, Sophia. In fact, you might be more alive than you've ever been."

"But how?" I asked with my mouth full. "I don't understand."

"You're free from everything that held you back, free from all your duties as a princess and daughter. The rules of the living world no longer constrain you. Everything you understood to be true—about life and death, and the nature of time, and the known and the unknown—is but half the story. There is so much more to uncover! There are a thousand worlds, and there are places *between* these worlds. Sophia, there is a Beyond. There is life after life—"

My mother's words were cut off by a thundering crash. The cottage door swung open and a cold wind came rushing in, sputtering the fire and extinguishing the rushes. I saw dark, looming shapes at the threshold—the glint of firelight on metal—and then an axe spun through the air, lodging in a wooden chest behind us and shattering it.

CHAPTER 21

My mother leapt up, knocking over her chair. With one hand she drew a knife from her waistband and with another she shoved me toward a smaller rear door. "Sophia, run!" she screamed. "Run! They want your immortal soul!"

"I won't leave you!" I said, even as she was pushing me, putting her body between me and the intruders.

Her green eyes were incandescent with fear. "Do what your mother says. I command it!"

And so, like a good daughter, I obeyed her. Stumbling, horrified, I flung myself through the back door and hurtled away into the night.

Blindly, I crashed through the underbrush. There was no path. Branches tore at my gown and blade-sharp thorns bloodied my face and hands. I couldn't see where I was going and wouldn't have known which direction to go even if I could. My only thought was to keep running.

Behind me I heard guttural shouts and the metallic clang of long swords being unsheathed. My lungs burned and my breath came in gasps. I was weak with hunger, and I didn't know how long I could keep going.

I crossed a tiny, frigid stream, and then—unable to run anymore—I dropped to the ground and scuttled under the leaning trunk of a dead tree. I held myself motionless as the woods exploded around me. Soldiers were everywhere, bashing through thickets, their swords slicing leaf and vine, searching for their prey.

Me.

I couldn't see their faces, but whether they were men or beasts made no difference—I would not let them catch me. I willed my ragged breathing to slow and edged deeper into hiding. My pursuers came ever closer, slashing their way through the forest, their footsteps shaking the ground. I hugged my knees and shut my eyes, making myself as small as possible.

They crashed past me, vanishing in the thick trees.

Their shouts faded, and the night grew quiet again. The air was knife-cold and still.

I waited for a long time, until the pain in my cramped legs grew too great. Holding my breath, I shifted ever so slightly in my hiding spot. A twig snapped.

I froze.

I waited, breathless, as the darkness pressed against me like something malevolent and alive.

Silence, still, except for the faint call of an owl somewhere off in the distance. I knew I was safe.

But then a rough hand slammed over my mouth. My arms were yanked brutally behind my back as a soldier dragged me backward through the forest.

I tried to bite my captor's hand, but my teeth couldn't pierce his calloused skin. Whoever or whatever he was, he only grunted as he heaved me, twisting and kicking, through the brush and fallen leaves.

I was pulled out of the woods, away from my mother's cottage and into the middle of another road, where a black carriage pulled by four wild-eyed horses stood waiting. My captor lifted me into the air, and though I struggled and writhed in his grip, I was no match for him. He threw me onto the floor like I was a sack of laundry. The door slammed shut, a whip cracked, and we charged forward.

I clawed my way up to the seat and tried to look out the window. It was small and covered with iron bars—as if I were in a traveling prison cell. As I screamed and pounded on the walls, the horses raced deeper into the forest, and the trees arching over me seemed animate with menace.

When we finally burst into the open, we galloped across a field of dead grasses, and then the ground rose up before us and we began to climb.

The road grew rocky and so steep it seemed as if it ended in the sky itself. I didn't know how the horses could keep their pace, but somehow they did. Soon we were high in black, barren mountains. There was nothing to see but rock and ice—it was a world so inhospitable that nothing could live here but a howling wind so cold it burned my lungs to breathe.

I sank to the floor of the carriage, knowing that I could never find my way back. Fear made my breath come in quick, sharp pants. But worse than the fear was my grief. After longing for each other for almost two decades, my mother and I had met for mere moments. I hadn't even told her of my father, hadn't asked if he might be in this other world, too. I understood nothing but this: being torn away from her now was almost worse than never having seen her at all.

CHAPTER 22

It must have been hours later that I woke from a disturbed half sleep. I peered out the carriage window and saw that it was early morning, and we were traveling over a wide, misty plain. Through the haze I could see hundreds of tiny fires floating high above the ground.

What kind of magic was this? My breath formed white clouds in front of my face, and I shook with cold. A moth-eaten fur lay on the bench beside me, and I wrapped it tight around my shoulders. It smelled musty and rank, but it provided some protection against the chill.

As the carriage pressed onward, the fog bank parted, and I realized that the suspended fires were in fact torches, set at regular intervals along the top of a looming stone wall.

With half-frozen fingers, I tried to open the carriage door again—first by pushing it, and then by kicking it as hard as I could. But it was locked from the outside and impervious to the blows of my feet. There was nothing I could do but watch and wait.

As we approached a massive iron-barred gate in the wall, it heaved open with a shriek of metal. The horses clattered through the opening, and then the gate slammed down behind us.

I pressed my face to the window's bars, half expecting to see a great prison yard. But instead we were inside a walled village. It was much larger than the village near Bandon Castle, and it seemed much older, too. The houses on its outskirts were grand and imposing, but they looked long abandoned. Towering chimneys listed sideways, holes gaped in limestone walls, and dying ivy covered abandoned doorways. Even the wind seemed lonely. Haunted.

Soon we came upon inhabited dwellings, though, and the horses began to slow. Smoke curled up from kitchen fires, and a flock of chickens, frightened by our approach, took to the air, squawking and flapping their white wings.

"Hello," I called out. "Hello? Can someone tell me where this is?"

No one answered. But I kept on calling, my voice cracking with desperation. "Please, someone, answer. Someone please tell me what's happening to me!"

Then I smelled roasting meat, and my stomach—empty but for a few bites of bread—twisted in agony. All thoughts vanished except for these: Who was cooking something so delicious, and how could I immediately get some of it for myself? I still wore my pearl earrings, and I would have happily traded them for the humblest warm meal.

As if to answer my question, an aproned figure carrying a large ladle stepped into the doorway of a nearby cottage. I gasped in horror.

The thing was not human.

CHAPTER 23

It—she?—had the height and the soft roundness of Jeanette, but there the resemblance stopped. Her long, thin hair was a sickly orange hue, and her skin was leathery and golden. Instead of a nose, she had two nostril holes, like those of a snake. Her eyes were a cold, iridescent violet.

The horses slowed still more, as if to give me a better look at this monstrosity. The beast snatched up a chicken that had been pecking about the yard. Then, holding the poor flapping thing by its throat, she glanced up at me. A hideous grin split her face. Her teeth were yellow and as sharp as daggers. Smiling, she snapped the chicken's neck with a quick, deliberate motion. A few downy feathers sifted to the ground.

I covered my mouth so as not to cry out. The whip cracked, and the horses trotted on.

We came to the village square, which was ringed by small white buildings with moldering thatched roofs. It was market day, and the square was full of shoppers, vendors, and stalls. My mouth fell open in wonder. From alleys and lanes streamed hundreds of creatures, the likes of which I'd never imagined. Under a multicolored tent, a one-eyed, blue-skinned crone sold baskets of huge orange eggs. A bearded butcher with a lizard's tail stood beneath hanging slabs of flesh, which slowly dripped blood into the dust. I saw something that looked like a giant bee, a wolf with a hawk's face, and a monster with fat pink flesh and hideous black wings: part human, part vulture, and part pig.

As the heavy carriage rumbled past, each creature turned toward it and stared, their hideous faces full of hate. Was this venom directed at me? I was a stranger and had done them no harm. Surely this was a nightmare!

I pinched the skin on my forearm, but I did not wake up. Nothing changed.

Except that then, out of the corner of my eye, I caught a glimpse of a figure walking along the road. He had a human face. A *familiar* one.

My breath caught in my throat, and I pressed my face against the bars covering the carriage window. I saw dark hair—a proud gait—

Could it be? A cart pulled by some kind of horned donkey stopped in front of the figure, blocking my view. I craned my neck. Long limbs, a defiant jawline . . . no, it couldn't be. The last time I'd seen him, he'd been deep in the bowels of Bandon Castle, sick, imprisoned, and waiting for death.

My fingers curled around the bars. "Raphael! Raphael, is that you?" His back was to me now. "It's Sophia, your Queen! I'm trapped! Help me, please!"

But the boy thrust his shoulders back and walked on.

I sank back into my seat. I'd imagined him, hadn't I? It couldn't have been Raphael. Surely he was a corpse by now, and Gattis would be preparing the pyre on which to burn his plague-marked flesh. It was ludicrous to think that he could be here.

And yet *I* was here. I'd had the Seep, too.

If this was life after life—if I had died and somehow arrived in this village of monsters—then might he be facing a similar fate?

The carriage shook as a huge, wormlike creature passed by too close, trailing a stench of rotting meat, and my stomach twisted in revulsion. I kicked at the carriage door until my heels were bruised. I stopped then, but not because of the pain: I stopped because I realized that I was likely safer inside my cage than out, amidst a teeming crowd of beasts.

Up ahead a gate loomed; we were coming to the far edge of the nightmare town. I closed my eyes and prayed.

I prayed that I wasn't actually dead. That this whole world was nothing but a fever dream. That any moment now I would open my eyes to the walls of my own bedroom, my body covered with the Seep's blisters. A little more time, a little more pain, and my heart would finally stop. There would be nothing, forever more. And that would be a relief.

CHAPTER 24

When I opened my eyes again, we were back on an open plain. The driver shouted and the horses picked up their pace.

I pulled the ratty fur closer around my shoulders and huddled in the corner of the carriage. It didn't matter what I'd prayed—I knew this wasn't a dream. I wondered how many miles I'd traveled since I first awoke to the mournful tolling of the Bells of Death.

Since I saw my mother.

Maybe dying didn't mean heaven, or obliviousness, or anything I'd ever imagined. Maybe death meant spending eternity on a journey I couldn't understand, a journey for which there would be no rest and no arrival.

I was kicking futilely at the carriage door again when one of the horses let out a high, bright whinny, and I recognized the sound that our own mounts used to make when they approached

Bandon stables after a long and grueling ride. Whatever lay ahead, the carriage horse recognized it.

Once again, I strained to peer out the tiny window. I saw low gray hills to my left, a barren salt marsh to my right. In the distance, a castle rose from swirls of mist, its dark, jagged form piercing the clouds like a cluster of knives. Its myriad towers, rising high over looming battlements, glittered as if made of obsidian, and flags the color of dried blood hung limp in the dead, salt-smelling air.

I prayed it was not our destination, though I knew with dread that it was.

Then came a shattering crash from above. The carriage shook, and once again I was thrown to the floor. A shrieking, bird-like cry, unlike anything I'd ever heard before, pierced my eardrums. I scrambled up to see what had hit us. A large shadow passed over the dusty ground, and I saw some kind of giant feathered creature, its wings black like a vulture's but three times larger, swing into the sky, bank, and then swoop back down, deadly talons extended. As it neared the carriage, I gasped. It was not a bird at all. It was a harpy, like the ones in my book, with a hag's face and a madwoman's scream.

"Treasure, treasure," she shrilled from the sky, "soft flesh and warm blood!"

Her green hair streamed out behind her as she swooped past. Two others joined her, and they circled above the carriage, all crying out. "Treasure, treasure!" and "Break open the egg!"

The carriage roof shuddered and cracked as one of them landed on top of it. The harpy began to claw at the wood, and dust and splinters rained down on my hair. All the while, the others urged her on.

"Yes, sister! Break it open and let us feast! I smell tender flesh and salty blood!"

I screamed and hit the carriage ceiling with my fists, but a harpy doesn't startle like a robin. The carriage had begun to swerve under her attack, and I shouted for the drivers to hurry. As always, they ignored me. The horses shied and bucked; the carriage lurched.

CRASH! The harpy had launched itself at the carriage again, and now her sharp, dirty talons had pierced the roof like needles. I cowered on the floor, afraid she'd pluck me up like a worm from the ground.

But then came another bloodcurdling shriek, and I felt the harpy lift off from the roof. Scrambling back up to the window, I saw her burst into the gray sky, howling, an arrow sticking out from her flank and drops of blood falling into the dust like black rain.

"That will teach you manners," yelled a great deep voice, as the harpies wheeled away, their terrible cries fading.

A centaur, not twenty feet from the carriage, dropped his bow and turned toward me.

"My apologies. They are a most unsavory welcoming committee," he said in a voice like thunder. His human torso was thickly muscled, but the body beneath it was that of a stallion. His hooves pawed the ground and his tail slashed the air.

"Who are you? Where am I being taken?" My voice was hoarse with fear, but his was the first friendly face I'd seen since my mother's.

"You'll find out soon enough, girl," he said, and then he galloped away, his hooves kicking up clouds of dust.

The carriage started up again, and we continued on our way toward the castle, rising out of its rocky promontory.

Let the carriage roll on forever, I thought, *never mind the threat of the harpies.* I didn't want to know who lived in that dark place.

We slowed as we approached. I saw no way in: no bridge, no gate, and no footpath up the sheer cliffs. But as we drew nearer, I could see, against the black of the rocks, an even deeper blackness. It was the mouth of a cave, a hundred feet tall and arched like a cathedral.

As I held my breath in horror, hundreds of misshapen, mongrel creatures streamed out of that black opening. They wore servants' livery—tunics of black wool with a small silver scythe embroidered at the shoulder—and they swarmed the carriage, tugging on its door. The sounds coming from their mouths were not like any language I'd ever heard—a cacophony of grunts and hisses and clicks.

A creature with a human body and a bat's head succeeded in wrenching open the door, and I cowered in the far corner of the cursed carriage. But dozens of paws and hands and hooves were grabbing at me, pulling me out of the carriage and into the cold, briny air.

"Don't touch me! Leave me alone!" I shrieked, but they merely muttered and growled in response as they tugged at my arms, urging me toward the mouth of the cave.

Struggle though I might, I was forced into the cave. Darkness surrounded me, as close and as horrifying as all these teeming beasts, and just as palpable. As I felt the press of claws on my cheek, I wondered if I was about to die again.

CHAPTER 25

B ut then the claws fell away, and there was nothing but cold blackness. Everywhere around me, creatures whispered and churned, seething like rats on a refuse heap and prodding me deeper into the cave. I was too afraid to scream.

Then, suddenly, the beasts stopped in a tight cluster, their stinking flesh pressed against me. I felt something slithery on my shoulder and I jerked away, colliding with cold, slimy skin. I gasped and righted myself.

The floor beneath us shuddered and heaved. I heard the creaking of great chains. And then we all began to rise.

The platform we were on creaked up slowly, lurching, like a giant tray hoisted by a huge, drunken servant. A scuffle broke out near me, and I heard a bellow of panic, and a moment later, the sound of a body landing on hard stone. I held myself as still as possible, praying I was not near the platform's edge.

Still, we were lifted in utter darkness. I heard the screams of at least two more falling beasts.

As we rose, the air grew less dank. And then we came up, through the floor, into the biggest hall I'd ever seen. Candles glowed all around, their light nearly blinding after the darkness of the cave. As I blinked, eyes watering, I saw long, empty tables, tapestries depicting gruesome battles, and a jewel-encrusted throne at the far end of the hall.

"What is this place?" I whispered.

The beast nearest me offered a sort of growl and flicked its brow, as if I should have known the answer.

We did not stop but kept on rising, hauled upward to the high ceiling and then past it. Finally the platform ground to a halt in a long, dark castle hallway, and a wave of beasts pushed me forward onto solid ground. To my left was a large, elaborately decorated door, its facade carved with roses whose blooms were larger than my head and whose sharp wooden thorns dwarfed my parrying dagger. I felt grotesque paws pushing me toward it.

Then the beasts parted as a woman—thank God, a *human!*—approached. Her face, once pretty, was tired and careworn. She pushed the rose door open and motioned for me to enter. Eager to escape the monstrous servants, I did.

Inside was a grand, luxurious bedroom. A blazing fireplace revealed a vast bed overlaid with velvet and furs, an ornately carved chair upholstered in purple brocade, and rich woven rugs covering the gleaming ebony floor. It was a chamber worthy of a queen. "Where am I?" I gasped.

"Please, make yourself comfortable," the woman said.

I was surprised by her voice, which was soft and lilting as a girl's. She took my arm and gently but insistently pulled me toward the warmth of the fire.

"Where am I?" I asked again. "Why have I been brought here? Who are you?"

"My name is Florence," she said, ignoring the first two questions. "Please, sit. Rest. You must be tired from your journey."

Though I was so exhausted I could barely stand, I was also too agitated to rest. In one corner of the room, I saw a bouquet of fragrant, bloodred flowers, and in another I spied a small desk, stocked with parchment and quills. Nearby stood a harp, its gilded curves gleaming in the firelight. I almost laughed out loud: I could not escape that awful instrument, even in death!

But then—treasure! On a table near the window I found soup, a goblet of ale, and a crusty loaf of bread, still warm from the oven.

I almost fainted at the smell. I reached a trembling hand toward it, afraid that it was some kind of mirage.

But no—it was real, and I fell upon it like a starving beggar. I was so engrossed that I did not notice Florence leaving the room. And I did not realize, until too late, that the door had been locked from the outside.

CHAPTER 26

I pounded on the carved wood until my hands were bruised and bloody. I screamed until my throat felt raw. It didn't matter. No one heard me. Or at least, no one came.

Later, after I had collapsed on the floor in exhaustion, I heard soft, shuffling footsteps in the hallway. They came to a stop outside my room.

"Open the door," I said to whomever was out there. *"Please."*

"Hush, child. You must rest," said a voice I recognized as Florence's.

I put my mouth to the thin crack between the wall and the door. "Where am I? Why am I here? Am I a prisoner?" I asked.

I heard her sigh heavily. And then I heard the click of her heels as she walked away.

I pushed myself up from the floor and began to pace the perimeter of the room. I stopped by one of the high, narrow windows and peered out. The sight was dizzying: black sky all around, and below me, sheer cliffs that fell away to a churning bay. Icy mists swirled around rocks jutting up from the water like teeth.

Another window on the room's opposite side looked down on a torch-lit castle wall walk, a path along the rampart between my turret and the next. What I saw there was more frightening than the frigid waters: a dozen creatures, each more horrifying than the next, streamed across it as if it were a market road.

Even worse, I recognized them.

There was the Inkanyamba, a brownish, serpent-like thing with small, useless wings and a heavy, horse-like head, and the Impundulu, a black-and-white bird, as big as a man, who was said to drink blood like water. Behind them came a small swarm of silvery, furred flying spiders. All these creatures I knew from my book of mythical monsters.

How could this be?

I ducked back inside the room, my mind spinning in confusion. Every moment seemed to bring some new, fresh terror— but never any clue as to where I was, or why I'd been brought here.

I walked over to the little desk. Writing was such a familiar habit—maybe I could get down a scrap of a song, a shred of a prayer, and maybe it would somehow calm me. I had just picked up the quill and gone to dip it into the ink when a flash of movement caught my eye.

I turned and saw another beast, there in the room with me! A cat-eyed, bruise-colored monster with two curving, pearlescent horns coming out of its head. I shrieked and backed up, knocking over my chair. The beast backed away, too, its own mouth open in horror.

I looked again at the creature: its sharp, silvery teeth, its glowing golden eyes. It wore a dress of blue satin. I took a step toward it now; it did the same. I held my breath and reached my hand out to it.

I touched the cold, smooth surface of a mirror.

CHAPTER 27

My mind seemed to extinguish itself. But an instant later, when I came to my senses again, I knew the truth but could not explain it. By some demoniac, mysterious bewitchment, I was no longer a princess.

I was a monster.

They are, for want of a better word, beasts. Never, ever forget that, my father had said of the villagers. What would he say if he could see me, now that it seemed that I was *literally* a beast?

Outside, gulls screamed as if crying out in shrill grief, and the ocean waves rumbled, as ominous as thunder.

I held on to the wall to steady myself, willing my pounding heart to slow. If possible, I wanted it to cease altogether. If this was what my mother called life after life, I didn't want any part of it. Locked in a great stone room, a monster surrounded by other monsters, the hostage of some unknown, malevolent lord—surely true death would be preferable.

I was certain that I was going mad.

I took up the quill again and wrote.

> *My name is Sophia, and I am seventeen years*
> *old. I have been kidnapped, brought to a fortress*
> *at the edge of a world I do not understand, and*
> *locked inside without explanation. I have no*
> *knowledge of what happened to my castle, to my*
> *village. Find Jeanette deCoeur, find Odo*
> *Fttum, and tell them I need them urgently.*

I let the pen drop to the hard floor. Who did I think would transport this note? A shrieking gull? One of the flying spiders? And how would anyone know where to look for me? I didn't know how to explain where I was. *Take yourself to the very brink of death, and there you will find a carriage pulled by stinking trolls. Ask them to drive off a cliff, and then they'll bring you to me . . .*

Anyone who found a note like that would think its writer unhinged. I might as well throw the words into the fire and ask the smoke to carry them away.

I crept to the mirror again. Though I was afraid of what I'd see, I peeked into it, one eye open—

A repulsive beast glared out at me.

Jumping back, I upset the remains of my dinner, ruining it. I ran to the door and called for Florence, and when she didn't come, I sank down to the floor and put my face in my hands.

What did this mean? Why was this happening? And would it ever end? These questions—which I obviously couldn't answer—were a torment.

After a while, I roused myself, pinched my cheeks, and went to look in the mirror.

Still: that horrible creature gazing out at me, teeth bared in a frightened grin.

This went on all through the night. I didn't sleep, and though I kept checking the mirror, I did not change back into myself. By the time the sun rose, pale and sickly, starved of warmth and light, I felt like I had always been here in this room, always been a captive, always been a monster.

CHAPTER 28

The sound of the lock being unlatched roused me from an exhausted stupor, and I was up and stumbling toward the door before my eyes had even focused. I couldn't stay in this room one more instant! But if I had expected to slip past Florence, or barrel over some short, furred beast into freedom, I was wrong.

I ran straight into the muscled torso of an eight-foot-tall chambermaid. With giant, seven-fingered hands, she firmly picked me up and set me back in the center of the room.

Florence clucked her tongue at me from the hall. "My dear, it isn't ladylike to run."

I laughed bitterly. Apparently I couldn't escape *that* bit of critique in this world, either. As Florence picked up her skirts and swept into the room, I assailed her with questions.

"What's happened to me? Why do I look like this? Am I

bewitched? Are you? You look human—but perhaps you're a monster, too. Was *she* once human?" I gestured toward the seven-fingered giant.

Once again, Florence ignored me, busying herself rummaging through the great wardrobe. The giant chambermaid shoved me—not exactly impolitely—toward the fire as a third attendant pushed in a giant wooden tub set upon wheels and already full of fragrant, steaming water.

Florence turned, saw my surprise, and smiled proudly. "Yes, a traveling bathtub! Our lord is very innovative."

"Who is he?" I asked. "Did he turn me into this?"

Florence swept her hand toward the tub. "Go on," she said. "You'll find it quite luxurious, I imagine."

I didn't want to accept any hospitality from my captor, whoever he was. But on the other hand—I was filthy.

"Don't stand there staring, child," Florence said. "You must bathe, dress, and go to breakfast in the Great Hall."

My legs nearly gave out beneath me. That sentence was so familiar! Hadn't Jeanette spoken a version of it every single morning after prodding me out of bed? Oh, how I missed her! I longed for Odo, too, and all my ladies in waiting, and my poor murdered father most of all.

And what of my mother? Seventeen years after her death, I had seen her, I had touched her, and it was the most wonderful moment of my…

My *whatever it was*. Life, death, heaven, or hell—I had no idea. I felt tears coming, and I fiercely wiped them away.

I was afraid I'd never see her again.

But Florence was growing impatient. She reached for the bodice of my gown, and I thought she was going to unbutton it.

But instead she pulled a knife from her waist and quickly raised it toward my neck.

I stumbled back and flung up my hands. "What are you—"

The giant chambermaid caught my shoulders and held me still as Florence, clucking her tongue in remonstrance, slit the front of my dress open with a knife. "There's no saving that old thing," she said brusquely, as it fell to the floor at my feet. She picked it up and tossed it into the fire.

And there I was. Naked. Monstrous. And yet I was supposed to bathe and be dressed like the princess I had once been.

"Go on and get in," Florence said, backing away. "I can smell you from across the room."

And so I sunk my wretched body into the bath. The water was briny but perfumed with the essences of orange and lime. I quickly turned it a muddy brown. Florence looked at me disapprovingly but made no further comment as my hair floated around me like seaweed.

The last time people tended to me in my bath, I'd been telling them that everything would be all right. That Bandon Castle was impenetrable and could withstand any attack. How wrong I had been! It had taken just one man to enter our castle and kill my father. I wanted desperately to know what had happened. Had Ares come? Were Elodie and Adelie safe? And what of little Faye, the chambermaid? Did our castle stand? Had our enemies breached its walls or laid siege from the meadow below?

I sank all the way under the water, wanting to wash away the scenes that haunted me—Sacheverell's ghastly face, my father's blood, the way the stranger's knife had nicked my own neck. I wished, instead, that I could see how things were now, both in the village and inside the castle walls.

Would they be worse than when I'd left?

There was simply no way to know. I stayed underwater until my lungs burned.

Florence finally pulled me up by my hair. "You won't drown yourself on my watch, Princess."

The giant chambermaid glared at me and I lowered my gaze and began to wash myself as best I could. Then Florence snapped her fingers, and a girl who seemed perfectly human except that she had no mouth came forward with linen undergarments she'd warmed by the fire. I stifled a gasp of horror as she blinked dumbly at me.

"Velvet for you today, I think," Florence said, more to herself than to me. "You still may not be clean enough for silk. Plus, I've not seen your manners, and judging by the state of you, they are not very refined. That is your dinner spilled on the carpet, yes? So let's find something dark. Something that won't show stains."

As I rose from the bath and slipped the linen over my mottled skin, the giant attendant held out a velvet gown, its violet color so deep it was almost black. It fit as if it had been made for me. Then she handed me a necklace of wrought silver, set with a stone I'd never seen before; it was pale and seemed to change with the light, sometimes pink, sometimes blue, sometimes flickering as though containing a tiny flame. It was beautiful, I thought as I fastened the clasp silently, but I would not relish wearing it. It lay close about my throat like a collar. Then came a cape lined with white rabbit fur and a thick bracelet of pearls.

"Mind that's still on your wrist later tonight," Florence said. "I'll not have it lost or . . . *borrowed*."

I shook the wrist it encircled; it was heavy. "Just because your master is a kidnapper doesn't make me a thief," I said quietly.

Florence looked at me out of the corner of her eye, but said nothing.

"Who is your master?" I asked. "Why did he bring me here against my will? When will he let me go?"

Florence turned her face to the window, where the cold, gray sea swelled below. "You'll know soon enough, I expect," she said.

CHAPTER 29

I'd begun moving toward the door, but I suddenly stopped. I realized that the thought of leaving the room terrified me. Freedom meant... *showing* myself. Revealing to the lord— whoever he was—the beast I'd somehow become.

"I don't want to be seen like this!" I said, pressing myself against the wall.

Florence frowned. "Like what? Don't you like your dress? It fits you perfectly."

I pointed to my cat's eyes, my little horns, my fingernails like claws. "Do you not see what's wrong?"

Florence calmly looked me over, head to toe, and then shrugged. "I have seen princesses more graceful," she said, "as well as more careful with their food. But you look perfectly fine. You no longer smell, which is nice, and the velvet suits you. Perhaps some vermilion for your cheeks, though, as you look a bit sickly..."

"But Florence, I need to know—"

"Begging your pardon," she said firmly, "but stop talking this instant and follow me to the Great Hall."

I wasn't used to being spoken to like this, and I opened my mouth to protest. But the giant chambermaid quickly stepped to my side, signaling quite clearly that she was ready to pick me up and carry me should I fail to make haste and follow Florence.

I shrunk under her look, and she, perceiving my new obedience, turned away from me. There was a lump under her dress that looked suspiciously like a thick, heavy tail.

Florence led me out of the bedchamber and down the vast stone hallway. A bear-like beast carrying an armload of laundry passed by, bowing obsequiously as it did. Pages—most of them human boys, but some far wilder, stranger creatures—scuttled here and there on errands for their knights.

Whoever owned this castle must have scores of noblemen under his command, and great riches, too, to feed so many, and to live in a keep ten times larger than my own.

Not that it was altogether luxurious. A cold, salty wind whistled through loopholes and narrow windows; beneath its briny tang was the scent of rancid oil and horse manure. Spiderwebs hung like ghostly lace from the ceiling.

Florence hurried me along, though my shoes pinched my feet. A maid trimming candlewicks in a hallway stopped to stare as we approached.

"Is she the one?" the maid whispered.

Florence silenced her with a look.

Was the maid referring to me? Was I the one *what*? But Florence would not tell me the answers if I asked—I'd learned that quickly enough.

We wound down a series of spiraling staircases and passed

through a dizzying maze of dim hallways until Florence finally
stopped in front of two huge iron doors. A pair of armored wolf-
men hauled these open as we approached. The way the iron
screeched against the polished rock floor sounded like a woman
crying out in pain.

"Go on," Florence whispered, nudging me in the small of my
back. "Inside."

I took a deep breath and entered. The room was even larger
than the one I'd seen the night I arrived. It was windowless, but
lit with thousands upon thousands of candles, and the air was
thick with smoke.

I could immediately tell who commanded the room. My captor
stood in the center with his back to the door. He looked human
from what I could see, though large and powerfully built. I had
expected a king's robes, but instead he wore armor of tooled
leather, studded with brass knobs. His glittering longsword lay
unsheathed on a table near him. A curved knife hung from his belt.

I knew, suddenly, that I did not want to see his face.

Stay there, I thought. *Don't turn around. Just stay.*

I reached for Florence's arm. "He seems occupied," I whispered. "I will come back—"

The man's shoulders tensed. His hands curled into fists at his
sides and then released. Slowly, silently, he rotated toward me. I
saw his forehead, high and cruel; his hair, a tight cap of black
curls; his cheekbones as sharp as blades; and his eyes, the clear
blue-white of ice.

His lips twisted into a sneer as he spoke. "I am Ares," he said.

My knees buckled.

My father's greatest enemy...and the cruelest of men. My
captor.

CHAPTER 30

I clung tight to Florence, who grimaced but did not try to shake me off. "This can't be happening," I whispered.

"Ares is the lord of this domain," Florence said out of the side of her mouth, "as well as your host. Stand up straight."

"You are surprised?" he asked me. He sounded almost... *amused*.

"This cannot be," I said, louder now. "You are—I don't understand—I refuse to—"

"Come, come," Florence urged, leading me to a heavy carved chair to the right of Ares's throne.

I felt as if all the air had been sucked from the room. There was no way to breathe. Standing before me, a goblet of wine in his hand, was the man who had vowed to destroy my castle, my family, and my entire kingdom.

And perhaps he already had.

I swayed on my feet. Was I dead, but Ares alive? Did he exist in two worlds at once? Would this nightmare ever stop getting worse?

"Sit, Sophia," Florence said, as if I were a dog.

Ignoring her, I stared at my captor, hoping in vain that his stony features would offer up some answers. Ares held my gaze, his own look so triumphant and cold that I shivered as if I stood in snow. Finally I could look no longer. My eyes fell to the long, oaken table before me, the surface of which had been scarred by knives and stained with wine. Or blood. Though the table could have accommodated fifty men, there were only two place settings: one for me, and one for my enemy.

"I thought we might enjoy a fine meal together," he said. "As proof of my hospitality, fair princess."

"I am queen." I tried to put iron in my voice, but I heard it falter at the last word. I did not want to be queen—I wanted my father to be alive and for this nightmare to be over.

Ares smirked. "What is your pleasure, Princess?" he asked.

I shook my head, my mind still reeling. Out of the corner of my eye, I saw Florence backing away. I tried to grab her sleeve. "Don't leave me," I pleaded.

But she curtsied, turned, and hurried out of the hall.

Ares hardly gave her a look. "Well?" he asked me.

I gripped the back of the chair for strength and steeled my will. I would not give into him, I promised myself. I would fight back if I could—even if it was just with words. "There is no pleasure for me here," I said quietly.

"Oh, don't be so quick to judge," Ares said. "I'm sure you'll find my keep very hospitable."

"If you are to show me hospitality, then let me go," I said, my voice stronger now. "Set me *free* from this hellish place, in whatever world this is. Send me back to my home, so that I may look after my people."

Ares pressed his hand against his heart and smiled. "You are the most charming creature when distressed," he said. "Your cheeks grow so pink! And indeed, you may ask me for many things. But that, my dear, is not one of them. I cannot let you go back to your charming little castle by the River Lathe. I have brought you here for a very special reason, which we will shortly discuss. In the meantime, have a seat."

I hesitated.

"Now."

His tone warned me that I should not disobey. So I sank down to the chair—but not before I swept my place setting to the floor, where it landed in a heap on the rushes. A childish act, I knew. But wasn't I as powerless as a little girl?

Ares looked on with chilly amusement. "I see your father didn't teach you basic civilities."

I stiffened. "Don't speak of my father," I said.

Ares shrugged, unperturbed. "Another time, then. He was an interesting man, wasn't he? A warrior king who suddenly set down his swords, all for a silly girl. Did you know it would doom him, Princess?"

The words hit me like stones. So he knew it, too: my girlish wish had killed my father. And if Bandon fell, that fault was mine. I bowed my head. What could I say to him? We both understood my guilt.

Ares stepped close to where I sat, bringing with him the chill smell of snow. "So you don't want to talk, my pretty guest? I was hoping for a pleasant chat to learn more about you. But if you will not cooperate, there are others to entertain me."

He rang a huge brass bell, and the great iron doors shrieked open again. An army of knights poured in, shedding battle armor as they came and throwing their weapons down to the floor.

"Of course, they are not as pleasant to look at as you are," Ares said.

My mind reeled as I watched them advance.

I knew them—every single one.

CHAPTER 31

elcome, friends!" Ares cried. He turned back to
me, and his voice grew confidential. "That's a term
I use loosely, of course. When one consorts with
monsters and murderers, the bonds of friendship are weaker than
a thread of spider's silk."

I couldn't speak, so overwhelmed was I by whom and what I
saw. And I couldn't say who produced the bigger shock—Ares,
or these fictitious monsters.

"I do hope you'll begin to develop and nurture the art of
conversation while you're my guest, Sophia," Ares said. "Otherwise you will not earn your keep. Now, shall I make the intro-
ductions? Everyone is very eager to meet you."

He pointed first to a giant: a man nine feet tall at least, with
hulking shoulders, a brutal slab of a face, and a massive closed
eye in the middle of his forehead. "That's Balor—we call him

the Smiter—and you'd better hope he keeps that eye shut, or else we'll all burn like twigs."

Balor bowed solemnly at me. He looked just as if he'd stepped from the pages of my book of monsters.

"And next, meet Hasshaku Sama, whose pastime is kidnapping children. We don't know what she does with them, but I expect it's unpleasant."

A pale, willowy woman, dressed all in white and almost as tall as Balor, glanced disinterestedly in my direction. "The girl is too old for my taste," she hissed. Her voice was like wind over dead grass.

"Then, of course, we have Seth, god of violence, Mordred the Traitor, and El Cuchillo, whose hands sprout knife blades upon his command. Have you met him before? He seems to like you."

Seth's jackal head inclined in my direction as his forked tail lashed. Shifty-eyed Mordred ignored me completely—but at least he looked human. So did El Cuchillo, who tossed his cape to the floor and blew me a lewd kiss.

I looked away—I didn't want to see any more of them. I knew all of them from *Myths: Demons and Monsters*. I knew their histories, their secrets, their deceits. But I had never imagined that I would see them in the flesh.

Is this what life after life would be for me? Kept like a pet in a castle full of villains?

"Pay attention now, Sophia," Ares said, snapping his fingers. "Why are you shivering? No one's going to bite you...not today, anyway. And we're not done meeting everyone. The Ekhidna's outside—we don't let her in; she's not housebroken— but here is two-headed Hesia. Make sure to say hello to both of her faces, or else one will get jealous, and that never ends well. And here's the demon Zozo—don't worry, I won't let him sit next to you."

Zozo, whose eyes were pools of blackness in his ghastly white face, slid into the corner of the room, silent and malevolent.

"And of course we have Reiper."

When I turned toward him, a terrible chill passed through me. Though in appearance, Reiper was no different than any other man, I could feel a pulsing, inhuman evil emanating from him, filling the air like a stench. He was handsome—beautiful, almost—with chiseled cheekbones and a cruel, sensual mouth. He bowed low, his body rippling with hard muscle.

Ares clapped his hands sharply. "Now that we are all introduced, let the servants bring us meat!"

The knights cheered as a hunched lizard in a bloody apron skittered forward from the shadows. In his arms he held a wriggling young pig, which he held out to Ares.

Ares produced a knife, the gleaming tip of which he pointed toward me. "Ready, Sophia?" he asked. And then, in a movement so quick I didn't even have time to cry out, he plunged the knife into the animal's stomach. He hoisted the poor thing, squealing in agony, high into the air.

"I don't know how much you know about cooking," he said. "Probably nothing at all, since you are a princess and not a scullery maid. So let me enlighten you. The best way to keep meat fresh, my dear, is to keep it alive until you want to eat it."

CHAPTER 32

res swung his arm down and thrust the stuck pig into the licking flames of the fireplace. Its piercing squeals grew even more excruciating. I tried to cover my ears, but Ares shook his head at me.

"In this castle we do not hide from suffering, girl," he said darkly. "We embrace it."

His terrible knights were deaf to the animal's screams. They found their seats and drained their wine goblets as if they'd not seen a drop of liquid for weeks.

I was crying now, hot tears streaming down my face.

"She weeps over a pig!" Ares exclaimed to his knights. "When her own villagers squirmed on their deathbeds like maggots in dung—oh, the irony is rich indeed. Did you cry for your people, Princess, or were you busy having your cheeks powdered and your hair plaited? Were you writing a pretty song? Were you trying and failing to play the harp?"

Furiously, I wiped my tears on my sleeve. The pig's squeals were growing weaker.

"Anyway," Ares said to me, his voice almost gentle now, "the fellow in the fire won't be ready until dinner. By then you'll be over your sadness and you can slice right into him. He'll be delicious."

"I'll do no such thing," I said.

"Oh, delight, our guest speaks again."

I hunched my shoulders and turned away. I would neither eat nor speak on his command.

"Here—have a sweet," Ares said. "What, you won't take it? That is a strategy that works only on children." He laughed. "Of course, you're practically still a child yourself, which is a large part of your rather limited appeal. The older queens get, the more ornery they become. By twenty they are good for little but target practice."

I shivered, and someone—or something—draped a fur coverlet around my shoulders. Pride told me to shake it off, but I was too cold.

More beastly waiters shuffled in, bearing great golden platters of meat. The knights stabbed the giant slabs of flesh with their daggers, bringing bloody hunks straight to their mouths without even bothering to make a stop at their plates.

"And he talks to me about my manners," I muttered, watching Seth gnawing on gristle like a dog and grease rolling down Balor's chin.

"What's that, my blue-eyed captive?" Ares said. "Speak up."

But of course I would not.

"You are an unwilling enchantress, I see that. Well, you will come to like us yet," Ares said. "Or else..."

I spoke through clenched teeth. "I would rather be starving in Bandon's dungeon than fed in your finest hall."

Ares sighed and turned to his army of monsters. "Would anyone else care to try their conversational luck with this she-cat? She is not pleasing to me at the moment."

"Come sit beside me, pretty thing," called El Cuchillo. "I promise you, I am very charming."

Hasshaku Sama whispered, in her voice of dry leaves, "Tell us a story, Princess."

Zozo gazed at me with eyes as black as space and beckoned me toward him with a long, skeletal finger.

Mordred's eyes glittered. "You are fairer than an angel. Perhaps you sing like one. Come sit on my lap and sing me a song."

Through force of will, I had managed to stop shivering. I drew the cloak closer around me and remained silent. I would not go to anyone.

Then Balor rose, stalked over to my side of the table, and placed a bowl full of brandy in front of me. "A game, then, Princess," he said. "Look into the bowl. Do you see the gold coin?"

Because he was nine feet tall, with fists bigger than my own head, I thought it wise to answer him. "Yes," I said. A fat gold coin, embossed with a raven's claw, shimmered brightly at the bottom of the bowl.

"Good." Then he opened his great eye, just one hair's breadth, and the brandy burst into flames.

"That's a nice trick he does," Ares said, "always entertaining." But Balor ignored him.

"The rules of the game are only this," the giant said. "If you can reach through the fire to take the gold, then it will be yours to keep."

I felt the flame's heat warming my cheeks.

Beside me, Mordred cackled and held up a hideously scarred hand. "I won an emerald ring this way. It was painful."

I held my breath. The flames licked and danced and the coin glittered. The pig had finally gone silent.

With a sudden swipe of my arm, I sent the whole thing flying into the hearth, where it exploded in a ball of white-hot flame.

Ares sucked in his breath. He narrowed his icy eyes at me. "I grow tired of the way you throw things, Princess," he said. "I will have to train you in matters of gratitude and decorum."

"No," said a deeper voice. "I will."

CHAPTER 33

I turned to see Reiper, who had risen from the table. His handsome face was unmoving, as if it had been cut from living stone. "I will take her as my wife," he announced. "Under my tutelage, she will learn what she must."

His *what?*

I looked wildly around the table. What was Reiper talking about? Ares laughed low in his throat, but his knights—even Balor—ate and drank as if my life had not just been claimed by one who had no right to it.

"I will nev—" I began.

My voice faltered when Zozo came out of the corner, drifting toward the table like a shadow carried on the wind, his eyes black and hollow. He pointed to me and rasped out but one word: "Mine."

Ares's laugh became a cruel bark. "That's the first sound I've heard from those ghastly lips in decades. Zozo the Nightmare is even worse at conversation than you are, Princess."

"Not that conversation matters much in a fight," Mordred whispered to me, trying to slip an arm around my shoulders.

I pushed him away as I looked from Reiper to Zozo in horror and confusion. Would they really fight — now, right here in the hall? The knights suddenly looked expectant, almost cheerful, like spectators at joust.

And for a moment, the whole hall was still. The only sounds were the crackling of the fire — the hiss of dripping fat from that poor piglet — and the wind, crying outside the walls like something begging to come in.

Reiper drew his sword and pointed it at Zozo. The demon seemed to flicker and grow fainter for a moment, but then he drew his own weapon: a morning star, with a six-foot wooden haft and a spiked iron head.

Reiper moved. He swung his sword so quickly that I saw nothing but a flash of shining steel. Zozo darted sideways and the sword tip hit the wall with a ringing clang. The demon swung his morning star at Reiper and caught the fabric of his cloak, ripping it open. A faint trickle of blood bloomed on Reiper's shoulder.

Reiper struck again; Zozo slid away, then countered with a fist to his combatant's cheek, splitting it open. Reiper let out a growl of pain and shook his head in fury. Blood spattered Hasshaku Sama's arm and she furtively licked it off. Reiper stepped backward, as if retreating, but then suddenly he lunged toward Zozo, bringing his sword from behind him and swinging it upward.

Zozo's left hand went flying into the air.

By reflex, Zozo looked down at his bloody stump, and in that moment Reiper advanced again.

He thrust his sword so deep into Zozo's stomach that half its length came out on the demon's other side. Zozo dropped his morning star and gripped the sword hilt with his one remaining hand, straining horribly, without any sound, to pull the sword out.

"That's not going to work," Ares said. "Poor Zozo."

Zozo stood, wavering, swaying a little. Slowly, he turned toward me, and my heart thudded in my chest. "Mine," he gasped, and then he fell down dead.

Reiper returned to his seat and took up his goblet.

I turned to Ares in shock. "Your knight killed his comrade!" I said. "Do you do nothing?"

"As I already explained, Sophia, we use words like 'friend' and 'comrade' very loosely in this kingdom," Ares replied.

"I agree with you, pretty thing," Mordred whispered. "A murder such as that one is bad table manners. But don't you find it exciting?"

"Stop speaking to me," I hissed.

Reiper raised his goblet to me in a toast as his eyes bored into mine. "I killed him in your honor, Princess."

"And anyway, what is a feast without bloodshed?" Ares asked. "It would be poor entertainment for a princess if she did not see something lively on her first day with us. Thank you, Reiper, for the show."

Zozo's body still lay on the rushes, his blood staining them black.

Ares spat on the ground near the corpse. "Pig food," he said, as the lizard came to silently bear Zozo's corpse away.

CHAPTER 34

W hy have you brought me here?" I demanded. "What is this world, and what makes you think I belong here among blackguards and beasts? I am not like you! I'm not one of you!" But then I saw my hand—a purplish fist—clenched on the table, and I remembered that I was more like them than I thought.

Still, I was a queen, kept against my will. "You have kidnapped me," I said, "stolen me from—" I stopped. I still didn't know what I'd been taken from: My life? My *death*? And what did it even matter? "I demand to know why I'm here!"

"Oh, pretty thing," Ares said liltingly. "Dear Sophia, dear Princess, dear *Queen*. I will tell you. It is time you were betrothed, isn't it? I expect your father wasn't wild about the idea, but his opinion no longer matters, does it?"

"I don't know what you're talking about."

Ares sighed. "You are here to marry one of my brave knights,

I should think that would be obvious. We can't fight and kill *all* the time. Occasionally we must stop and celebrate beauty. Love. *Lust*." Then he smiled lasciviously. "And we must birth more knights, of course. To replace those who leave us, whether on the battlefield or in the Great Hall." His eyes flicked toward Zozo's empty place. They held not a hint of remorse.

I could hardly comprehend what I was hearing. The same man who sought to destroy my castle also desired to arrange my marriage? "You cannot make me—"

Ares held up a hand. "I can make you do anything I want, Princess. But we won't let it come to that. Bandon Castle needs a ruler on its throne, and having you joined with him will likely spare us from any pesky revolts your farmers may plan otherwise. I prefer my subjects working obediently for me, not wasting my time with ridiculous loyalties. So. You may choose your husband from these fine candidates. I would rather not pick for you, as you seem to have a mind of your own. I regret to acknowledge that Zozo is out of the running. I'm sure you would have had a nice time being silent together, and no doubt he could have taught you table manners as well as anyone. So which of my brave knights will you choose?"

Reiper stood. His cruel, beautiful mouth held the flicker of a smile. "She chooses me. I have won her."

I, too, rose trembling from the table. "You have done no such thing. I may be a captive, but I am not a prize! You cannot win me the way Mordred wins an emerald ring."

"You may feel that way now," Ares said. "But everything can be won, whether it is a ring, a kingdom, or a *girl*."

"I choose to leave this cursed place," I said. "*That* is my choice!"

Ares put his hand on my shoulder, and my skin felt as if it were being burned with a cold, raw flame. "What's so fascinating is that for all your faults, you are growing on me. I hardly know why!" He turned to his men. "Maybe Sophia should be my ninth queen. It is so unfortunate, what happened to the others. Perhaps, though, she would have better luck than her predecessors?" His fingers tightened their grasp. "For a little while, anyway."

The knights—all but Reiper, that is—laughed and shouted their approval.

But Ares turned back to me. "No," he said, "your teary blue eyes would soon bore me. So—the choice is yours, Sophia. You have until the new moon to make it."

"No!" My voice echoed against the stones, and I shook off Ares's hand and started running. I raced toward the far end of the hall and flung myself against the huge iron doors. To my shock, they swung open, and I stumbled, collapsing with a gasp onto the flagstones in the corridor.

CHAPTER 35

lorence sat waiting on the other side of the great iron
doors—as if she'd expected me to burst through them.
She gave me her hand, helped me stand up, and briskly
brushed the dust from my skirts.

"Did you have a nice meal?" she asked as she led me through
gloomy, labyrinthine halls back to my bedchamber.

I stared at her. "How could you even ask such a question? I
watched a man die, and Ares tells me I must marry one of those
monsters."

Florence sighed, and when she spoke her voice held a note of
reproach. "There's nothing to be done about that, but you should
have at least filled your stomach." She reached into the pocket of
her apron and gave me the heel of a piece of bread. "Here," she
said. "I won't have you starving to death on my watch."

Numbly, I ate it. It was dry and stale and tasted like dust.

After what must have been a mile of hallways, we arrived

back at my bedchamber. I immediately removed my jeweled satin slippers and rubbed my pinched feet.

"I need a pair of boots," I said.

Florence looked startled. "Whatever for?"

"I wish to go outside," I said.

"Ares has strictly forbidden that you leave the castle," she said.

"I'm sure he has," I said. "And yet he calls me a guest." I opened the doors to the great wooden wardrobe and combed through its contents, finding nothing but satin gowns, embroidered cloaks, and opulent, fur- and jewel-trimmed tunics. "Am I a guest? Or a prisoner?"

I knew she wouldn't answer me, but I didn't need her to—I knew the truth.

She laid a calming hand on my arm. "Child," she began.

"Do not call me a child!"

She sighed, and when she spoke again her voice was full of regret. "I don't want to lock you in this room again, Sophia, but I will if I must."

I pulled my head out of the wardrobe and turned to face her. I was several inches taller than she was, and I also knew that I was stronger.

"You will not," I said quietly. "I have no way of returning to my home and Ares knows it. I will go outside and *you will not stop me.*"

Florence shrank back ever so slightly. "It's dangerous outside," she said urgently. "Storms may come without warning. Half-wild creatures roam the cliffs. There isn't even anywhere for you to go, unless you fancy a swim in an ice-cold bay—"

"I will leave the castle," I said. "And I will go to the village."

And maybe, just maybe, I'll find Raphael.

Florence fell silent. I peered into the wardrobe again, seeking something warm, something woolen. I pulled out dress after beautiful dress and tossed them to the floor.

The dark-eyed attendant who had been making my bed gasped. She picked up a velvet cloak and clutched it to her breast.

"Do you like it?" I asked. "Take it—it's yours. But give me your dress and your boots."

She looked at me as if I'd gone mad. And who was to say that I hadn't? Maybe I had lost my human mind when I lost my human shape. Maybe I was now more beast than girl. Well, so be it.

Her eyes never leaving my face, the maid began to disrobe, taking off her humble shift as carefully as if it were made of cloth-of-gold.

I shook off my velvet gown and flung it onto the bed. "Take that one, too," I said as I slipped her dress over my head. "I never want to see it again."

Florence no longer tried to stop me, though she made sure to collect the jewels I removed, tucking them away in a fold of her apron. Then she sank down to the stool beside the dreadful harp and watched me, fear in her eyes. And I saw a flicker of something else, too. It was sorrow, I thought, or maybe...guilt.

Had she waited on other prisoners, in other grand rooms? Had she kept them locked up tight? Maybe she had served Ares's eight queens. And maybe, somehow, she had played a role in their demises.

Dressed in a servant's rags, a princess no more, I stood before Florence. When I touched the strings of the harp with my small, sharp claws, she grabbed my wrist and held it tight.

"If you don't come back, he'll kill me," she said.

I felt myself softening. I didn't want another death on my conscience. And what I'd told her was true—there was no road home to Bandon.

"I'll come back," I promised. Adding, in my mind, *this time.*

CHAPTER 36

After I offered her a few other bits of finery, the dark-eyed attendant agreed to show me a secret way out of the castle. I followed her through servants' passages so narrow and dark they seemed more like tombs than hallways, at every turn stopping to listen for Ares's guards. By the time we emerged in a small courtyard, where a two-headed bear-man was polishing swords, I was dirty and frightened and disoriented. I looked up to the square of gray sky visible above the castle walls. The sun was so pale and cold it looked like the moon.

The girl gave me a quick shove. "Go through the postern there," she said, pulling the cloak I'd given her tighter around her shoulders, "and you'll see the path down to the village. Hurry."

I darted out and slipped between the rusting bars of the small back gate—and then just as quickly, flung myself back against them. I was now balanced, just barely, on a tiny, craggy outcropping in the middle of a sheer wall of stone. One wrong step, and I'd plummet into the gray, frigid waters of the bay. Was the servant hoping I would die?

But then I turned around, still clinging to the bars, and I saw them: tiny, serpentine stairs, carved into the vertical face of the cliff itself. Heights terrified me, but I couldn't turn back now that I was so close to being free. And so, ever so slowly, I picked my way down the crumbling steps, as rocks slipped from underneath my boots and went spinning into the bay.

The going was torturous, vertiginous; I had to remind myself to breathe. My hands — my ugly, lavender hands — were scraped and bloody by the time I leapt the final feet down, to land on a marshy plain near the water's edge.

And where to now? I almost laughed. What did it matter? I was alone, I had not plummeted to my death, and, for a moment, I was free. The wind whipped my hair around my head and my warm woolen skirt flapped like a flag. I turned away from the water and began to walk.

I passed underneath stunted trees, then hurried through tall, waving grasses, hoping that my escape had gone unnoticed. I'd begun to breathe easier when I felt a sudden sharp rush of wind. An instant later, a ridge of grass next to me burst into flames.

I whirled around. Crouching not twenty feet away was a tatzelwurm. It looked exactly as it had in the pages of my beloved book, except that it was infinitely more terrifying. Its giant cat's head was a dark, tawny yellow, its body scaled like a snake's. Flames licked around its lips and fangs, and, as I watched in shock, another ball of fire burst forth from its throat, missing me by a hand's breadth.

I flattened myself against the grass, but a spark flew up and landed upon the sleeve of my dress, burning it through and singeing my skin. "Stop it!" I demanded without thinking.

The tatzelwurm roared, and then it blinked at me with a dim, wordless apprehension. Absurdly, it reminded me of my own cat, Cotton—a thousand times larger and more threatening, but with the same look of worry when it knew it did something wrong. *The beast is not cruel,* my book had said, *merely wild.*

"There's nothing to be afraid of," I said, uncertain if I was talking to myself or to the fire-mouthed monster. I took a step toward it. It watched, still and wary, as I approached. Flames crackled at my back, and the salt wind blew smoke around us in swirls.

When I drew close enough, I reached out my trembling hand and touched the tatzelwurm's fur. It was bristly, rough, and warm. The creature held itself motionless—not even its huge eye blinked. I could feel it, tense and waiting, as I began to stroke its cheek.

"No one has ever been nice to you, have they?" I whispered, as my fingers brushed its dusty face. "They're not particularly friendly to me, either," I added, "if it makes you feel any better."

Smoke billowed from the tatzelwurm's nostrils. I knew that if it wanted to, it could char me like that poor pig. But somehow, I felt that it wouldn't.

"You're just a big cat," I said soothingly, "aren't you? Yes, I know, there's something a little odd going on with your back half, but look at me—I've got horns instead of plaits, and claws where I used to have fingernails. Nobody's perfect, isn't that right?"

Still my hand moved gently along its great cheek. I felt, first, a vibration beneath my palm. Then came a thrumming, rumbling sound.

The tatzelwurm was *purring*.

There on the barren salt marsh, I pressed my forehead against its fur. I felt its awful loneliness, and I understood it completely.

"I would love a pet," I told it. "But you're too large for the castle. And anyway, I won't be staying. I'm not going to let Ares keep me here—somehow I'm going to find my mother again." I leaned against the tatzelwurm's side and felt the deep vibrato of its purr in my bones.

But then, suddenly, came shrieking voices I recognized.

"Prey, pretty prey!" called the biggest harpy. Her smaller sisters cackled, echoing her. "Pretty, pretty, let us eat!" They circled above us, diving low, spiraling up on salty gusts of wind and then swooping down again.

Frightened, I pressed myself closer to the tatzelwurm. I cursed myself for not listening to Florence—I should have stayed safe in my castle prison!

"The egg is out of its shell," shrieked the green-haired one, and her sisters squawked, "Feast, feast, pretty feast."

"Don't leave me," I whispered to the tatzelwurm. "Please."

As if it understood, the tatzelwurm coiled its tail around me. It bared its teeth, lifting its heavy head, and the harpies raked its scalp with their claws. It roared, sooty smoke pouring from its mouth.

"Feast, prey, eat!" the harpies cried, plunging toward us.

I screamed and ducked. Bellowing in rage, the tatzelwurm sent a huge blast of fire skyward. The harpies spun higher, dodging it, their huge wings beating like drums. One of them dove down again, claws extended, then swooped up as her sister dove.

Summoning my courage, I picked up a rock and flung it, but it merely grazed the tips of her feathers.

The tatzelwurm's tail tightened around me, knocking against my legs and sending me sprawling. As a harpy plunged toward me, I scrambled forward on hands and knees, then dove underneath the tatzelwurm's belly. As I lay on the ground, panting with fear, I realized it had knocked me to the ground on purpose. I was safest *here*.

Still roaring, the tatzelwurm shot another fireball into the air, and then another, as the harpies continued their attack. I was sure it would run out of fire or give up, leaving me to be torn to shreds by their beaks and claws. But then the tatzelwurm launched a huge orb of flames skyward, and this one found its mark, engulfing the biggest harpy and holding her in the air inside a red-hot cage. I watched in horror as she burned, blackened, and plunged to the ground.

Her sisters flew screaming into the distance, and the dragon resumed its purring.

CHAPTER 37

I crawled out from beneath the tatzelwurm and planted a grateful kiss on its rough, furred cheek. "That was my second death of the day, but I cannot entirely be sorry for it."

The creature blinked and uncoiled its tail, freeing me.

"Goodbye, my wild friend, and thank you," I said.

The tatzelwurm settled down onto its front paws, as if to wait for me to return, and I found the path again and began to walk.

The land soon became so featureless and barren it looked like the white face of the moon. But, in the distance, I could see the walled village shimmering in and out of the mist.

Suddenly, I was nearly overcome by sadness. I thought of our own little village, which I'd visited every week. I wished there were any way to know how it fared, now that neither my father nor I was there to protect it. Did the families have enough food? Did funeral pyres burn? Did Fina still live?

I fretted for miles, but eventually the slow monotony of the walk calmed my thoughts. As the ceaseless wind whistled its high, lonely notes, I began to hum along. And after another little while, I started to sing—a song that seemed plucked from the wind itself.

> *Above a cruel and fallow land*
> *A dire castle looms.*
> *I try but cannot understand*
> *Why monsters haunt its rooms.*
> *Some dread spell its master speaks*
> *To make such beasts as these:*
> *Maids with tails and wolves with beaks,*
> *Purring dragons, mammoth bees . . .*
> *Ares named me the honored guest*
> *At his splendid, deadly feast,*
> *But I am a prisoner, I protest—*
> *And worse, I am a beast.*

By the time I reached the walled village, my throat was parched and my boots were gray with dust. The gate stood open, and the two troll-like creatures guarding it hardly glanced at me as I passed through.

At the nearest inhabited cottage, I smoothed my hair and stepped into the barren yard. "Hello?" I called out. "Please—I beg your pardon—may I have some water?"

There was no answer.

I tried not to recall how in my old life, I had wanted for nothing at all. Anything I desired was brought to me, almost before I even had to ask for it. The accusation Raphael had flung at me— what stung more than the manure—was true: I'd never known hunger or thirst or deprivation of any kind. And such luck that had been, back in my old, entitled life, when I did not even know enough to appreciate it.

A loud crash came from inside the cottage, and a hulking man peered out of the doorway. I gasped at the sight of him. He had eyeballs, dozens of them, circling his brow like a crown, and when he saw me the expression in each turned to loathing.

He spun on his heel and went back inside. I turned to leave. But before I'd gone two steps he reappeared with a pewter mug of water, which he thrust at me as if it were a weapon.

I took it carefully, gratefully, from his hands. "Thank you," I said.

He bowed low, but I could see his shoulders shaking with rage.

I drained the cup and hurried away. Why did he hate me and yet bow down before me? Did he know me? Who did he think I was?

As I followed the rutted road toward the heart of the village, a gray, six-legged fox began to follow close on my heels. And everyone who watched me pass by, whether they were beast or human, looked at me with that now-familiar blend of deference and abhorrence.

In the village square, several dozen sheep grazed, and I was comforted to see that they were perfectly average sheep, white with black legs and faces. An old man juggled apples listlessly by a dry fountain. He, too, looked human, though for all I knew his dirty shawl hid the stubs of wings. I was very hungry but afraid to ask him—or anyone—for food.

The fox darted forward and began worrying the sheep, and a voice called from somewhere, "Call off your animal!"

I turned around and saw a woman with a pinched, rodent-like face shaking her fist at me.

"He's not mine — I've never seen him before!" I said.

The woman's eyes went dark. "Forgive me, I did not know who you were."

"What do you mean?" I asked. "Who do you think I am?"

She didn't answer, but she bowed low, just as the many-eyed man had. And then I saw her spit quickly into the dust.

I could not imagine who she thought I was, or why she seemed to hate me, too. I might have asked her, but then I saw something that made me catch my breath.

Not another terrifying beast. But Raphael, for certain this time.

Human.

Beautiful.

Alive.

CHAPTER 38

Part of me was still convinced that this could not be real—that it was somehow a dream inside a nightmare. But hadn't I seen him here last night, during that mad carriage ride to Ares's castle? And Raphael seemed so substantial now, striding across the far side of the square with an armload of sticks.

And unlike me, he looked exactly like himself. He hadn't sprouted wings or horns or turned a strange color of blue. Nor did I see the shine of fever sweat on his brow or the blisters of the Seep on his hands. How had we both ended up here—and why was he unscathed?

I ran giddily across the grass, the six-legged fox nipping at my heels, and I pulled up short before him, breathless. I pushed the hair from my face. Would he recognize me? Or would he turn away in horror?

"I know you," I said urgently. "Do you remember me?"

He looked me up and down, saying nothing, his dark eyes unreadable.

"This isn't a dream. Am I dead? We're both dead. Are the two of us in hell? Or is it possible that this is a hallucination? Is it life after life? Are we ghosts? Help me understand." My words tumbled over one another. "Your name is Raphael, I know it. You're proud of your name, you told me so!"

He slowly shook his head at me, still without saying a word.

"Can you explain this...place to me? You said maybe we'd meet again in a different world. Is that where we are? Please, tell me what you know!"

Raphael shifted his burden of sticks to the other arm. "What I know is that firewood is heavy, and I don't get paid to stand still holding it."

"You don't recognize me," I whispered, and a feeling of desolation swept over me. Of course we'd only met twice before — and my own father had thrown him into the dungeon — but somehow I thought he might be glad to see me.

We can keep each other company while we wait for death, he'd said.

But now he just shrugged.

"Tell me what you see when you look at me," I begged.

One of Raphael's sticks dropped, and the little fox snatched it up and ran away with it in his teeth. "Come back, you dumb mutt!" he called, and the fox seemed to grin at him before vanishing down an alley. Raphael sighed and looked at me again, his brow slightly furrowed. "You're a princess — anyone can see that. Doesn't matter the rags, they don't fool anyone. You're pretty in a princess sort of way. Is that what you want to hear?"

"But I think—"

"Everyone knows that princesses don't think," he interrupted.

"Their heads are full of airy nothings, and they like music and embroidery. Oh, and they believe themselves to be better than the rest of us."

Raphael's words made me flinch. He was wrong about what I liked — but maybe not about what I had once believed.

I took a step closer to him. "So I don't look like a beast to you?"

Raphael shook his head and began to walk away.

"Do you mean I look human? When I look in the mirror, I see a monster! And I don't think I'm better than you, Raphael. When I last saw you, we were dying of the same thing."

He turned around. "Then why are you still living in a castle, being waited on hand and foot? While those in the village can barely eat?"

"I don't know. I'm a prisoner here!"

"You look pretty free to me," he said as he began to walk away again.

It was true that I wasn't behind bars in some rank dungeon, but I was undoubtedly trapped. As he turned a corner, I cried, "Raphael, stop! You must come back. Raphael!"

He ignored me, but the monstrous villagers stared at me with contempt. I felt my voice die in my throat. My commands meant nothing here.

Don't go, I thought. *Please don't leave me alone.*

But of course that was exactly what he did.

CHAPTER 39

Standing there, bereft, I could feel the cold, glaring eyes of the villagers on my neck. Hadn't Raphael defied me before, in my old life? Perhaps I should have expected it now, in this new and terrible one. At least he hadn't thrown horse manure at me again.

"Go back to the castle, Princess," someone shouted, "or else we'll all suffer the wrath of the tyrant Ares."

I spun around to see who had spoken, but no one would meet my gaze. So they feared my jailor as much as I did. "I'm not on his side," I said. "He had me *kidnapped*."

"Leave!" someone else called.

And so I turned to go. I didn't want Florence's death—or their suffering—on my conscience.

The wind was with me on the way back, making my journey quicker if not more pleasant. I looked in the marsh for the gentle tatzelwurm, but he was nowhere to be seen. Instead, waiting for me at the bottom of the narrow stone steps, was a man without a head.

I froze, every muscle in my body taut with terror. I knew this monster, too. But no painting in my book of gods and beasts could have prepared me for the Blemmye in the flesh. His shoulders were broad and bare; his chest was a great big wedge of chiseled muscle; and a man's ugly face leered at me from the center of it.

The Blemmye took a step toward me and I leapt back. He stopped his advance and bowed. "Welcome back, Princess," he said. "I've been waiting for you."

"I'm sorry to hear it," I said, trying to keep the tremor from my voice. "I do not seek company."

"Is that so?" He moved a little toward me again. "But what if company seeks you?"

"If you touch me, I'll scream," I said.

The mouth in his chest offered me a false smile as his bloodshot eyes cast about the empty plain. "But there's no one to hear you."

Again I looked for the tatzelwurm. Why hadn't I given it a name? Then I could call it to my side! It could protect me from this monster as it had protected me from the harpies. And where was the centaur? He had saved me from them, too. But today he was nowhere to be seen.

"Let's take a walk," the Blemmye said. His arm shot out, and he'd grabbed my wrist before I could react. "It's a fine day to stroll along the water with a beautiful girl."

His grip was so strong I knew I could not shake him loose. I managed to smile back at him. "All right," I said. "The more I think of it, the more it sounds like a fine idea. I could use a stroll."

He looked surprised by this response. I supposed it was unlikely that many girls, whether human or beast, would go anywhere with him willingly.

"What are you waiting for?" I asked brightly. "Come on. Let us walk."

We took a few steps toward the water's edge. A seagull floated, screeching, above us. "Do you live in the castle," I said, "or are you a visitor? I didn't see you in the Great Hall—"

And then I stumbled forward in the sand, crying out as I fell. The monster's hand on my wrist tightened. "My ankle!" I gasped.

He let go of me as I clutched my boot, moaning. He dropped down to his knees, his horrible chest-face full of concern. "Are you—" he began.

The instant he was down, I sprang to my feet and began running. I couldn't believe my trick had worked. But perhaps I shouldn't expect a monster with a brain squashed somewhere between his lungs and his stomach to be a paragon of intelligence.

I reached the tiny cliff stairs and began to scramble up them. Roaring, furious, the Blemmye followed me. I knew that he was faster, and I knew he would catch up to me. I hoped to be ready.

I clambered upward, using my hands and my claws as much as my feet, feeling loose rocks sliding away and ricocheting off the jagged cliff. The trail turned sharply up ahead. In that moment, when the steps doubled back across the vertical rock face, the Blemmye would be able to reach up and grab me.

When I came to the switchback, rather than speed up, I slowed, as if hesitating. I clutched the rock with all my strength. The Blemmye grinned his terrible, squashed grin. When his hand reached for my ankle, I kicked it away as hard as I could.

His arm flew backward, and this was just enough to unbalance him. He wavered on the tiny step. His hands grasped madly at the air, and then, roaring still, he fell.

I didn't wait to see him land on the rocks below. I scurried up and up, panting with triumph and fatigue, and then I slipped through the narrow gate into the castle courtyard.

And here, someone else was waiting for me.

CHAPTER 40

O r perhaps I should say some*thing*. In a narrow patch of dim, silvery sunlight, just before the castle stables, crouched a Sphinx.

Its great eyes were closed, but it knew I was there. I could hear its breathing, calm and heavy. Patient. Inquisitive.

It's not as big as I'd imagined it would be, I thought—and then that thought struck me with its absurdity. Had I ever, thumbing through my old beloved book, *really* imagined what size a Sphinx would be? No—because a Sphinx didn't exist.

Except, of course, that it did.

The Sphinx had shared a page with the Bennu, and I looked up, halfway expecting to see a huge, blue, heron-like creature gazing down at me from the castle wall. But it was just the two of us here: serene Sphinx and panting beast.

The magnificent thing opened one eye. "Good afternoon,

Princess." Its voice was a low rumble, the sound of some ancient, primordial thunder.

And I didn't know why I did it, but I curtsied! Did I think that politeness would earn me passage? I had no idea how a Sphinx preferred to kill a girl, and I did not intend to find out. I began to inch away.

The creature laughed. "Surely you know the rules," it said.

I swallowed. "No."

But this was a lie—of course I knew. I'd read them in my book.

"You cannot deceive me, and you cannot pass me unless I allow it," the Sphinx said. "Come, answer me a riddle. If you answer correctly, you are free. If you do not, well...it's best not to discuss it."

"You will eat me," I said.

The Sphinx nodded. "That I will, and I'll enjoy it thoroughly. Are you ready?"

What choice did I have? "I am ready," I said. It was another lie.

"I cannot speak, yet all understand me. I swallow, goldbright, the breath from a king's bosom. When I am alone, I am silent. When I am kissed, I sing. Who am I?" It settled back and looked at me expectantly, neutrally.

I exhaled quickly and with relief. "That's easy," I said. "You are a battle horn." My father had taught me that riddle when I was small. I felt a pang of grief, thinking of him. What world was *he* in now? Wherever he was, I hoped he was free.

The creature looked only mildly surprised. "You did smell clever," it allowed. "Let us try another riddle, then. I am featherlight, yet it takes four to move me. My path twists and loops, yet it always runs straight. Though I tell you great secrets, I have no mouth."

I had to think about this for a moment.

"You also smell delicious, in case you wondered," the Sphinx added, licking its lips. "Tender. Delectable."

My mind raced—a path that turned and yet was straight? And then, like a gift, the answer came to me. "You are a quill! Four fingers to hold you. The letters curve, but the written lines are straight. The words are your secrets."

The Sphinx sighed. "A pity you guessed it, as I am hungry. There is one more, less a riddle than a question. Who, dear girl, killed your father?" It stared at me now. Waiting. A thin rope of saliva dangled from the corner of its beastly mouth.

"*Reiper.*" The name came without thought, and I realized what I was saying only as it came out of my mouth. How did I know? I didn't, I couldn't—and yet at the same time I was certain of it.

Was it in a book I read? How did I know? I had to pay attention. I had to remember everything; I had to learn what mattered.

It all still felt like a dream. So why couldn't I wake up?

The Sphinx moved its great paw out of my way. "Ox for dinner again, I suppose," it said glumly.

So I was right.

CHAPTER 41

Florence greeted me at my bedchamber door with obvious relief.

"Yes, I'm back," I said, unable to keep the bitterness from my voice. "And no," I added, "I would not have you killed on my account."

She smiled a little then. What low expectations for kindness she must have! She was *grateful* that I hadn't wanted to be the death of her.

I sank down on the stool and glared in indignation at the harp. "Meanwhile I was nearly killed myself, by what, three monsters? Four? I've lost count. And everyone in the village looked at me as if I'd eaten their children. Why?"

"You must try to make the best of things, Sophia," she said, ridiculously.

How would that be possible? Did she think I could resign myself to this fate?

"Why do they stare?" I asked her. "Why do they hate me?"

Florence brushed dust from my sleeves. "I will not speak ill of my lord, but..."

"But what?"

"The villagers find his reign a cruel one, and they know you are here as his guest."

I gave an unladylike snort at the word "guest."

"Here, let us remove those rags," Florence said. "I've run a bath for you. You must bathe and dress and do your hair."

"I am tired, and I want to go to bed."

Florence shook her head. "I'm afraid that is impossible. You are to join Ares for dinner."

"I won't."

"You will." Her voice was firm.

One look at her told me that I could not talk her into letting me go to bed the way I'd talked her into letting me leave the castle.

"I will help you, of course," she said. "It has been too long since I have brushed a girl's hair."

I stood up quickly. "Thank you, but I don't need your help," I said, and she silently bowed and left.

I didn't mean to be cruel—only honest. I couldn't bear to be waited on, not the way I once had been by Jeanette and my attendants. Such kindness and attention belonged to a world that had vanished.

A world that was stolen from me.

I removed the servant's dress and hung it carefully in the wardrobe. Then I bathed quickly and dressed with equal speed, selecting the first piece of clothing my fingers touched: a rich, red satin gown with a fitted bosom and flaring, gold-tipped sleeves. I didn't bother looking in the mirror.

The dress fit me perfectly, just as the previous one had, which I found strange. Whose clothes were these, anyway? I wondered if the gowns had been made just for me—or for another, prior princess. If they had been sewn for me, how had Ares known the size of my waist, the length of my legs? And if they had once belonged to someone else, who was she, and what had happened to her?

Though I'd hurried through my ablutions, I was the last to arrive in the hall. Ares and all his hideous knights were already at the table, and already, it seemed, half drunk on honeyed wine served in exquisite golden goblets. They were not wearing armor, but richly embroidered cloaks instead, and rings glittered on many a rough finger.

Ares smiled as I took my seat. "Ah, speak of the *angel*. The surly enchantress from afar returns to our company. We have been discussing you, Sophia. Some of us find you more charming than others, but we can all agree that the castle is much enlivened by your presence, and by the friendly competition it has inspired. Again, using the term *friendly* very loosely. Look, we even dressed up for you." He gestured to Seth, who wore a golden vest, and Hesia, whose two necks were hung with heavy, jeweled chains.

I gave them all a curt nod of acknowledgment—it was the least and most I could do. Then I took an empty seat next to Mordred, who leaned in and whispered, "Hello, beauty," which I ignored.

"And how will you dine this evening?" Ares asked. "Pheasant? Duck? Venison? Perhaps your friend the pig? I do believe we have some of his face left."

"I will have vegetables only," I said.

Mordred shuddered. "Too much vegetable matter harms the guts, Princess. Tomatoes, in particular, are better to look at than to consume."

"Some might say the same of little piglets," I said.

He placed his hand over his heart. "*I* didn't kill it," he said innocently.

"But you are eating it."

He nodded in agreement. "It's hardly the worst thing I've done," he said. He speared a piece of it with his knife. "Would you like to —"

"No."

A stew of boiled potatoes held inside a hollowed-out bowl of bread was set before me. Though I didn't want to eat — I wished to take nothing from Ares — I was so hungry that I couldn't resist. I ate quickly and without relish. The potatoes tasted of dirt and loam, and the broth was as briny as the ocean.

Ares watched me thoughtfully. "I see your manners have not improved since this morning. Was it because you had no mother? I must remember to keep my expectations low." He drained his goblet and held it out for a lizard servant to refill. "In any case, you will not race off as you did earlier. You will remain here, and you will enjoy an intimate meal with your chosen suitor. Remember our agreement? You must pick one of my knights and get to know him." He looked at Hasshaku Sama and Hesia. "Or her, I suppose."

"We had no agreement," I said, "and a choice between these monsters is no choice at all."

"Be that as it may," Ares said, "*make* it." His voice was like a blade of ice.

I looked around the table in fear and desperation. Whom should I pick? Who was the best of the worst?

The only one of the knights who was not staring at me was El Cuchillo. He was carefully slicing his meat with the knives that had sprung from the tips of his fingers. If my book was right, he was far from the worst of the lot. They called him the stealer of light, the bladed shadow.

"Him," I said, pointing. "I choose him."

Chapter 42

As soon as I said it, the lizard servant took my soup bowl away, skittering it over to a small table at the far end of the hall. With a pointed look, Ares made it clear that I was to follow the creature. And so, reluctantly, I did, and then I seated myself there on a small dais, ringed by candles and bedecked with roses the color of spoiled wine.

El Cuchillo brought his own plate to the table and sank into the chair across from me. "Do not be afraid of me," he said. "Underneath this fearsome exterior is the heart of a poet."

I looked at him, dressed all in black, an obsidian brooch at his neck. His eyes were deep-set under heavy dark brows.

"A poet, you say? You are dressed in the garb of a hangman," I said.

I was surprised when he laughed.

"Rope is not my weapon of choice, Princess," he replied, as

his gaze traced the low neckline of my gown. No man had ever dared look at me like that so openly.

I leaned forward. "So you admit you are a killer."

"We are all killers here, Sophia! That's why we get along so well."

"You make it sound...so ordinary," I said.

"There is nothing more ordinary than death, Your Highness. It comes to king and serf alike, to dragon and sparrow and gnat." El Cuchillo gazed up at the ceiling thoughtfully for a moment, and then he began to speak again.

> *A princess with hair as black as mine,*
> *With melodious voice and features fine,*
> *I would like to hear her laugh and sing—*

I thrust my face close to his. "Who killed my father, the Warrior King?"

Startled, El Cuchillo looked at me with grudging admiration. "It is rude to interrupt a poet," he scolded me. "But your rhyme and meter were well chosen."

"I am not interested in your poetry," I said. "Who is responsible for the death of King Leonidus?"

I had to know if I was really right.

El Cuchillo exhaled. "It was Reiper," he said. Then he shrugged, as if it didn't matter. "Or maybe it was Zozo. Or could it have been Seth? Possibly it was all of them." He took a long drink from his gilded goblet. "They are all terrible—they have no soul. It wasn't me, I can tell you that much. I am the only one in this dark castle you can trust." He paused and took another sip. "Trust, rust, dust...lust. Yes," he said to himself, "I feel another poem coming."

I laughed, I couldn't help it, and his face twisted in anger.

"You mock me," he seethed.

"I do no such thing," I said. "I admire poems and those who write them well. But I do not choose you. Go back to your leader and tell him this. Tell him I choose to be alone, tonight and every night."

For a moment, El Cuchillo stared at me. Then he rose from the table slowly. I let the breath I had been holding out. Alone, I would finish my humble meal in peace.

But then he flung his arm forward, his fingertips flashing with knives, and he struck at me. By some miracle I moved out of the way—almost. A single blade sliced my cheek and pain flared up, hot and urgent. I fell backward onto the floor, knocking over candles as I did. The rushes quickly ignited. I began to crawl backward like a crab, blood running into my mouth and flames licking my gown as my poet-suitor advanced on me, murder in his eyes.

"You will be alone for all eternity," he whispered.

Terrified, I felt the wall at my back. There was nowhere else to crawl.

He lunged at me. And then he stopped, midair.

Reiper's sword had run him right through, like a pig on a spit.

El Cuchillo's limbs spasmed wildly and then went still.

Reiper tossed his body onto the fire, extinguishing it. "In your honor, Princess," he said, and bowed.

CHAPTER 43

Once again, a knight had died because of me. And this time, I was sorry for it. I could hardly say that I had liked El Cuchillo, but I'd felt a shred of kinship with him. A sliver of respect. He'd loved words and rhyme as I did, hadn't he? He was a killer who wished to be a poet, and I had watched him drown in his own blood. Because I had dared to laugh.

And selfishly, I understood that his death complicated my situation further. Reiper had saved my life, and surely he believed his claim to me had now grown stronger.

These were the thoughts that troubled me as I rose the next morning and dressed in the servant's clothes, which were warmer and sturdier than my own. I was going to the village to find Raphael again, and I'd demand to know where we were, and how we'd gotten here, and if it was possible to ever go home.

Florence was nowhere to be found, and no one seemed to

notice me as I made my way out of the castle. Nor did I have Jeanette to tell me that my hair was messy, or a father to tell me I couldn't consort with beasts. In a way, there was a strange freedom in being Ares's prisoner—just as Raphael had said.

In the dusty courtyard, the Sphinx sunned itself in the pale early light. As I tried to slip past, it sat up and blinked sleepily at me.

"You'll let me go, won't you?" I asked. "I don't need to answer three questions every time I want to leave or return?"

The Sphinx shook its great head in a slow, dignified manner. "No, my small, delicious-smelling girl, you have earned free passage. But for the sake of conversation, do you know what comes each night without being called?"

"Not at the moment," I said. "If you'll excuse me. I hope you have a nice day."

"And you as well," it said gravely.

I picked my way down the twisting cliff to where the tatzelwurm lay curled in the sand. I was glad to see it.

"Hello, you enormous kitten," I said. "If the Sphinx ever asks you the riddle about what comes each night without being called, the answer is 'the stars.'"

The dragon huffed gray smoke and ducked its head so that I could pet its cheek.

"Maybe I should train you to let me ride you," I said teasingly. "It's such a long walk to the village."

The dragon leaned into my touch, a low rumble beginning in its furred throat.

"That would be a grand thing, wouldn't it, to show up at the gates of the beast village with a dragon as my mount! What would the troll guards think of me then?"

But the tatzelwurm didn't answer; it only purred.

"Perhaps I'll call you Leo," I said softly. "Leo for lion—and for my father." I scratched it for another few moments, then kissed it goodbye on its nose and began walking along the dusty track to the village. I didn't see the harpies, the centaur, or any other fantastic creature; I was trailed only by a seagull, circling high in the cold gray sky and calling out in sad, lonely squawks.

When I came to the village gates, the trolls who stood guard ignored me yet again. Hurrying past the decaying, abandoned part of the town, I made my way to the square where I'd last seen Raphael.

I had made up my mind last night: if he did not know me from my past life, then he would know me in this one.

But Raphael was not in the square, and neither were the sheep. The lonely old juggler was the square's sole inhabitant, but he was asleep beneath the empty fountain. Standing there, uncertain of what to do—how would I find Raphael now?—I heard something that made my heart clutch.

Metal ringing against metal. The clash of striking swords. A gruff shout. And then, like a bell, a bright peal of laughter.

Somewhere, not too far away, friends parried their weapons, the way I used to do with Odo.

Without thinking, I ran toward the noise. I turned down an alley and nearly collided with a winged man in a butcher's apron. "Excuse me," I gasped, hurrying past him. Laundry flapped above me and chickens, scratching in the alley dust, fluttered out of my way. An old woman standing in her doorway glared at me and hissed like a cat. Probably she was part feline, with a furry tail hidden under her dirty smock.

The alley grew wider and then opened onto a courtyard.

Neat, whitewashed cottages ringed it, their shutters closed against the chill breeze.

And there he was: Raphael. Shirtless, his brown chest polished with sweat, he wielded a heavy dull sword against a man with a dog's face. Behind him, a mix of men and beasts engaged in practice combat with blunt knives and axes, while in the courtyard corner, four ragged children—boys or girls, I couldn't tell—took turns firing arrows into a target made of straw.

I quickly realized that this was not simply play. Everyone in this courtyard was preparing for battle.

CHAPTER 44

B ut which enemy would they strike against? What kingdom was at stake?

Still unseen, I watched Raphael. He was graceful with
his footwork, skilled with his blade—though I thought Odo
could still teach him a thing or two.

Beside me was a bucket of water, with a cup lying next to it in
the dirt. I picked it up, and before I dipped the cup into the water,
I saw, in its still surface, my reflection: cheeks the color of storm
clouds, tiny pearlescent horns peeking out from my dark hair. No
wonder Raphael didn't know me—or pretended not to.

I filled the cup and walked slowly toward him. Still dodging,
dancing, and thrusting his peasant's weapon, Raphael took no
notice of me. Standing close, I could hear his heavy breathing, the
strain of the fight, the clash of the swords. The opponents were
evenly matched: one light and quick, the other stout and strong.

After a few moments, Raphael turned and saw me. He leaned

his sword against a cottage wall. "What are you doing here?" he asked. His tone was far from welcoming.

I should hardly be surprised by his capacity for insolence, I thought to myself. *It's how we met, after all.*

"I had thought to give you water," I said stiffly. "But never mind." I held out the cup, tipped it, and let the water spill into the dust. "You can get your own."

A smile seemed to flicker at the corners of his mouth. "That I can, if I want it," he said. He reached out and took the cup from my hand, but he didn't move to fill it. He just gazed at me silently. Curiously.

It unnerved me.

So I stood taller, summoning a shred of my old, royal pride. "Why are all of you sparring?" I asked. "Even the little ones?"

"This is our work now," Raphael said. "We have been conscripted."

"By whom?"

"We are Ares's men," he said flatly. "We are training for combat."

I felt my heart begin to pound. Did Ares seek war in this world, too? I thought of Faye, my chambermaid, crying out that she didn't want to die. "With whom does he have such grave quarrel?"

Raphael laughed bitterly. "Everyone," he said.

"But what kingdom? Who is his enemy?"

He looked at me in disbelief. "Does it make any difference who it is? We swing our swords unwillingly. The target hardly matters."

"Of course it matters!" I said. "It matters to *them*—to those you would seek to kill."

Raphael shrugged, his expression dark, as he kicked his foot in the dirt.

Then the dog-faced man spoke up. "We're going to attack a castle some days west of here. It's well defended, they say. An outright fortress, encircled by a moat..." And as he spoke of its size, its defenses, and the way it loomed over a wide river valley, with snow-tipped mountains in the distance, I felt a prickling chill creep up my spine.

I *knew* the gatehouse he described. I had climbed those great towers and imposing battlements; I'd once been safe behind those massive stone walls.

He was speaking of my home.

Under Ares's command, Raphael and the villagers were preparing to attack Bandon Castle.

I couldn't fathom how this could be true. Ares had been on his way to destroy Bandon as I lay in bed, wracked with the burning fever of the Seep. That was days ago now. Surely he had already stormed its gates! Its proud towers must now be piles of rubble.

Unless, by some miracle, the fortress still stood.

Perhaps Odo and his men had repelled Ares's first advance, and now he was mounting his second. Hope bloomed in my chest: Bandon stood! Odo had been victorious.

And yet it seemed impossible.

Or what if the attack had somehow not happened yet? Perhaps I wasn't trapped in a different world, but instead held captive in a different, earlier instant. Maybe, somehow, there was still hope to save my home.

I knew this was a ludicrous thing to wish.

But was it more ludicrous than me—a princess, a queen—turning into a purple-skinned beast? I still didn't even know if I was alive or dead, so what did I know of anything? Who was to say that time was a line instead of a circle? Maybe, like a melody played on a harp, time repeated itself, its refrains echoing forever and ever—

"I don't understand," I said.

Raphael lifted his head. "Well, like I told you, princesses know nothing."

"I'll ask you to stop saying things like that," I said sharply. "It's not as if *you're* any paragon of knowledge. And you might be proud of your name, but you should hardly feel pride about your sword-fighting skills."

Then Raphael surprised me by offering me a true smile. "That's why I'm practicing, Your Highness."

I held out my hands, almost pleadingly. "Do you understand what's going on? What *is* this world we're in?"

His smiled faded. "Again, I might ask you why it matters. Some things are different, but most remain the same."

"But—"

"What of that old life of squalor and shit? Good riddance, that's what I say."

"How did you get here? I must know!"

Raphael stabbed the tip of his sword into the dirt. "I don't know," he said quietly.

Then a familiar, hateful voice rang through the courtyard. "This is not the time to be idle!"

CHAPTER 45

I whirled around to see Reiper striding into the courtyard. He made his way toward Raphael and the dog-faced man, his cruel mouth twisted in a sneer and his fist clenched white around the hilt of his sword. "What is this—tea time? Ares bade you wretches fight."

I ran forward to stand between him and Raphael. "It's my fault," I said. "They were sparring. I interrupted them."

He didn't even glance at me. "Does the wench speak true?" he asked them.

"Yes," said the dog-faced man, bowing and panting nervously. "We were at practice, sir."

"But do not blame her," Raphael began—and then, in an instant, he crumpled to the ground. Reiper had struck him across the face.

I gasped, falling to my knees beside him. Raphael's cheekbone was already turning purple, like my new skin. "That was uncalled for," I said, glaring up at Reiper. "Do you forbid your men to even *speak*?"

Reiper's lip curled. "I do not need the peasant to tell me who I should or should not blame. I asked if you told the truth—if they had been sparring."

"You have no right," I said. I ripped a corner of my dress and pressed it to Raphael's now bleeding cheek.

"You are incorrect there, girl," Reiper said. "He is under my command. His life is mine." He smiled cruelly. "As is yours."

Raphael was shaking his head, clenching his fists, and lifting himself from the ground. He spat into the dirt and took a step toward Reiper. I reached out to stop him—he should not make Reiper angrier. But he shrugged me off and stood, his dark eyes fierce and blood trickling down his face.

"My life is my own," he said, and his voice held the same defiance it had the day I met him. The day he flung manure in my face.

Some people never learn, I thought.

Raphael lifted his sword and swung, and Reiper's blade met his with a clash.

"Stupid boy," Reiper hissed. His blade flashed, and he sliced Raphael's fighting hand. Raphael's sword fell to the ground as he clutched his wounded hand to his chest.

Once again I put myself between them. "Stop," I pleaded. "Spare him."

Reiper lowered his sword. "I will spare him," he said, "but not because you asked."

"Ares must have told you to stop murdering his men," I said.

Reiper ignored this. "Do you see how quickly I defeat my opponents, Sophia? *In your honor,* of course," he said.

"You don't even know what that word means," I said.

His expression was so cold it seemed to turn the sky to ice. I turned away from him, shivering, as the dog-faced man and I tended to Raphael's bleeding hand.

"Don't worry," I told him as I wrapped another piece of my skirt around the cut. "It's just a scratch. Everything's going to be fine."

Raphael laughed bitterly. "Everything? Fine? Lying doesn't become you, Princess."

"Queen," I reminded him.

"Prisoner," he returned. He smiled a little, and then winced in pain as I tightened the makeshift bandage around his hand.

He closed his eyes, and I looked at the dark, handsome planes of his face, his worried brow, his full mouth tense with wounded pride. I wondered how it was that we two had come to be here together, and what it all meant, and if we'd ever be able to leave.

"We'll get out of this," I said softly. "Don't worry."

Raphael kept his eyes closed. "How?"

"We'll kill him," I said. I was surprised how calm I felt about it. How certain.

Raphael opened one eye. "You don't look like a killer."

I shrugged, thinking of the Blemmye and my lack of regret at his death. "I don't look like a queen, either. And yet I am."

Raphael didn't answer, and I rose to go. But he reached out with his bandaged hand and caught my wrist. "I will see you tomorrow," he said. "I hope."

I felt my cheeks flush. "Hope is a good thing," I said.

CHAPTER 46

When I returned to the castle, gaunt, pale-skinned Mordred was waiting outside my bedchamber. A giant, funereal lily dangled loosely from his hand, and its scent filled the corridor with a sickly sweetness.

"You are smiling," he said. "A lily for your thoughts."

Had I been smiling? I'd been thinking of Raphael. But Mordred certainly didn't need to know that. "What do you want?" I asked. "I'm in no mood for company."

He licked his thin lips as he pushed off the wall he'd been leaning against and managed to tuck the flower into my hair, though I stepped back to avoid his touch. "It's not what I want," he said, "it's what Ares wants." He reached out to touch my cheek, and I flinched away from him. He smiled. "Though I suppose I want it, too."

"Stop being vague," I said. "Tell me what you're doing lurking in the hallway."

"We are to spend a little time together," he said.

I shuddered at the thought. "Ares still thinks I'll choose one of you," I said.

Mordred's smile was sly. "He knows you will. Let us talk, Princess. Perhaps you will come to like me."

I plucked the flower from my hair and threw it back at him. "I highly doubt it."

"You must admit, I am better than some," he wheedled.

"Considering the scum you call your friends, that's hardly saying much," I said.

He grabbed my arm and thrust his face close to mine. "I was hoping for a friendly conversation," he said. His fingers were cold and his breath smelled like a tomb. "Or perhaps a kiss."

I yanked myself away. "I'd sooner cut out my tongue," I said.

Mordred's face darkened. "Watch what you say to me, girl."

But I knew from my book that Mordred was greedy and weak, and his only true power was that of deceit. "I'm not afraid of you," I said.

"But perhaps you should be."

"You're a sycophant and a coward," I said. "If you are kind, it is only because you are not strong enough to be cruel. Had you more power, you would be more despicable than any of your fellow knights. You are a worm who longs to be a cobra."

As I spoke, Mordred grew paler and spots of color began to bloom on his cheeks. He raised a hand—he wanted to strike me. But this time I did not flinch, and he lowered his hand on his own.

"You spoiled, insolent *girl,*" he hissed. "Ares made a mistake in taking you. He should've left you to die like the rest."

And then he turned on his heel and stormed away. Die like the rest? What did he mean?

I hadn't even put my hand on the door to my room when a tall white form appeared at the end of the hall. It was Hasshaku Sama, wafting down the corridor like a ghost. "I suppose Ares has sent you as well," I called to her.

She said nothing, only bent her head in acknowledgment.

"But you don't like me," I said. "I'm too old for you."

Hasshaku Sama's laugh was the hiss of a snake. "You are too old to be eaten, true. But as a companion you may show more promise."

"You will not get a chance to find out," I said. "Float away, back to Ares, and tell him I refused you. Tell him I refuse you all."

Hasshaku Sama inhaled slowly. "I will," she said, "but not because I obey you. I go because I can sense that I will not enjoy your company." She looked me up and down. "You look like a charwoman," she said.

"And you look like a piece of muslin hung to dry on a line," I answered.

Hasshaku Sama seemed to shimmer and vibrate with rage. "I will not tolerate this insolence!"

"By all means, don't. Leave me," I shouted, and then I pushed my door open, stalked into the room, and slammed it closed behind me.

I went to the fire and prodded it with the iron poker. It flared up, bright and crackling. I put my head in my hands. I was tired and drained; I craved the oblivion of sleep. I could not stand these monsters, and I could not stop thinking about the fate of my beloved kingdom.

Cold and exhausted, I kicked off my boots, turned to my bed, and gasped.

Reiper lay sprawled across my pillows.

CHAPTER 47

H ello again," he said. He leisurely gathered himself into a
sitting position, a demon with the face of a god.

I could feel the blood drain from my cheeks. My
pulse beat hard in my throat. I pressed myself against the wall. I
was afraid if I opened my mouth, I would scream.

Reiper took note of my reaction, and the tiniest hint of a
smile flickered on his terrible, perfect face. "This is a cold welcome for a suitor."

I struggled to control my voice. "Who let you in?"

His smile inched wider. "Silly, beautiful girl," he said, so quietly it was almost a whisper. "I do not need to be let in anywhere. I think you of all people should know that."

That vile, soft voice.

I thought back to that awful night at Bandon Castle, when
the air was thick with fear and panic. I remembered my father's

men running madly through the hallways, shouting in terror, desperately trying to prevent a horror that had already happened.

I saw my father's lifeblood spilling onto the floor.

I put my hand on the smooth curves of the harp. Somehow it steadied me. "You were in my castle that night, weren't you?" I asked. "It was you who found me in the hallway. Did Ares attack my people? Does Bandon still stand?"

Reiper said nothing.

My voice was a whisper. "Did you kill my father?"

His eyes, black as depthless space, flicked away toward a narrow window. Moments of tense, cold silence passed, and then he turned to look at me again. His face was utterly emotionless, his eyes unblinking, and I had the sense that I was being somehow evaluated. Judged. He was trying to decide what I knew, and what I deserved to know.

I refused to speak or look away from him.

Eventually Reiper broke his stony gaze. "Has no one told you, Your Highness, that it is better not to ask questions when you will not like the answers?"

"My father did not teach me to honor ignorance," I said, "but rather honesty. Bravery."

"You certainly seem to care a lot about him," Reiper replied. "He was a killer, too, you know."

"He was a warrior, not a murderer," I said.

Reiper rose from the bed and went to stand by the fire. I wished that it would explode from its grate and consume him. But it flickered pleasantly, and its quiet crackling seemed to speak of warmth and comfort.

It was a lie.

"Did you kill my father?"

"I don't know why it matters," Reiper asked. "Does a tree care which axe felled it?"

Chillingly, his words reminded me of Raphael's when I'd asked him whom they were planning to attack. "Stop evading my question. You seek to be my suitor, and so you must give me what I want."

Reiper nodded. "Of course. I know what a princess wants. Gold, priceless gems, perfumes from lands beyond the sun—"

"I want the truth."

He folded his arms across his chest. "Stubborn, aren't you?"

"I have been called worse," I said.

"I am an honest man, and so I will tell you," Reiper said. "Perhaps you should sit down."

"I will not."

"Suit yourself." He began to walk the perimeter of the room. "I can kill with a look, or with a wave of my hand, did you know that? And you've seen for yourself how easily I can slay a speechless demon or a knife-fingered killer with a sword. But I prefer the intimacy of a knife," he said. "I like to feel the blade going into the flesh. Did you know that it makes a sound like tearing? Like threads ripping? Did you know that it feels different to kill a man than it does an animal? Physically, I mean— emotionally there is little difference. As far as I am concerned, a man is but a pig on two legs. But there is more fat on a man, especially a rich, well-fed one. The skin can be tough, but the knife goes through fat like butter."

Reiper stopped and turned to face me. "Oh, the great Warrior King, he begged for his life just like any peasant. He wept. He even spoke your name—as if I would be moved to pity by an orphaned princess! I had brought my sharpest dagger, with a blade so thin and evil it could cut the eye that merely looked at it." He paused. "But for your father, I chose a duller knife."

My pulse quickened. I could almost hear my blood rushing through my veins. "Stop now," I gasped. "I don't want to hear any more."

But Reiper went on. "You asked for the truth, and now you shall have it, Princess. There's no changing your mind when it gets unpleasant. You see, I wanted it to hurt. I wanted it to last. What satisfaction is there in death if it comes too quickly? Murder should be a leisurely process. There's more to savor that way."

He threw another log onto the fire and I — I just stood there, paralyzed with horror.

"And so, Your Highness, I found your father in a midnight hallway, and there in the darkness he pleaded with me to spare his life. As the words poured from his gasping, gluttonous mouth, I slowly plunged the knife in so deep that even the hilt was inside his body. My hand drowned in blood. I could have grabbed his entrails and wound them around my wrist like a rope had I wanted to. Oh, the sounds he made! The agony he knew in those moments...it was one of my best kills."

I couldn't bear it anymore. I covered my ears, but I could still hear his voice.

"The honest murderer is the most dangerous," said Reiper, "for he has no fear, or guilt, or shame. Pride, perhaps, in the savage death he brings. I did take a bit of your father, you know. Here — here is a little slice of his heart. Would you like to hold it? Dried, it makes a fine talisman."

He moved toward me in the flickering half-light.

No, no —

I stumbled backward, throwing up my hands, trying not to see the small, shriveled, brownish thing he held out to me.

"Hello, my beautiful princess," he whispered, just as he had on that horrible night. *"I think I'm in love."*

The room spun around me, and then everything went dark.

PART THREE

CHAPTER 48

I woke in my bed with Florence standing over me, her pale face lined with worry. "I found you in a heap on the floor," she said. "Whatever happened? Are you ill?"

I sat up stiffly. My throat felt parched and my head throbbed. I rubbed my eyes and then looked quickly around the luxurious room, as if Reiper might still be lurking in the shadows. There was no one but me and Florence. But Reiper's presence seemed to linger in the air, poisoning it.

My breath caught at the memory of his vile words.

"How do you stay here?" I sobbed. "How do you serve such monsters?"

Florence handed me a steaming mug of milk, spiced with cinnamon and clove. "You are hardly a monster," she said.

Gasping, I took a sip. It was warm and soothing. "You know full well that's not what I meant."

Florence sat down on the edge of my bed—a liberty Jeanette

would have never taken. "You are so young still," she said gently. "There's much you do not understand."

"I'm seventeen, and my mind is hardly deficient."

Florence smoothed the silk coverlet and then looked up at me. "But you have not yet had to make a terrible bargain," she said quietly. "You have not had to give up one thing in order to keep something else."

"I think I've given up a lot," I said. "My crown, my freedom—"

"But not willingly," Florence said. "And that difference— between what is forcefully taken and what is voluntarily sacrificed—is a great one, my dear."

She stood up quickly and turned her back toward me. It was clear she didn't want to talk about this anymore. I wondered what it was that Florence might have given up. What secret was she keeping?

"Will you go to the village again today?" Florence asked, her tone falsely bright.

I swung my legs over the bed and dug my toes into the fur rug, just as I used to at Bandon. "Yes, of course. If I have to stay here, fending off suitors all day, I'll go mad." *And,* I thought, *Raphael wants me to come back—and there is a matter I must discuss with him.*

Florence smiled. "Mad? Then perhaps you will be more like the rest of us." She handed me another woolen dress, well worn but clean. "I think Lelia, the servant girl, hopes you will keep exchanging garments with her."

"So I will," I said. "I have little use for satin."

Florence paused at the door. "Why, child, were you on the floor?"

I took a deep breath. To say out loud what I had learned—it

made my heart ache all over again. It was as if I could still see the pooling blood, still watch my father's face grow slack and gray in death. "He killed King Leonidus. He killed my father," I finally said.

"Ares?"

"No, Reiper."

Florence nodded almost imperceptibly. She did not look surprised. "I am sorry, my dear. I hope the knowledge..." She seemed at a loss for what to say next. "...brings some peace," she finally said.

"It has done the opposite."

"Ares holds the throne by Reiper's will," Florence warned. "I must beg you. Do not test either of them, for each is worse than the other."

I didn't answer. I would do far more than test them—I had already made that vow.

Florence gathered up an armful of soiled linens and made for the door. "Be careful when you leave the castle, child," Florence said as she shut the door. "And do not forget to return."

I dressed quickly and hurried to the village, meeting neither harpy nor tatzelwurm on my way. I asked the dog-faced man, who was plucking a chicken in his yard, where I might find Raphael, and he directed me down a narrow lane to the blacksmith's workshop.

The shop was dimly lit but blazing hot inside. An inferno of flames roared inside a giant forge, and Raphael was right in front of it. I watched as he pulled a glowing red piece of iron from the heat and then began to beat it into shape over a metal anvil. His chest was streaked with dirt and sweat, and the fire made a halo around his dark head. As my eyes wandered over his strong jaw, tense with concentration, the ropes of muscle straining in his arms, I felt a flare of heat rising from my core. I did not think it was from the forge.

I dragged my eyes back to his face and I yelled as loudly as I could above the clang and din, "I'm glad to see your wounds have healed so quickly!"

He looked up, caught sight of me. "Perhaps because I had such an excellent nurse yesterday," he said.

The flare in my body rose higher at his cheeky smile. "A–Are you making a sword?" I stammered. "I'm not sure you're doing it correctly. Is it supposed to curve like that?"

Raphael laughed and set his hammer down, wiping his brow of sweat. "I'm not making a sword, Your Highness. It's a blade for a plow."

"But why a plow? You've been conscripted into Ares's army."

"I assume he will provide his soldiers with fighting weapons." Raphael held up the crude tool. "In the meantime, we must eat. Food doesn't magically appear on a plate, you know. We must grow it." A smile flickered in the corner of his mouth.

"You tease me," I said, smiling back. "I'm not so ignorant as all that." I stepped closer to him, my voice lowering. "But how can you do it? How do you go about your daily work, while waiting to be called to bloodshed?"

He looked down at me, his dark eyes boring into mine. His voice was barely audible over the din of the forge. "What do you think I should do instead?"

What *did* I think he should do? Suddenly unsure of myself, I turned away from the intensity of his gaze. Through the grimy window of the smithy I saw a narrow lane and a girl skipping down it, her tattered skirt far too short for her coltish legs. Her wild, curling hair was the same bright copper as Fina's—and as Rosa's had been. My fingers twisted in the rough wool of my skirt. As she bounced out of sight, I knew, suddenly and certainly, that I could not let this girl's village suffer as my village had.

I felt my heart beat faster because of what I was about to say—and because Raphael and I stood so close together that our bodies almost touched.

"Take matters into your own hands," I said urgently. "Into *our* own hands."

Raphael frowned in confusion. "I don't understand, Your Highness."

I waved my arms around the room. "You have fire, you have metal, you have hands. Make yourself swords!"

And then he laughed. "All right, I admire your spark. But this is iron. Ares's blades will be steel."

"I'm sure yours could kill just as effectively when wielded by brave men. And women," I added. "When they fight not for Ares, but *against* him."

Raphael stared at me for a long moment—it seemed as if he couldn't comprehend what I was talking about. But wasn't it obvious? The best way to stop the attack on Bandon Castle was to mount an attack of our own.

Then he spoke. "I think you've lost your mind," he said.

"There are more of you than there are of them," I insisted.

"More of who?"

"Villagers," I cried. "There are a thousand of you! Ares doesn't have a vast legion of knights."

"He doesn't need a legion with the killers he's got," Raphael said.

"But they aren't invincible—put a sword through their bodies, and they die like anyone else. I've seen it."

By now some of the other smiths had stopped their work to gather around us. I saw, with some surprise, that there was no hate in their eyes. Instead there was curiosity.

"What does she want with us?" asked a man with an eye patch.

"Nothing," Raphael said quickly.

I looked the man in his one good eye. "What Raphael means to say, actually, is nothing—except *revolution*."

CHAPTER 49

At that, Raphael flung his arm around my shoulder and all but dragged me outside.

"Excuse me," I said, trying to shrug him off. "You can't just haul me around like a stack of firewood."

Raphael's eyes flashed. "It's just as I feared, you really have gone mad. Or maybe you were always mad. You can't wander into a room of men and talk about rising up against Ares and his knights."

"Should I speak to the women instead?" I asked.

Raphael looked as if he'd like to shake me, but I had to make him understand. "Don't tell me these villagers want to be on Ares's side," I said. "They all hate him, I know it."

"What makes you so certain?"

"Because they hated me when they thought I was his."

"You *are* his, aren't you?" Raphael's tone was light, but there was a challenge in it.

"He imprisons me, but he doesn't control or own me, and I won't have you suggesting otherwise." I put my hand on his arm. "If we join together—*all* of us—we stand a chance against him."

"'Stand a chance'?" Raphael repeated. "Those sound like impossible odds."

"You are preparing to attack Bandon Castle," I practically shouted. "Where I live—*lived,* I mean. In whose shadow you grew up. Please. Do not fight against innocent people whom you likely know. Fight against our common enemy."

"Sophia, neither you nor I are war leaders," he said. "We can't ask the villagers to die for this cause of yours."

"In battle, hundreds will die, no matter whom they fight for."

His handsome face was grave—sad, even. "So that may be. But it is not for us to decide. I will help you, though."

"You, alone." I couldn't keep the disappointment from my voice.

"Two is twice as good as one, Your Highness." He reached down to the bench outside the workshop and picked up two swords, one of which he gave to me. "Ready?" he asked. "I'll teach you to fight."

I hefted the blade in my hand. It was heavy and crude.

"Have you held a sword before?" Raphael asked. "Or only an embroidery needle?"

I heard the teasing tone in his voice, and in answer, I lunged at him. He flung his blade up to block my blow, but just barely. I stepped back, crouched, and then came at him from the side, my sword tip plunging down as if to slice into his thigh. Again he barely avoided my strike.

"Beginner's luck, clearly," he said. He danced backward and held his blade with both hands, extended toward me.

I smiled, knowing already he was more of a beginner than I was. "The inexperienced fighter stands with his arms out, to keep his opponent at a distance," I said—this was something Odo used to tell me over and over again. "But he cannot strike without pulling back. And when he does, his enemy's blade finds its mark."

"So you have been taught a little," Raphael said. He was already a little breathless, and he seemed surprised at my skill.

"I have held a sword more often than an embroidery needle," I said. I faked a thrust and then stepped back.

"So it would seem," Raphael said, letting his sword drop to his side. He looked at me thoughtfully.

Several of the men had come out from the sweltering smithy, and they called for us to keep sparring. I gathered that it wasn't every day that a princess crossed blades with a blacksmith.

"With wrapped swords we need not be so careful with one another," I said.

A bearded man offered us wooden roundels and dull swords wrapped in cloth, so a blow could hurt but wouldn't draw blood. We squared off, and then we began to spar, surrounded by a group of cheering villagers.

Though untrained, Raphael was a natural fighter, swift and clever. I had to summon all Odo's teachings, and soon my chest was heaving and my breath was coming in painful gasps.

When I could barely lift my sword any longer, I dropped it, as if in defeat. But then I clutched the practice dagger and darted forward, twisting it in the air so quickly Raphael couldn't block it. I ducked low and came up fast, thrusting the dull wooden blade into his armpit. Raphael yelped in surprise and pain.

"That," I said, gasping, "is a deadly strike." Then I shoved him, and he landed in the dirt, much to the delight of the whooping, cackling smiths.

He looked up at me in what actually seemed like admiration. "You are...unpredictable," he said.

"Thank you," I said, for the adjective pleased me. "I owe it to the knight Odo. He taught me, though it was against my father's wishes. The king wanted me to be a proper princess, to walk gracefully and play the harp."

Raphael brushed the dirt from his ragged pants, and then he held out his hand. I took it in my own—it was warm, strong, and filthy—and pulled him to his feet. For a moment, our fingers stayed entwined, and I felt my cheeks flush.

"And did you do such things?" Raphael asked.

"I certainly tried. But I wasn't very good at either one," I said. I smiled ruefully. "Once upon a time, having to practice that infernal instrument seemed like the worst sort of hardship. It's funny how much things have changed since then."

"What's so hard for you now?" Raphael asked. "You still live a life of luxury."

"I am under an enemy's roof," I said, and I heard the note of bitterness creeping into my voice. "It's worse than being in prison."

Raphael raised an eyebrow. "I might venture to disagree with you," he said. "And unless I'm mistaken, only one of us has been locked in a dungeon—so I know of what I speak."

I saw the hint of a smile on his face. "In your father's cells," he went on, "I recall a distinct lack of proper manure clumps. But the rats were rather cute and friendly, actually, especially if you gave them a bit of moldy bread and hid them from Gattis's hungry eyes..."

He was trying to cheer me, I knew that. And I was grateful for it. But he couldn't understand what it was like to live in Ares's keep. To be less a princess than a plaything, or a prize for a killer.

"How would you like to share a table with the man who murdered your father?" I asked, feeling my throat constrict at the words. "Because that is what I must do, every single day."

Raphael looked thoughtful. "I never knew my father," he said.

"And I am sorry for that," I said. "But I knew mine, and I loved him deeply, and now Reiper, his murderer, courts me." I swung my sword in agitation and Raphael, caught off guard, leapt back.

"Careful, Your Highness," he said, "unless you wish to maim your allies as well as your enemies."

"Sorry," I said, setting the weapon down. "But any day now, Reiper will lead the charge to attack my castle."

"I told you, I will help you," Raphael said.

"Help me how?" I asked, more sharply than I meant to. "Will you fling manure in his face?"

Raphael's answer was calm and matter-of-fact. "Sophia, I'll help you kill him."

CHAPTER 50

The next day, when I returned to the village to spar with Raphael, he seemed glad to see me. "We'll see who beats whom today," he said, strutting around in the dust, and I laughed to watch him puff out his chest in a parody of cruel Ares himself.

I drew my sword. "Shall we take a bet?" I asked him.

"Yes," he said. "I'll bet you—ah, see, I have nothing to offer!" But then he shrugged. "No matter, I don't plan to lose." He grinned slyly at me. "You'll wager your crown, though, won't you?"

"I already lost that," I reminded him. "So perhaps I have nothing, either."

"Let us spar, then!" Raphael said, lunging at me and taking me by surprise.

Our match that day was long, but I bested him again. And so it continued this way for days. I journeyed to the village, found him wherever he was, and summoned him to a duel. Sometimes a small crowd gathered to cheer us on, and other times we fought in an alleyway, alone.

Though I'd never admit it, I had come to enjoy his company. He teased me, tested me, and yet when I returned to my room at night, tired and bruised, I missed him. But I couldn't bring myself to ask him if he felt the same way. Maybe, like me, he experienced a spark of heat when we clasped hands to help each other up. Or maybe he felt nothing at all. That brilliant, lightning-flash smile of his—perhaps he bestowed it on everyone.

And though we were getting stronger with practice, it was impossible to imagine that he and I alone could take down some-one like Reiper. But every time I tried to speak of a larger revolt, Raphael's face darkened and his mouth grew small and tight.

Meanwhile, at Ares's castle, the forge turned out gleaming new weapons, and knights and their pages practiced at the pell, striking the heavy wooden post with swords and battle-axes. Florence, slipping past Ares's chamber one night, had heard Mordred whispering of pack animals and plunder.

"I should not tell you this," she had whispered, "but they will ride out in three days."

So I hurried to the village to tell Raphael. The old man by the fountain gestured vaguely to the west with a bony, withered arm. "I saw the boy go down that way," he croaked. "Try the baker's."

Thanking him with a curtsy, I set out along the dusty streets. When I saw the man with the crown of eyeballs, I sped up—I hoped to spare myself his glaring ocular hostility. But he stopped me, gripping my shoulder while his many eyes searched my face. "Forgive me for thinking you were on their side," he said. The largest eye blinked earnestly at me.

"It is no matter," I assured him. I looked around—we were the only two people in a narrow side street—and then I whispered, "Especially if you would join me in rising against them."

The man shrank back as if my words had burned him. Then, without another word, he scurried into a building and slammed the door shut behind him. I felt my shoulders sag. It seemed more clear than ever that Raphael and I would be alone in our fight. I couldn't imagine how it would end well for us.

I found the baker's after several wrong turns and dead-end alleys, but Raphael was nowhere to be seen. The warm smell of fresh bread made my mouth water, and, fascinated, I watched a woman take a soft lump of dough, punch it down, and then begin to knead it vigorously, all the while sprinkling flour over its surface.

Eventually she looked up at me. "Why do you stare?" she asked.

My cheeks flushed. "I've never seen anyone making bread before," I admitted.

Her eyebrows lifted in surprise. "A strange life you must lead," she said.

I thought of my throne—and then of my sickness—and now, of my imprisonment in this strange and inexplicable world. How I still didn't even know if I was half alive or all the way dead. "I suppose you could say that."

The fire in the great stone oven crackled and roared. Rising loaves lined the shelves, wrapped in towels like swaddled babies.

"I heard you were looking for me," said a soft voice in my ear.

I whirled around to see Raphael with his hands on his hips and a playful grin on his face. I was as glad to see him as if it'd been days instead of mere hours since we'd last been together.

I smiled back at him. "I've come to best you in a duel again, obviously."

"I distinctly remember our last match being even," he said.

"Perhaps, after so many blows to the head, your memory has suffered," I teased.

He gave a little snorting laugh. "I doubt it. But let's not fight yet. Let's take a walk." He looped his arm through mine and steered me toward the door. "Goodbye, Bryn," he said, calling over his shoulder. "Save me one of those sweet buns, will you? I'll pay you tomorrow, I promise." He leaned into my ear again. "She knows I won't," he whispered, and I shivered at his breath on my neck. "I don't have any money at all."

Outside the air was brisk, but the morning mist had burned away, and in the distance was a small patch of blue sky. I was acutely aware of Raphael's touch, the solid warmth of his body next to mine, as together we strolled down the winding streets of the town. I felt suddenly shy, but the villagers, humans and beasts alike, called out in greeting to him, and he called right back. He knew everyone's name.

Then I felt a nip at my heels, and I turned to see that the little six-legged fox creature had reappeared. "Hello again," I said. "Where have you been?"

"I think he likes you," Raphael said, as it twined around my ankles.

I gave it a pat on its bristly head and it fell into step beside us. The sun came out from behind gray scraps of clouds, and for a moment, I felt almost happy. I knew it didn't make sense—I was a beast, I was possibly dead, and Ares was preparing to destroy what was left of my kingdom—but there it was. A glimmer of hope. For the first time in my life, I finally didn't feel alone.

"Why are you smiling?" Raphael asked.

"Life is strange, isn't it?" I said.

"Or death is."

"Or whatever this is," we both said at the same time.

Then Raphael unhooked his arm from mine, and I felt suddenly bereft—until he took my inhuman-colored hand in his and squeezed my fingers tight.

CHAPTER 51

Though we should have been sparring, or should have been making plans to destroy Reiper, we kept walking through the town's narrow streets. Beside me, Raphael began to whistle a high, lilting tune.

"How do you do that?" I asked.

"Do what?"

"Whistle," I said, flushing a little in embarrassment.

He laughed. "Your tutors neglected to teach you such a common skill?"

"Yes," I said, "probably because it *was* common."

"It's simple. You make a little circle with your mouth"—he demonstrated—"and then you blow air through it. Like this." His song was as lovely as a bird's.

I tried to do as he instructed, but I could hardly even make a sound.

"I see," he said, with mock gravity. "Perhaps your lips are too noble for it." He bent closer to me and peered at them. "Yes, I do believe I see the problem."

"What? What is it?"

"Do you really want to know?" he asked.

"Yes," I said, even though I was afraid he'd tell me something cruel. *You have the mouth of a monster.*

But he didn't say anything. He put his hands on my cheeks, and then before I even understood what was happening, Raphael was kissing me. Not shyly, not gently, but urgently, his lips somehow soft and hard at the same time. My heart began to bang against my ribs and I swayed on my feet. It felt delicious, frightening, overwhelming. After a moment, I broke away, breathless.

Raphael blinked at me. "I'm sorry," he said. "I shouldn't have presumed."

"No, no, it's all right," I stammered. "I—you—" My thoughts were scrambled, my cheeks aflame. I'd wanted such a thing to happen, and I hadn't even known how much.

He took my hand again. "Strange, isn't it? A princess and a beast," he said, shaking his head.

Whether he was calling himself the beast—or me—I didn't ask. I put my hand on the back of his neck, lifting my lips to his. "Not so strange at all," I said.

As his arms tightened around me, I let myself sink into him. I wanted to stay that way forever. But I knew that I couldn't.

"Ares's army rides in a matter of days, and I am to marry one of his knights," I whispered into his chest.

I felt him start, and then pull away. He stared down at me. "*Marry*? I don't understand."

I explained to him about Ares's command and all the knights

I had to choose from against my will. "Ares stole me, and he seeks to make a gift of me — as if I have no more mind than a fur stole or a ruby ring. That's bad enough. But what's worse is that Reiper seems to think that I'm already his."

Raphael had begun to pace in circles in the road. Suddenly he stopped and turned to me. "The solution is right in front of you, Princess, even if you don't want to see it."

"I *know* what the solution is. We must rise up against him."

"No," he said. "You must marry Reiper."

I felt as if I'd been punched in the chest. "How the hell is that a solution?"

Raphael didn't seem to think he'd said anything surprising. "Who is better positioned to wound a devil than the woman who marries him? Think of it, Sophia. You pledge your loyalty, and then you strike when he's most vulnerable." He avoided looking at me. "On your wedding night."

"I-I can't," I whispered. Each time I looked at Reiper, I felt the breath sucked from my lungs and fear crawling up my spine like a snake. The thought of pledging myself to him and entering his bedchamber made me shudder.

But Raphael was insistent. "What do you have to lose? You're probably dead anyway." He waved his arm around. "Likely we all are."

"And we speak and we walk and we breathe! This is *some* kind of life, and though I don't relish it, I don't want to forfeit it by marrying a murderer."

We continued toward the square in silence. The sweet moment of our kiss had been ruined, and I mourned its loss. The sheep ran bleating away from us as Raphael took his place opposite me, holding his practice sword loosely in his right hand and his shield in his left. Unlike Odo, he didn't worry about hurting me or risking my father's wrath, and I had blue-black bruises to prove it.

I planted my feet and raised my weapon. "Ready," I said.

Raphael brushed a loose strand of hair from my cheek, sending shivers down my whole body. "What is it he says to you? *In your honor, Princess.*"

"Don't mock me!" I said, swatting his hand away.

"I'm not. I'm trying to help."

"Then raise your sword," I said sharply.

Raphael shrugged, but he did as I asked. Our fight was particularly vicious, and it was not me who walked away more bruised.

CHAPTER 52

I returned to the castle to find Seth lurking where the Sphinx usually basked in the weak sunlight. He said nothing as I approached, but he raised his jackal nose and sniffed inquisitively at the air. I pretended that I didn't see him. Pretended, too, that I didn't notice him fall in step behind me, and then trail me through the halls the way a wolf tracks its prey.

As I passed through an interior courtyard, he drew closer, until I could almost feel his panting breath on my neck.

I quickened my pace. I was a better fighter than I had been, but I had no weapon with me. And even if I had, would it protect me against a demigod? My book of myths called him the first murderer—a creature who'd killed his own brother to steal his throne—and it didn't seem wise to turn around and challenge him.

We were coming upon the Great Hall. The doors were flung open, and I could hear laughter and strange, discordant music from within. I entered, already breathless, with Seth close at my heels.

Ares and his knights were drinking mead and watching the musician, a woman with a bird's beak who played a stringed instrument fashioned from a monstrous skull. When Ares saw me, he grinned in leering welcome. "Ah, you are coming to like us after all! I didn't invite you to our little party, and yet here you are. Would you like a drink?"

"I would like you to call off your hound," I said, gesturing to Seth.

Ares narrowed his cold eyes at me. "You speak boldly for one so...defenseless," he replied. "I take it the jackal is not to your liking? Fine. Seth, come join us by the fire. Leave the princess alone for now." His smile grew threatening. "So who will it be for you, Sophia? To whom will you give your heart?" He glanced at his men, all of whom had turned to stare at me. "Metaphorically, of course," he added, "though there are some who would enjoy it in a more literal, gustatory sense."

Reiper, who had been lurking in the corner once occupied by Zozo, advanced to my side. "We know whom she will choose," he said, in a voice that sent shivers down my spine.

I could feel waves of malice radiating from his body, the way heat rippled out from a flame. My hands began to tingle and my heart thrummed with dread. I knew that I should play along, as Raphael had suggested—the plan, as awful as it was, made sense. I opened my mouth. I only had to speak one single syllable: yes.

Instead the words came out rushed, unbidden. "I would sooner die than marry you."

And though I spoke softly, everyone heard.

Reiper nearly shook with rage. "You will have me," he said.

"Or I will slice you open like a melon. But first," he added, "I will kill your little human companion. Slowly, while you watch."

I said nothing—I didn't want to provoke him further—but his livid face was horrible to behold.

"Oh, yes," he said. "I know all about the little friendship you have with the peasant boy." He leaned so close that his lips touched my hair. "Just for the fact that you desire him, his death will be even more painful and terrible than your father's," he whispered.

Though it took all my will, I kept my face expressionless as I turned my back to him. "If you will excuse me," I said to Ares, "I should not have come to your gathering. I will retire to my chambers."

"Perhaps you can return when you have become more agreeable," Ares said.

"There is little chance of that," I muttered under my breath.

"Or else..." he added. He let the sentence end there.

The music started up again as I left the room, and Seth did not follow me. Nor did Reiper. But I knew I had stretched everyone's patience to the breaking point. If Reiper didn't kill me soon, I felt certain that Ares would.

CHAPTER 53

I could sense him as I lay in bed that night: Reiper, in the darkened hallway outside my chambers. Not prowling, not pacing, just...*waiting*. Was he guarding me from the other knights? Or was he there to prove that he would not be denied—that he had laid claim to me, and so I would be his?

I couldn't know his thoughts, but I knew that I wasn't safe. He had easily breached Bandon's defenses. If Reiper wanted to come into my bedroom, he would; there was no lock in the world that could stop him.

I stepped to the door and placed my hand against it. It was icy cold, and the very air in my room felt prickling, charged, the way it did before a thunderstorm. Drawing a knife that Raphael had given me from its sheath, I sank down to the floor and leaned against the stone wall. If Reiper was going to let himself into my room again, he'd be met with a dagger.

The minutes ticked by, tense and interminable. Outside, a

chill wind whistled through the castle's jagged towers. The fire flickered and dimmed, and mice skittered in the corners of the room. My eyelids grew heavy.

Hours later, I awoke on the floor, my cheek against the flagstones and every part of me stiff and cold. My first thought was that I could no longer sense Reiper nearby. Tension drained from my shoulders, and I exhaled in relief. I was safe — for now. It was Florence who stood above me, her brow furrowed and her hands on her hips.

"What, again?" she said. "This is the second time I've found you on the ground, and this time it looks as if you slept there on purpose. You came here a princess," she admonished me. "And what are you now, sleeping in the cinders like a scullery maid? Ares will not approve."

Blearily, I stood. My very bones ached. "Then we will be even, since I do not approve of being his so-called guest."

Florence reached out and gently touched my cheek. "Poor child," she said. "You are still under the impression that what you want matters to him."

I shook my head. "I know full well that it doesn't."

"Shall I help you dress?" she asked hopefully.

"No, thank you," I said.

But unlike in recent days, I took time with my preparations. I bathed in rosemary-scented water and washed and carefully combed my dark hair. From the wardrobe, I chose a velvet gown of midnight blue, its sleeves twined with gold vines. And from a small chest of jewels, I selected a golden necklace with a luminous single pearl that nestled in the hollow of my collarbone.

I stood before the mirror and gasped at my reflection. Was it possible? I reached out to touch the cold glass as my pulse quickened in excitement and disbelief. The mottled purple of my skin had faded to a lavender shade that was nonetheless closer to my real coloring, and my horns had shrunk to small, shimmering nubs. My old self seemed to flicker there underneath the beastly surface. Was I really becoming human again? I ached to be the girl I once was.

Florence, who had slipped back into the room, sucked in her breath. "You look beautiful," she said. "Like a true princess. Are you going to the village today?"

I shook my head. "I'm going to see Ares."

"You have made your choice of husband, then." She smoothed the coverlet on my bed. "Good girl." But then she saw my expression, and she came to me and took my hand. "If you don't decide, he will do it for you, child." She paused. "Or he'll do much worse."

"Why do you serve him?" I asked her again.

She looked hard at me, as if weighing whether or not to speak. "Ares saved her," she finally said.

"Who?"

"My only child. My daughter. Balor came for her on her birthday. He wanted her."

"To be his bride?" I whispered, horrified.

She nodded. When she spoke, her voice sounded far away and hollow. "She was only twelve years old. Soriah—a name not so unlike yours. I threw myself at Ares's feet and begged him to take me instead. I was young then, and I had my charms. I told him that if he let her go, I would serve him until I died."

Florence took a deep, shuddering breath. "I lay in the dust a long time. He said nothing. But when I finally looked up at him, he just...*nodded*. And I knew that she would be spared." She turned to me, her eyes searching my face. "So I am his, as long as I have breath. And I am not sorry. There was a time when Ares had a human heart, and my daughter is alive because of it. Balor took another wife."

"And is his wife content?" I asked. "I have not seen her."

Florence seemed to shrink a little. "She died in a fire" was all she said.

I leaned closer. "Don't you see that Reiper is coming for me the way Balor came for Soriah?" I couldn't help prodding. "Except I have no mother to intercede on my behalf."

"I am on your side, child," Florence whispered.

But how could that be true when she served my jailor?

"I am going to appeal to Ares myself," I said.

Florence wiped her eyes. "I wish you luck, child," she said. "Though I suspect you will not have it."

CHAPTER 54

I found Ares in his library. He was reclining on a low tufted bench underneath a huge tapestry, whose faded, ancient wool depicted fierce-faced men battling axe-wielding trolls.

Though my fate lay in his answer to my request, I couldn't help marveling at his books—this wasn't a treasure I'd have expected to find in such a place. I touched a nearby leather spine, and my fingertip came away feathered with dust.

When he looked up at me, I gave him my most graceful, dig-nified curtsy.

Ares's icy eyes narrowed. "Your politeness is suspicious," he said. "I doubt Florence has been giving you lessons in queenly comportment. So, tell me why you have come to disturb my solitude."

I swallowed and found my voice. "I did not ask to come to your castle. But nevertheless you are my host, and I beg for your protection," I said.

"Now what is that supposed to mean?" Ares asked. "I feed you. I clothe you richly. You are already protected."

"I ask protection from Reiper. He is a demon and a butcher."

"Your most ardent suitor? The best possible match?" Ares returned his gaze to his lap, where his empty hands clenched and unclenched themselves. "How is it that you fail to understand your duty, Sophia?"

"All night he waits in the hallway outside my room. Have mercy," I begged. "Send him to haunt some other door."

A servant tiptoed in, bringing a tray of fruit and a flagon of wine, which she set down on a little table near Ares. He didn't seem to notice. Several moments passed in silence, and I allowed myself to hope for a nod, like the one he'd given Florence.

But when Ares looked up again, his voice was choked with rage. "I showed you mercy when I did not tear you limb from limb the first time you defied me. Or the second, or the third," he said. "You have no idea how you have tested my patience. Were it not for your beauty—and the novelty of your presence— my hounds would already be fighting over your skull. But beauty grows stale, Princess, and novelty, by its very definition, *wears off.*"

I dug my nails into the palm of my hand, and the pain centered me. If Ares wouldn't protect my life, that was a hard blow. But I had still more at stake. "Then my castle, sir. I ask—"

"Have I not made myself clear? You have no right to ask me anything!" Ares shouted. "You have taken so long, with your sniffling and whining and running off to the village, that the choice has been made for you—you will marry the very man you're here to beg against, I'm exceedingly satisfied to tell you. I would sooner put you to the sword myself then deny Reiper his claim to you— or deny my knights their charge against your precious castle."

His words hit me like stones, and I nearly fell to my knees as he pointed one pale, hooked finger at me. "You will wed Reiper tomorrow morning and then journey to his keep for the rest of your forgettable life, or you will be executed in the evening."

My throat constricted, and I felt like I couldn't breathe. Which fate could be worse? As I gasped for air, Ares seemed to enjoy my anguish. He leaned forward and spoke softly, almost confidentially.

"If you refuse to take Reiper, I'll let my men choose the method for your execution, as decisions are clearly very difficult for you. Will you be flayed alive, or pierced with red-hot pokers, or gutted and then burned on a pyre? Whatever method they select, you can be sure it will be slow, bloody, and exceedingly cruel."

He gestured to a guard, who took me roughly by the arm and began to drag me from the room. I was too stunned and horrified to struggle.

"I can fill my fountains with wine or blood, girl," Ares called. "Shall we drink to your marriage or your murder? That is the only choice left to you now. Each, in its own way, is a celebration. Now get away from my sight. I have a battle to prepare for."

CHAPTER 55

Later that evening, Lelia the maid knocked lightly on my door and then, without waiting for permission, stepped into the room. In her arms she held a gown of pale and lustrous gold. Its shimmering, embroidered train was so long that two other attendants followed her, carrying its heavy folds. When they laid the beautiful garment on the bed, it glowed as if embers had been sewn inside it.

I didn't have to ask Lelia what it was for, because I knew. It was my wedding dress.

Pearls shimmered at the neckline, and I ran my fingertip along the seams, stitched in fine silver thread. Lace edged the sleeves, and embroidered roses twined around the waistline. The gown was exquisite, a thing of almost indescribable beauty. But it was also a reminder of Ares's ultimatum: I was to be wed, or else I was to die.

Sinking down to the bed, I thought of my mother, who'd

married my father when she was only sixteen years old. Had she gone to him willingly? Had she been trained to accept that her sacrifice was the lot that all women had to bear?

I thought achingly of the rest of my days, unfurling endlessly before me, each of them owed to a man I loathed. If I had hated being captive here, how much worse it would be in Reiper's castle. There would be no Florence, no Raphael, and I would be forced to sit beside him on his throne of skulls—and lie beside him on his bed—until my poor wretched heart finally stopped beating. How long would it take for death to find me there?

As I loosed a single pearl from its thread, I thought of the gruesome song I'd first heard amidst the stench and horror of the plague-ridden village.

> *Now Death will be her husband,*
> *No jewels but worms she'll wear!*

I dropped the little pearl to the floor and it rolled away into the corner.

"Try it on."

The booming voice came from the hall. Peering underneath the door, I saw the massive feet of the eight-foot-tall chambermaid I'd met the night I was brought here. Where was Florence? Why had she sent this monster in her stead?

"I will not," I said.

The door heaved open, striking me in the head. My vision blurred as the huge maid loomed over me, her face dark and gnarled like a tree root. Reaching down, she gripped my neck in one seven-fingered hand and roughly pulled me upright. She held me as I struggled, yanking off my clothes with her other giant hand. "You *will,*" the maid said.

At her command, two lizard-women, hissing like adders,

brought the golden garment from the bed. My strength was no match for the giant, and soon the bridal gown hung heavy on my shoulders. Its jewel-encrusted bust pressed against my chest like cold, lifeless hands. The arms felt as though they had been sewn from lead. I staggered, and the maid roughly pushed me upright.

She pinched a fold of silk roses at my waist. "It needs taking in," she muttered.

The lizard-women removed the dress's heavy train, laid it back on the bed, and then skittered into the hall. The giant took my chin in her hand. "Stay where you are. Do not undress. I will return with the tailor."

She bolted the door behind her, and I was alone again.

For a moment I stood paralyzed, my mind a black cloud of despair. Then a log in the fire popped, sending up a shower of sparks, and it startled me back into myself. I had only moments to act.

I ran to the window and flung open the casement. Clouds amassed on the horizon, illuminated every few moments by flashes of lighting, and thunder rumbled in the distance. Below me was the wall walk, where I'd first seen the Inkanyamba and Impundulu and all their fellow monsters.

Right now it was deserted, its torches dark. It was a twenty-foot drop to the pathway, and if I broke an ankle, I wouldn't be able to run. I ducked back into the room and tore the covers from my bed—the beautiful silk coverlets, the soft furs, the bolsters stuffed with goose feathers. Then I threw them all out the window.

Would it be enough? I wouldn't know until I'd landed.

Moments later I was balanced on the outside ledge like some

awkward, flightless bird. I was afraid to jump. A mound of blankets—*this* was my idea? But when I heard a sound in the hall, I closed my eyes and leapt.

A plummeting, whirling sickness filled my body—this was a terrible mistake! I stifled a scream as I plunged downward and the ground rushed up to meet me.

I landed hard on the wall walk. The bedding had cushioned my fall, but the breath was knocked from my lungs. I crouched in the darkness, gasping. My vision spun; the lump on my head from the door flared with pain. Squinting, I stood up, trying to get my bearings to find the best route of escape.

Before I had taken a single step, a giant shape lurched out from the shadows. Lightning burst all around me, and I saw one huge eye, held tightly shut. I saw fleshy lips part in a contorted leer, a grimace meant to be a smile.

"Where do you think you're going, little Princess?" Balor asked.

CHAPTER 56

My heart beat so hard and fast it felt like I was being stabbed. The only way to escape was back through the turret, the bottom of which arched over the wall walk like a bridge. So I spun around and ran.

Balor let out a roar of rage and charged blindly after me. I heard a stutter step and a curse as he stumbled on the hill of bedclothes. Icy rain began to fall as I sprinted down the narrow walkway in my heavy gold wedding gown. Up ahead, the path split, with the left fork leading back into the center of the castle and the right continuing along the perimeter of the cliffs, high above the churning bay.

I turned left, burst through a door, and then frantically bolted the lock behind me. Now I stood in a long hall, its cold stone walls flickering with rushlights. Already I was disoriented, and panic made everything look unfamiliar.

Which way was the Great Hall? Which passage led to the servants' corridors and the secret gate to the cliff?

The lights guttered as Balor banged on the door. I didn't know which way to run, but even as I hesitated, I smelled the acrid scent of burning wood. I turned to see flames licking at the door's base, casting contorted shadows on the wall as Balor burned it to cinders.

I dashed down a hallway that soon curved inward toward the center of the castle. It grew darker and narrower as I went. I ran until my legs nearly gave out beneath me, and then I stopped to listen. I tried to breathe slowly, calmly, but I inhaled in ragged gasps.

Silence. Had Balor gone in the other direction? Maybe he couldn't fit through this hallway. I closed my eyes and prayed.

And then I heard footsteps, careful, creeping toward me in the dark.

Once again I ran, nearly as blind as Balor in the dark hall. Ahead lay a twisting staircase, and I paused for just a breath before hurling myself down. Stumbling on the craggy, crumbling steps, I spiraled lower and lower into the shadowy castle. Balor crashed behind me, too big for where I led him but too bent on capturing his prey to give up.

At the bottom of those countless stairs, I fell forward onto hard-packed dirt. When I lurched up again, I staggered through the castle's vaulted undercroft and into the main courtyard.

Through the slanting rain, I could see the stables near the curtain wall—and closer to me, a storage structure half collapsed from neglect. I scrambled inside, and there, amidst the dust and spiders, I felt the gritty scabbard of a long sword. Grabbing the hilt, I pulled with all my strength, and the blade screeched itself out. It was blackened and rusty. This was a poor weapon or else it wouldn't be here. But it was better than bare hands.

I held the blade out to feel its heft—it was well balanced, and heavy enough to cut off my leg if I wasn't careful.

I peered through the doorway and saw Balor stalking in the courtyard, his heavy head turning blindly from side to side. His clenched fist was the size of a boulder.

"Show yourself, Princess," he shouted, "and maybe I'll spare you."

Feeling along the shed's wall, I found the shaft of a broken axe. I picked it up and flung it as hard as I could, and it thudded into the ground behind Balor. When he turned around, I rushed toward him across the rocky courtyard. With all my strength, I swung the sword low and sideways. The blade bit into his calf and he roared in anger, twisting back around. His giant fist caught me in the shoulder, and I went sprawling, my blade sliding away across the dead wet grass. I scrambled to my knees and lunged after it, pain exploding in my shoulder.

Balor's laugh was louder than thunder. He didn't have to see me—he knew exactly where I was. "The little gnat stings," he said. "No matter. It's over. Do you understand, Princess? I will use you as a match to light the village on fire."

I had the sword in hand again, though, and I swiped it at him. But my aim was off. The brittle metal glanced off the hard leather of his boot, smashed against a rock in the courtyard dirt, and shattered.

I saw Balor's great bristled lashes tremble, and slowly his huge eyelid began to open. A blinding ray of light streamed forth, as if a piece of the sun itself had suddenly fallen to the ground. Behind me, the storage shed burst skyward in a pillar of fire.

The flames hissed in the rain but only grew higher, and in seconds the courtyard seemed as bright as day. Acrid smoke stung my eyes. Balor pivoted toward me, and I threw myself out of the way as a trail of flames followed me. They caught the hem of my dress, and though I stomped them out, I knew I couldn't outrun the fire.

Then, suddenly, the giant bellowed out in shock and pain. He flung his head back and forth, a channel of fire still streaming from his forehead as he clawed madly at his back.

I saw a silhouette, teetering high on the curtain wall. As I squinted through the darkness and the rain, I felt my breath catch in my throat. It couldn't be!

And yet it was.

Raphael.

Why had he come? How did he know?

He stalked high above the courtyard, taunting Balor, goading him into fury. "Over here, beast," he shouted. "Turn around and face me!"

When Balor did, howling with rage, I saw what pained him: the spear that Raphael had thrown stuck out between the massive planes of his shoulder blades.

A river of flames poured from the giant, arcing up to where Raphael stood. Raphael jumped away, ducking behind the shelter of a drum tower. Balor's fire ignited the castle's flags and the wooden hoarding that ringed the upper part of the tower. The courtyard flickered yellow and red in its glow.

"Balor," I shouted. "I'm here! It's me you want." I tightened my grip on the broken sword.

The giant turned back around, burning a path through the stubbled grass. Flames leapt and danced between us. He looked back and forth, and I realized that he couldn't see me through the smoke and fire. I, on the other hand, saw him perfectly.

I crouched low and took aim, thinking of Odo, who could do this blindfolded. As Balor staggered forward, I hurled the broken sword right at him. Like the dagger Odo had trained me to use, it went whirling through the air, end over end. I held my breath.

And then it found its target: the center of Balor's eye.

The giant let out a shriek that seemed to rip the sky in half. His head became a corona of light. I watched in shock as his arms shrunk, curling inward, and his legs twisted and shriveled. His enormous, herculean body began to collapse, as if he was being devoured, sucked into oblivion by his own terrible eye.

After a few horrible moments, Balor was only cinders, and I lay shivering on the ground.

Raphael clambered down into the courtyard on a thick, knotted rope. He held out his hand. When I took it, he lifted me to my feet, and I felt his other hand press close in the small of my back with an intimacy that made me gasp.

I wanted to kiss him again, but something about his expression stopped me. So instead I spoke. "You came for me," I said.

"I did," he said. "And I'm not alone."

CHAPTER 57

W here are we going?" I cried as we ran.

Raphael didn't answer but pulled me toward the castle postern—the secret back gate that led to the treacherous cliffside stairs. Tonight, it stood wide open.

"See for yourself, Princess," he said.

Though the rain had stopped, lightning flashed above the wet sand and the roiling bay. I peered dizzily over the edge and saw dark shapes scrabbling up the stone steps, weapons strapped to their backs. There were dozens—hundreds—of them, scaling the monstrous crags like beetles.

"The villagers," I whispered, amazed. *The beasts.*

"They're coming," Raphael said, "all of them." Then he pulled me away again, and we hurried back toward the inner stronghold. "More came across the mudflats and are being hoisted up on the platform," he said urgently. "Any minute, they'll come streaming through the undercroft, and we will be here to meet them."

"But I don't understand——"

Raphael unbuckled a short sword and a dagger from his waist and thrust them at me. "Revolution," he said. "Isn't that what you were after?" He glanced at my opulent gown, now torn, dirty, and sopping wet. "Although you're hardly dressed for it."

"Perhaps you should have warned me?" I inquired. Though I was glad to see the villagers' uprising——and had even urged them to do it——I'd had no idea it was going to happen.

Raphael looked away and said nothing.

"Wait——you weren't sure you could trust me," I whispered.

"Sophia, now's not the time——"

"You're right," I interrupted, "it isn't. So I will take the matter up with you after our victory."

"I look forward to it." Then his fingers gently, fleetingly, touched my cheek. "Do not enter the fray too early," Raphael said. "The first assault is better left to stronger, larger soldiers."

And I knew enough about battle not to be offended by his plea.

The courtyard lay peaceful and open beneath a towering mountain of thunderclouds. No torches flared, no alarms had sounded. Wherever Ares and his men were, Balor's death hadn't summoned them.

A castle's defenses depended on its walls remaining unbreached—— my father had taught me that. But even now, someone was raising a platform of soldiers into its understory. What traitor to Ares sought to bring his enemies inside?

Whoever it was, I hope Ares never found him out.

I reached for Raphael's hand. "Remember, the inexperienced swordsman stands with his arms out—"

Raphael gave me a wry half smile. "Are you still calling me inexperienced after all our practice?"

But before I could answer he went on.

"I know, I'm not a seasoned fighter. But perhaps, when the inexperienced swordsman fights, he does exactly what he *isn't* supposed to do, and it catches his enemy by surprise."

I looked at him in concern. "I hope that isn't your actual strategy!" I said. "You'll be killed."

"I'm not afraid of dying," he said. "I've done it before, remember?"

And then suddenly, like a huge, clamorous wave, the villagers poured into the castle courtyard, sweeping Raphael along with them. Some ran into the castle itself. From the black sky came the warning screech of the harpies, and a battle horn sounded its ringing notes. For another moment, the castle was dark and still. Then shouts rose from all ranks as flaming arrows rained down from its windows.

I couldn't see Ares's knights—only the villagers with their swords raised, taunting them to come down from the castle and fight. A stone crashed in the center of the crowd, and I heard an agonized cry as someone was crushed beneath it. A moment later, another stone landed not ten feet from where I stood. A trebuchet on top of a flanking tower had pivoted toward us to fling down missiles from above.

Servants rushed from the castle, metal clashed against metal, and screams rent the air when arrows found their mark. From some dark underground lair, the Ekhidna uncoiled herself, her beautiful face made hideous by anger and her snake tail lashing with lethal force. I watched from a helpless distance as she attacked the villagers, sending their ranks into disarray. When Ares and his men finally charged into the courtyard, the villagers fell back.

But even as I despaired that I was now responsible for still more deaths, the villagers regrouped and surged forward again. They had but rudimentary shields, and their weapons were crude swords and even simple wooden clubs, but they ran at their enemy with a ferocity I could never have imagined.

I saw Mordred, dressed head to toe in gleaming mail, hacking at them with his broadsword. The dog-faced man, caught in the head by a sideways blow, howled as he fell.

A billhook caught in Mordred's mail and pulled him sideways. A horned man threw himself at the knight, as Mordred, screaming, tried to claw out his eyes. The old man from the village square, bearing a lance so heavy he could barely lift it, staggered forward to aid his horned friend, as behind him the giant chambermaid stomped through the melee, an axe clutched in her fist.

I saw a flash of white along the base of the curtain wall: Hasshaku Sama, trying to escape.

I ran toward her, my sword held high, and she rose in the air as I approached, her laugh like dry leaves rattling in the wind. "You cannot kill what you cannot touch," she said, fitting an arrow into her bow.

I threw the sword aside and grabbed the dagger Raphael had given me. Before Hasshaku Sama could loose her arrow, I sent my blade flying, and it found its mark in her throat. She gave one gasping, watery gurgle before falling to the ground.

I stalked over to her body. "My knife can touch you well enough," I told her. But she was beyond answering.

I grabbed my sword again and ripped the bloody knife from Hasshaku Sama's throat. And then I felt it: the icy pull of evil, tugging at me with a force like the dark suck of a whirlpool.

Reiper had come.

CHAPTER 58

He was nearly incandescent with fury, and I watched in horror as he stabbed his sword through two men at once. He left them writhing there on the blade as he advanced, pulling another sword from his waist. And then, suddenly, he stopped. His head swung around as his cold, narrow gaze passed over the battlefield.

I knew he was looking for me. I crouched near the castle wall, waiting. My sword seemed to shiver, as if eager to make its blow.

And yet—

I was no match for Reiper. Perhaps I'd wound him a little, and then what?

A villager staggered by me, one hand clutching a bleeding gash in his leg. "Stop," I hissed, "give me your bow."

He looked at me like I was mad. Shaking his head, he careened toward the shelter of the stables, listing sideways because of his wound. I lunged after him. "I'm sorry," I said, as I ripped the bow from his hands. Then I grabbed an arrow that had buried its tip in the ground. It hadn't hit its target the first time, but I hoped it would now.

Kneeling in the mud, I pulled back the gut, feeling the string cut into my fingertips. The bow wasn't my weapon of choice, but it was the one that kept me farthest from my target.

I held the pull, waiting, my arm shaking with effort. I didn't breathe. I didn't blink. I tried, even, to still my heart, as I aimed the arrow at Reiper's back.

Yes, I would kill him without warning. It was the only way I could. As my father had once proclaimed: there is no honor among beasts.

And I knew whose side I was on.

The sounds of battle seemed to cease. There was only me and Reiper, and the arrow that would soon travel between us. I felt like a bolt of lightning about to strike. I tracked him with the point of the arrow, and then—I let go.

My breath and the arrow rushed into the night at the same time. The gut twanged; the shaft spun through the air, its path straight and true as it flew toward Reiper's unsuspecting back. A perfect, deadly target. In another instant it would bury itself in his flesh.

But suddenly he moved, pivoting sharply, and the arrow glanced across his shoulder and skittered away.

The blood pounded in my ears—for an instant, the world went black.

I had *missed*.

CHAPTER 59

Reiper whirled around, and this time, he saw where I hid. His eyes bored into mine and his mouth twisted in fury. "You thought you couldn't bear to be my bride." His voice was quiet, but I heard every word perfectly. "Now you will wish you'd said yes."

I grabbed my sword and fled along the curtain wall, sliding on the wet ground and nearly falling over prostrate bodies. Reiper came after me, slinging his sword like a scythe. Above us, the trebuchet heaved another jagged piece of obsidian that shook the ground on impact.

I saw an opening in the wall ahead—it was the door of a cavalier tower. I flung myself inside and raced up the stone steps, spiraling upward until I found myself on one of the wall walks. Wind screamed through the battlements. On one side of me was the din and chaos of combat, on the other, hundreds of feet below, the frigid waves of the foaming bay.

The wall arced out, following the curving line of the cliff. I raced along it, lungs heaving, every muscle screaming in exhaustion and terror. Something caught my foot and I fell forward. My sword flew from my grip and went spinning over the wall as I slammed into the ground, striking my chin on the stones. I heard my involuntary cry of pain. Dizzy and breathless, I staggered to my feet. My jaw ached, my palms were shredded and bloody, and now I had no weapon.

Behind me, Reiper smiled coldly. As he strode forward, he drew a curved knife along the hard, smooth leather of his armor.

He was sharpening his blade.

"This is my gift to you, the girl I thought I would marry."

"Your forgiveness?" But I said this knowing it could not be true.

"No. Only a promise that you will not suffer too much."

I wasn't interested in suffering, no matter how brief. Using what was left of my strength, I clambered to the top of the stone wall that bordered the walkway. And then I flung myself into the air.

Another sensation of sickening, spinning dread before I landed on the roof of the courtyard smithy. As I lay there, stunned from the impact, rain began to fall again. The icy drops revived me and I crawled to the edge of the roof. Did I dare risk another leap?

Below me the battle still raged. I saw Seth sinking his teeth into the cheek of a villager, and the air smelled of blood and smoke and burning tar. The stench of bowels slit open seemed to come from hell itself.

I turned to look at Reiper, who was balanced on the wall, about to jump after me. A shadow raced toward him in the downpour.

"No!" I screamed, and then clapped my hand over my mouth. Too late. Reiper spun around and saw what I had: brave, foolish Raphael, rushing toward him with his blade raised.

Swiftly Reiper dropped down from the wall to meet Raphael's attack.

Raphael pulled up short—he'd lost the element of surprise.

And it was my fault.

The two of them squared off. They held their swords at long point, the tip of each aimed at their enemy's heart. For several seconds neither spoke nor moved. To lunge from this position opened one's body to counterattack—would Raphael remember that?

I held my breath as he suddenly skittered backward, ducking his body low and then shooting forward, bringing his blade up from below to strike at Reiper's leg. Reiper blocked the attack with a clash of ringing steel.

"Pitiful," Reiper shouted, as Raphael backed off, readying himself again. "Did I not best you once already? You are such an amateur that I could simply wait for you to impale yourself on my sword! Who trained—"

Raphael, lunging forward again, sliced his blade through the air, and the tip caught the back of Reiper's sword hand.

Blood flowed from the wound. Reiper looked down at it in surprise, and Raphael used that split second to attack again. But once more Reiper deflected the blow, and then he laughed. "Slightly better," he said.

And then, quick as a striking snake, he slashed at Raphael's chest. Raphael spun his sword and blocked the blow, but its power shoved him backward and he reeled, off balance.

"You're getting worse again," Reiper said maliciously.

I watched helplessly from the roof as Reiper feinted left, smiling. Another strike, which Raphael warded off. They stood close together, and for a moment their crossed swords seemed to rest against each other. But then Reiper lurched and drew his blade upward along Raphael's, and when it came free, the point sliced deep into Raphael's cheek.

Reiper lifted his sword for another blow just as Raphael pitched to the side and disappeared from sight. Desperately I tried to climb the stones back up to the walkway, but my hands couldn't find purchase. I fell back to the roof, just in time to see Raphael struggling to his feet. He lifted his hand to me, as if to say, *Everything will be fine!*

But this was so clearly not true.

"Go," he shouted. "Run!"

Reiper tossed his sword aside. "You are brave, boy," he said, "but you are also stupid. I could kill you with my bare hands."

And then Reiper cuffed him on the side of the head, as if Raphael were nothing but a stray dog. Raphael stumbled and nearly went down. Reiper brought up the curved, gleaming blade of his knife. He paused, waiting for Raphael to regain his balance. "On the other hand," he said, "a knife is so much more efficient. Ready?" But he didn't wait for an answer. He plunged the blade into Raphael's chest.

I heard myself screaming, a horrible, piercing shriek that collapsed into a sob.

Raphael stood still, his fingers grasping helplessly at the hilt of the knife, and then he swayed.

Staggered.

Fell.

CHAPTER 60

Still screaming, I crawled to the edge of the roof and heaved myself off, onto the ground. When I stood up from the mud, I grabbed an axe from a dead man's back and ran blindly into the center of the courtyard, swerving every which way. First Reiper had killed my father, and then he had killed my only friend.

Mad with grief, I was ready to cleave in two whoever came within reach of my weapon. But suddenly Ares's men weren't fighting anymore—they were running away.

A woman with scaly lizard skin stood beside me, a broken sword in her hand. Her right eye was swollen shut and a lattice of blood tracked down her face. She slipped on the slick mud, and I grabbed her arm to keep her from falling. "What's happening?"

She let her breath out in a rush. "They're *retreating*. There are too many of us."

"Is it over?" I felt a surge of hope.

Wearily she shook her head. "Ares has a hunting lodge two hours' ride from here," she said. "He'll rest. And when he chooses, he'll return to attack the village." She looked me up and down, and then she smiled grimly as she removed her arm from my grip. "It is far from over."

But for now, at least, the fighting had stopped. Exhausted villagers laid down their arms and the air filled with weak cheering. They clapped one another on the back as they staggered toward shelter. The rain had turned to mist, and our enemies had fled.

I stood frozen, unable to feel any relief. Grief weighed on me like a stone. I wanted to collapse right where I was. But I needed to go see Raphael. I had to prove to myself that he was really gone.

And so I trudged up the tower steps, back to the wall walk where he had saved my life a final time. Where, if I hadn't cried out, he might have won the fight.

No more war, I'd begged my father. *Revolution,* I'd whispered to Raphael. In both cases, I'd thought I was doing the right thing. But somehow each time I'd been wrong, and they had both paid the price for my errors.

I felt like I'd been gutted, the way Ares suggested I should be, but I was somehow still alive. There was nothing left inside me but pain.

The wind had grown stronger, and it drove against me as I walked along the stone path. Below me, the courtyard was slick with blood and mud. Bodies of the dead lay where they had been struck down. Flames devoured the empty stables.

Wiping my streaming eyes, I came to the place where Raphael had fallen. I felt the blood drain from my heart.

It was empty.

CHAPTER 61

I stared at the stones in shock until I felt a hand on my shoulder. The villager with the crown of eyeballs stood behind me, his cap clenched in his hand. My mouth opened and closed without sound. Where was Raphael? Had Reiper thrown his bleeding body into the waves? I peered over the edge at the black water, churning and crashing against the cliff. Even if the knife strike had not been fatal, Raphael could not have survived the fall.

Wearily the man shook his huge head at me. "I am so sorry, Princess," he said. He pulled me toward his chest, dark with dirt and blood, and wrapped his arms around my shoulders. "Florence cared so much for you."

I pulled away from him in shock. "What?"

His eyeballs rolled nervously in his head. "She was killed," he said.

"In battle? Did she fight?"

He didn't answer right away, and so I grabbed his collar and shook him. "What happened?"

"She let us in," he said quietly. "She raised the platform."

Stunned, I let my hands fall, and he straightened his filthy jacket. And then he told me how she had been found: near the platform, murmuring something about *bargains,* stabbed —

"Stop, I cannot bear it," I said.

Gone: first Raphael, and now Florence. How could it be? The world wasn't big enough to hold my sorrow. My knees buckled.

I am on your side, child.

But this strange, beastly man lifted me up and steadied me. "Go rest, Princess," the man urged. "We will tend to the villagers." He paused. "The tired, the wounded, and the dead."

Someone began to lead me away. I didn't know what I'd done to deserve such kindness.

"Raphael told me to look after you," the man called.

In my room, the fire had died down to just a few embers. No attendants would come bearing wood tonight, and so I broke the little writing table into pieces and threw them into the fireplace. They quickly caught. I would have thrown the harp in too, but I wasn't strong enough to break it. I touched its strings; a mournful trill sounded. A single, shivering note lingered in the air like a ghost.

Without thinking, I began to sing:

I met you first in my old life —
I found you again in the new.
Though bid to become a demon's wife,
I long to be with only you.

My voice broke off. It was only now — now that it was too

late — that I understood how much Raphael meant to me. Why did I have to keep losing everyone close to me? Everyone that I loved?

I could hear the hiss of rainwater outside my window, pouring down from the gaping mouths of the castle gargoyles and splashing to the wall walk below.

Ares and his knights were gone, Raphael and Florence dead. The castle belonged to the people now.

Which meant that I could leave it — for good this time.

I thought back to my first wild journey, when I woke to darkness inside a speeding carriage. I hadn't known if I was being kidnapped or rescued; I didn't know if I was alive or dead. I still didn't know the answer to that last question.

Thunder rumbled overhead, reminding me of the Bells of Death, sounding their grim notes over the sleeping world. How had I heard those bells, if indeed they rang for me? What if they had rung only within a dream?

There was so much I didn't understand.

When I met my eyes in the wavering glass of the mirror, I cried out at my final transformation. No longer golden-eyed and silver-toothed, I was blue-eyed and black-haired, the way I'd been born. In the room's cold half-light, I saw a human princess with a dirty, tear-streaked face and a ripped, ruined wedding dress. It was yet another thing I couldn't explain. But there I was, shocked and blinking. Alone again.

I met my gaze, wiped the tears from my cheeks, and steeled myself. It was time to go.

CHAPTER 62

In the dank cavern beneath the castle, the darkness was so thick it threatened to suffocate me. I felt along the cold, slimy wall, unsure if I was moving toward the cave's mouth or deeper into its lightless chambers. Around me water dripped ominously and the air whistled and whispered; I jumped at every sound. What if one of Ares's knights hadn't fled with the others? What if Reiper waited in the shadows, that terrible curved knife in his hand?

My footsteps resounded against the stones no matter how softly I meant to tread. I fell over a pile of rubble, and the sharp rocks cut deep into my palm. Stunned, I lay on the wet, gritty floor.

Just get up. Keep moving, I told myself. I squinted in the blackness, as if it would help. I could see just as well with my eyes closed.

I was bone-tired, but every time I stopped to rest I began to shake in grief and anger. This was not over.

Then something exploded above me. The air was filled with

shrieking, clawing, thrashing bodies. I covered my head with my arms and felt claws rake my skin. Was it the harpies? I screamed, and the sound ricocheted through the darkness as high-pitched squeals echoed all around me. Something tore at my hair and I threw myself back to the ground.

Wordless chittering, and the appalling, cold touch of leathery wings: I realized what was happening only as the myriad tiny bodies twisted and flapped away into the blackness. I had frightened a colony of bats.

And they, I realized, would lead me to the mouth of the cavern. I followed their shrieks in the blackness, creeping forward, falling, and then creeping forward again, until I could make out the yawning opening that led to the salt flats.

I was free.

But I wasn't alone. The pus-fleshed ogres who had first borne me away from Bandon Castle crouched at the entrance to the cave, peering toward me in the darkness.

I stopped and pressed myself against the wall. There was just enough moonlight to see that the carriage, too, stood behind them. The wild-eyed horses pranced in their harnesses, almost as if they were waiting for me.

Then a torch flared, and the nearest ogre turned to me in its fiery glow. "Get in," it rasped.

I shrank back from the light. Did I dare? It could be that this was a trap. Maybe Ares had ordered them to bring me to his hunting lodge. But what if he hadn't—what if the carriage and its drivers were somehow mine to command?

It was like deciding to jump out the window: maybe I'd survive the journey, and maybe I wouldn't. And there was no way to know until it was too late.

I opened the carriage door and climbed in.

The ogre slammed the door behind me and then hoisted himself up to the bench. I heard a shout and the crack of a whip, and the carriage surged forward, flinging me back against the cushioned seat.

I shouted, "Take me to my mother!"

I felt a quick stab of guilt as we picked up our pace. Maybe it was wrong to leave an uprising I myself had inspired. But this was not my world, and I told myself that it was better to run away after victory than after defeat.

Or maybe I couldn't bear another day here, not with Raphael gone.

As Ares's castle receded behind us, I pulled the satin curtain from the window and tore it into long strips, which I wrapped around the palm I had bloodied in my fall. My dress was stiff with mud and gore, and I smelled like the pit at the bottom of a privy.

The horses settled into their gait, moving quickly over the sand. Exhausted, I lay down on the bench. I didn't cry—I couldn't. I felt as if my heart had been carved out of my chest. But I slept then, as dreamless as the truly dead.

Later I awoke to the lurching rattle of carriage wheels over rough road. We were in a forest of dark and numberless trees. Were these my mother's woods? They looked different somehow. Grimmer, more desolate.

I leaned my head out the window. "Are you going the right way? Take me to my mother!"

The forest seemed to swallow up my voice, but the standing ogre, the one who swung his torch like a flail, turned back to me and sneered, his yellow teeth gleaming deadly sharp. "Shut up, stupid girl," he hissed.

The driver yanked the reins, the carriage swerved, and a branch slapped me hard in the face. I yelped and ducked back inside. As I wiped my bleeding cheek, I almost welcomed the pain. It was better than being wracked by grief.

Far off thunder rumbled. The horses leaned into their harnesses, and thorny underbrush tore at the sides of the carriage. We swerved again, then turned down an even narrower track.

We had been traveling for what seemed like hours, but the woods were endless. The night, too, seemed never-ending, and despair threatened to overwhelm me. But then we rounded another curve, and up ahead I saw bright squares of light, beaming golden through the trees.

The windows of my mother's cottage.

CHAPTER 63

The driver pulled the reins to slow the horses, and I leapt out of the carriage before it even stopped. In another moment I was at the cottage door, and then I was flinging it open and rushing inside.

My mother stood shocked in the middle of the little room. "Sophia!" she cried. "I thought—"

She broke off, hurrying toward me, her face so bright with relief that it glowed like a candle. She pulled me tight against her soft, strong body. "I can't believe it, my precious daughter, you've come back."

She smelled like summer, like warmth and sunshine, and suddenly I was laughing and crying at the same time. Exhausted, dazzled, I said the first thing that came to mind. "I didn't get any soup."

She wiped the tears from my filthy cheeks and looked at me in wonder. "Whatever do you mean?"

I smiled. "Remember? The night I first saw you. You made

soup, but they came for me before I could eat any." I laid my head on her shoulder and tightened my arms around her. How could I explain what had happened, and what was still happening?

"Are you all right?" my mother asked. "You're bleeding."

The words came out in a rush. "Ares kidnapped me, and he said I had to marry one of his men, but I refused. Then there was a great battle, and the villagers stood with me against him. But Raphael was killed and I ran away, and somehow here I am again, and, Mother, I really don't understand anything."

She held me for a long time before gently stepping away. "You will, child," she said reassuringly. "We will talk. But first…" With a smile, she handed me a square of warm, damp linen, which I used to clean my face and hands. Then she took the cloth back, now bloody and dark with grime. "There, that's better, isn't it? And here, you must have something else to wear." She draped a garment over the back of a chair.

I disrobed and slipped into the homespun dress. The fabric was a soft gray wool, plain, with neither ornament nor lace. But it was comfortable and it fit me well. I held the ornate, stinking wedding gown over the fire. "May I?" I asked.

"Even the pearls?" my mother asked, looking wistfully at the shimmering line of them.

"Yes," I said.

"Forgive me," she said, smiling. "It's been a long time since I have seen jewels of any sort."

"These are cursed," I said. I let the dress fall from my fingers, and I watched as it turned black in the flames. "May the memories burn with it," I said fiercely.

"What need have you of jewels anyway?" my mother asked. "You are so beautiful the moon gleams white with envy."

I felt myself flush. My cut cheek burned. "Mother, please—"

"Does it embarrass you to be so fair?" she asked, her smile even bigger now. "You must get used to it. I fear you have a life-time of loveliness ahead of you."

My own smile was more wry. "If indeed I am alive," I said.

"Oh, child," she said. Then she laughed. "Why am I still calling you child? You are grown now." She brushed a strand of hair from my forehead. "And you have seen much—perhaps too much."

I thought of Reiper's cruel eyes and the knife plunging into Raphael's chest. "Things I wish I could unsee."

"You can tell me everything, my darling, and I will listen. But now is not the time."

"What do you mean?" I asked. "Why not?"

"I wish you could stay," she said. "I wish we could talk for-ever. But you must go home, Sophia. You are needed there."

"Home? Where is that, and how am I to get there? And if I must go, then come with me," I begged. I couldn't bear to leave her again.

"I'm sorry," she said. "But I can't. Please, don't look so sad, love. Please."

How could I hide my sadness? I had seen monsters, plague, and murder; I had watched the one I loved stabbed through the heart. And now I was supposed to say goodbye to my mother again, having been with her for only a matter of moments.

My mother straightened up, her eyes bright, as if something had just occurred to her. "Wait a moment," she said. She ducked outside the cottage, and when she came back in, her arms were full of flowers. Huge, perfect blooms of pink and yellow roses glowed as brightly as a sunset gathered into a bouquet. She placed the great pile of them on my lap, and I touched their velvety petals in awe.

"They're beautiful," I exclaimed. "But how do they grow in a forest in winter?"

"There is beauty—and there is hope—in wholly unexpected places," she said. "That's what these flowers tell us. And that is what you must try to remember."

"But I don't understand," I said stubbornly.

"You don't have to understand it," she said. "You just have to believe it. Remember it. Trust it. Life is impossible to understand, isn't it? And so, my child, it must simply be lived."

"But is this life?" I asked. "Or life after life? Or is it a dream? If it's a dream, I want to stay sleeping. I want to stay here."

My mother took my hands in hers. "It is not a dream."

"But how can I be sure?"

My mother's smile grew wistful. "I see now. You don't know if you can trust me. And why should that be surprising? When you were first born, I held you in my arms, and I promised you that no harm would ever come to you. And yet much harm already has. So why would you believe me when I tell you anything? The first words I spoke to you were a lie."

"Oh, Mother," I began.

She held up her hand. "No, no—that's not right. The second words were a lie. The first were 'I love you,' and words more true were never spoken, in this world or in heaven. I breathed them right into your heart."

"Just let me stay here," I pleaded.

"You are needed at home, my darling," my mother said. She squeezed my fingers and her expression changed. Her voice became low and urgent. "Listen to me, Sophia. Ares and his men march to destroy Bandon Castle."

I stood so quickly I knocked over the chair, dumping the perfect roses onto the floor. "But we defeated him. He fled in the middle of the night!"

"He rides toward Bandon even now." My mother stood, too, and now she took my face in her hands. "You are no longer just a princess. You are the queen now, Sophia. Your people depend on you. You must go now. Go *home*."

"Come with me," I begged again. "If I can go back, why can't you?"

Slowly, sadly, she shook her head. "The journey is yours to make alone."

Though I didn't want to believe her, I somehow knew that she spoke the truth. And so I dragged myself from her arms and climbed once again into the dark carriage. Grief tore at my heart. The whip cracked, and the horses began to run, and the light from her windows grew smaller and smaller. And then it was gone.

CHAPTER 64

Exhausted as I was, sleep was impossible. Relentless jolts from the racing carriage tossed me up and down like a sack of grain. I held on to the windowsill as best I could, trying to keep my head from smashing into the walls.

Eventually the forest thinned. We careened through scrubby brush, then burst onto a stubbled meadow scattered with giant slabs of black stone. As dawn slowly broke, clouds billowed in the east, and a sprinkling of stars glittered overhead.

Our path led us into barren gray foothills. As we climbed, the track grew narrower and steeper, but somehow the strength of the horses never flagged. Their hooves pounded, the carriage shook and rattled, and still we rose. The air grew thin and cold, and the gusting wind felt like fingers plucking at my hair, my dress.

Terrible noises began to spill from the ogres' hideous mouths. I covered my ears as I tried to lean out to see what troubled them. It took me a moment to realize that they were *singing*. But the song had no words I knew. Their language was dark, primordial—the sound of ancient boulders grinding together.

The path suddenly leveled and widened, and now we galloped across a rocky plateau. The horses' hooves sparked each time they struck down, and the ogres began howling even louder. Our speed increased. And up ahead, I saw it: the yawning blackness of empty air. The trolls shouted and loosed the reins, and the horses careened straight toward it.

Then one of the wheels struck a rock and the door flew open, crashing against the side of the carriage. Below me, the ground rushed by in a dizzying blur. I held on as best I could as we raced toward the edge of the precipice.

I had made a plunge like this before, but fear gripped me nevertheless. I closed my eyes as the edge grew nearer and nearer. I was frozen—

And we drove off the cliff.

I choked back a scream of terror. The trolls no longer sang. We hung suspended in the night, silence all around us. And then, like a silk blanket, a great calm settled over me.

We began to rise, as if the clouds were stairs we could climb. We pressed through a veil of mist, through wisps of pulsing, flickering colors. The sky was a jewel box of black velvet. The air grew warm and soft as summer.

I heard notes ringing high and clear, like an infinite number of tiny brass bells: the sound of the heavens singing. I knew that the answers to all my questions floated there in the sky, and all I had to do was reach out and touch them. Any minute, I would know if I'd ever see my mother again. In another breath I'd know what happened to Raphael.

I leaned out the window. Above me, the stars; below me, the dark, spinning world. The beauty took my breath away.

And then, all of a sudden, there was nothing.

The darkness was deeper than the blindness of the cave. The carriage was gone, I was set adrift, and I could feel myself coming apart. Being... *unmade*. I had no sight, and no mouth to cry out. I could feel no limbs. I tried to assemble what I felt were the pieces of myself, but I was floating away like dust. Unfurling, evaporating, vanishing into eternal nothingness.

Maybe this, finally, was death.

CHAPTER 65

I awoke with a heaving gasp. My eyes snapped open to light—bright, yellow sunlight—but everything was blurry and jumbled. Shapes wavered, and colors smeared and bled into one another.

"She's awake," a woman whispered.

Was she talking about me? I blinked rapidly and the fog began to clear from my vision. I saw a stained glass window, a tapestry of blue gentians, and the gleaming curve of an old, all-too-familiar harp.

A figure moved toward me. Was that...Odo? Jeanette? Was I really home?

I struggled to sit up as Jeanette hurried toward me, tears streaming down her face. "You've come back to us," she whispered.

"We thought we had lost you," Odo said, sinking to his knees. "Sacheverell said there was nothing more he could do, but Jeanette never once left your side."

"My mother was right," I said, my voice full of wonder. "She said I could come back!"

Jeanette frowned and turned to Odo. Their expressions, so briefly full of joy, were now haunted by worry. "Perhaps the fever is not gone," she said to him.

"I feel fine," I insisted, but even as I said it, I began to grow confused. If Jeanette had never left my side, did that mean I had never left this bed?

That was impossible. Wasn't it?

Jeanette turned back to me. "Your Highness, you should rest—don't speak. Here, let me fix your pillows." She tried to reach behind me but I grabbed her wrist.

"It's all true," I said. "It happened, I'm sure of it. I felt myself die. I was taken to a black castle. There were beasts, just like the ones I read about in my book. And I saw my own mother, Jeanette. She was so beautiful, just like you said." I shook my head and felt tears sting the corner of my eyes. "But she told me that I had to come back. She said that Ares was coming to attack us."

Jeanette went pale and opened her mouth to speak, but just then Adelie came running in, kicking up the rushes. They had been strewn with dried lavender, and the smell of summer bloomed in the air. Adelie dropped low in a curtsy. "Your Highness," she said, "I'm so glad to see that you are better." Worriedly, she glanced over at Odo to see if he was watching her. "They won't kill us all, will they, Your Highness?" She bit her lip and waited for me to comfort her, the way I once had.

"They won't," I said, trying to sound certain, but already Jeanette was pulling her quickly from the room.

I turned to Odo. "You must tell me where we stand," I said. I looked down at my arms, unmarred by blisters. "And what of the Seep? Did Sacheverell find a cure? Does little Fina live?"

His eyes were troubled. "He did, Your Highness, and she does, and that is our lone good news. But if you will know what we face, you must come with me. Can you walk?"

I'd barely even managed to sit up all the way, but I said, "I think so. Why?"

He cleared his throat, and his glance flickered away from me.

"I know this habit of yours," I said. "It means that you don't want to tell me something, but you know that you must. Odo, tell me. I'm not a child. I am your queen."

"You are needed on the battlements," he answered curtly. "Ares's army masses on the plains east of Bandon. And we must meet them there in battle."

I nodded as I struggled out of bed. I didn't try to tell him that I had already fought Ares once. I didn't think he would believe me, and perhaps with good reason. I didn't understand it myself. But it hardly mattered now: my duty was to rule my kingdom. My army.

At least in this world, Ares's soldiers would be mere men, I told myself.

My legs were weak, unused to their own weight, and I leaned on my hated old harp to keep from falling over. Odo gently cupped my shoulder—steadying me without reassuring me.

There could be no reassurance with such an enemy outside the gates.

It is not over.

I gathered myself for a moment, and then I looked up at my father's knight with resolve. "I will need my sword," I said. Then I turned to Jeanette. "And I should not fight in my nightdress."

Odo bowed, handing the blade to me, and then went to wait in the hall. Without any armor of my own—my father would have been furious had I asked for it—I dressed in a soldier's garb of a rough tunic and leggings, with the sword girded at my waist. I straightened my shoulders and felt blood returning to my limbs in slow, prickling waves. I clenched my fists until they throbbed. Soon I would need all the courage I'd ever possessed and more. I had been a princess, a beast, and a captive. And now I must be a warrior queen.

I went into the hall and smiled grimly at Odo. Together we turned to go.

CHAPTER 66

B ut my thoughts were of Raphael, not Ares, as Odo and I climbed to the ramparts. If the Seep hadn't actually killed me, it meant that he might still be alive, too. Perhaps he was cured, and he needed rescue from Gattis's foul underground kingdom. I felt my pulse quicken with hope. If Raphael had saved me in that other world, then maybe I could save him now.

Odo put his hand on my shoulder, bringing my attention back to the present. He'd stopped at a stone embrasure along the battlement, and now he gestured for me to look out. What I saw took my breath away.

Ares's army, thousands strong, amassed on the plains beyond Bandon Castle. It was as if a city had sprung up where there had been only hillocks and meadow grass: a city of tents, shouting soldiers, and fluttering flags the color of dried blood. Bonfires burned throughout the camp, sending black smoke curling into the sky.

Every part of me flared with mortal fear.

What sort of world was this, where a thousand mercenaries marched on a lone castle? We had so little compared to Ares. Ours was a fiefdom of fields and hills, a twisting river, a village of a few hundred souls. What did he hope to gain?

Beside me Odo stood grim and still.

"Can our marksmen reach them?" I asked.

He shook his head. "They are out of arrow range."

Toward the camp's edge, I saw a knot of men cooking meat over a fire while two giant carrion birds wheeled and shrieked above them. As I listened, the birds' piercing cries seemed to turn into words. "Blood!" I heard them shrieking. "Flesh!"

I gripped the wall so tightly I cut my fingers on the stones.

The harpies.

Trembling, I watched as the green-haired monsters of that other world dove, rose, and then dove again, daring each other to snatch a piece of roasting meat from a fire.

I squinted, peering more closely at the soldiers. Would I now see what—or who—I dreaded most?

Yes. There was Mordred, prancing around the perimeter of the camp on a black-maned charger, while the long shape of the Ekhidna cut through the crowd of soldiers like a knife.

"All the monsters," I whispered. My lives—my worlds—had joined into one. To fight the coming battle would take more strength than our men possessed.

I leaned over the battlement so far that Odo grabbed the back of my tunic to keep me from falling. There were knights I'd never seen before, but recognized from my book: Bael, a toad-like creature with eight jointed arms; Aexe, the burned man, whose limbs looked like the blackened trunks of trees; and Vermis, a huge, segmented monster with fangs sharper than arrowheads.

I felt Odo trying to pull me back in. "Your Highness," he said, "please, you'll fall." I scanned the throngs for other faces I knew. Near another bonfire, I saw the sharp, savage face of the jackal god, Seth, and elsewhere I spotted more men I recognized from Ares's halls. But I didn't see Zozo or Balor. I couldn't find Hasshaku Sama or El Cuchillo.

I turned to Odo, and he saw the shock on my face, but he didn't understand its source. It wasn't just the strength of our foe, or my fear of the coming battle. It was this awful realization: an army of demigods and monsters had followed me into the real world, but the ones who'd died during my time with Ares were not among its ranks. So had the wild events I'd witnessed actually happened? Had it not been a dream after all?

And what did that mean for a certain human boy?

The thought hit me like a fist in the stomach. There was no point in going to the dungeon now. I felt the blood drain from my limbs.

"Your Highness," Odo said again, "they are waiting for us."

I could barely speak for sorrow. Raphael was gone. "What do you mean?" I managed.

"Ares waits for us to accept his invitation to battle," Odo said.

"They invite us to battle, as if it were a royal ball?"

"He is giving us a choice," Odo said. "We can come out and fight, or we can barricade ourselves in the castle, and he will lay siege."

"That is just like him," I said bitterly, "to offer a choice between options that we can only find abhorrent."

Odo turned to me in surprise. "What do you know of Ares?" he asked.

"More than I wish to," I said fiercely.

"Your Highness, I do not understand."

I didn't know how to explain it, and so I just shook my head, gripping my sword until my knuckles whitened.

"That's not how you hold a blade, my Queen," Odo said gently. "Your clasp must not be so rigid."

I loosed my fingers a little. "I know. I was remembering someone."

Reiper. My greatest enemy was down there somewhere, in that sea of men, and soon I would come face-to-face with him again.

"There is some honor in Ares if he does not attack without warning," Odo said.

"Honor? Hardly. He is only trying to make us tremble, so that we go to fight certain of disaster already. Our deaths are not enough for him. He must have our fear, too."

Odo said nothing.

"It's inevitable, isn't it?" I asked as I watched the harpies wheeling over the camp. A soldier tossed bread to them as if they were pets. "The villagers—all of us—we will be slaughtered like cattle."

"We will not."

"How can you say that, Odo? Remember that my father is no longer here to scold you for your honesty. Admit it. We are over-matched. We will be massacred."

"Many of us will die, yes. But we will not die like beasts, Your Highness. We will die like warriors. With honor."

My eyes swept over the city of soldiers. I remembered seeing my father's knights ride home after a conquest, and though I knew little then, I think I still understood: even a battle won is hard. I shook my head. "Was it my fault, Odo? I asked my father not to fight. And when he stood down..." I gestured to the plains.

"When Leonidus was no longer a warrior king, others were more than ready to take his place," Odo said. "Blame rests on many shoulders, including yours, but war and conquest are as much a part of our lives as birth and love."

"And death," I said bitterly.

"And death." Odo stood silent for a moment, his hand on his sword. Then he bowed, ever so minutely. "Battle is at hand, Your Highness. Our lives are yours to command."

Fate had put the crown on my head too soon, and now I must be worthy of it. *I know what is best,* my father used to say to me.

Now I hoped that I did.

CHAPTER 67

That night I asked Jeanette to braid my hair in intricate, twisting coils. She asked—her kind voice feigning lightness—what might be the occasion for such a splendid style. "There is none," I lied. I didn't want to speak of my decision to anyone. It was too terrible to voice.

I sent her from my chamber when she had finished, and then, alone, I dressed in the raiment of a queen. The gown had been my mother's, kept in a sealed wardrobe after her death, its folds still fragrant with cedar and dried roses. It was ivory silk, encrusted with opals and mother-of-pearl, its design as exquisite and refined as she had been. The blue gentians of our family crest were worked into the bodice in sapphires and golden thread.

When I looked at myself in the mirror, it was almost as if I saw *her*—how I'd imagined her all my life, and how I'd seen her in all my father's portraits. A fainter, paler version of the beauty I'd met in that impossible dark forest.

Then I pressed my hands together over my heart and said a prayer of protection, for all those in Bandon Castle and in the village not far away, all who would go to sleep dreading the bloodshed the dawn would bring.

But what if I could stop it? To demand that nearly everyone I ever knew and loved—Odo, Jeanette, Adelie, and even irritable, disapproving Abra—march to their own slaughter, and give up their lives in my name, was not the order of a queen. It was the command of a tyrant.

I knew that it was my duty to protect them if I could. I took a dark, hooded cloak from the wardrobe and covered my gleaming dress, and then I slipped from my room, easily avoiding the guards stationed at the end of the hall. Of course, I had no idea if my plan would work. But even the faintest glimmer of hope was better than the pitch-black of despair.

The halls were unlit, but I knew them so well that I did not need a torch. At the gatehouse, the guards stopped me with brandished swords. Showing them my grim, determined face, I bade them return to their posts, and then I slipped across the bridge.

Fires flickered in the field, but the camp was quiet. A chill wind from the north rustled the dry branches of the trees along the river. My feet crunched on dead grass. I walked to my fate as a thief goes to the gallows: frightened, unwilling, and yet knowing that he must.

I heard a snuffling breath behind me, and I whirled around in panic. But it was only Dogo, my father's half-wild hound. This brute had torn the throats from deer on many a hunt, but now he looked up at me and whined. I held out my hand, and he licked it.

I felt the prickle of tears in my eyes. "You can walk me to my doom," I whispered, touching his warm head gratefully. "I will be glad for the company."

I looked back at my castle for what was possibly the last time. A few torches flickered along its battlements, and they seemed as distant and as cold as the stars.

I had to keep going. If I hesitated any more, I could not trust myself to go on. I skirted the perimeter of the camp, waking no one. Ahead of me I saw a large tent, and I felt that dark, familiar, terrible pull.

For a moment I was still, taut as a bowstring, outside Reiper's tent. Then I went in.

CHAPTER 68

Reiper was sitting on the edge of a low cot, his back to me. As I entered, a candle guttered and then flared back to life, and my shadow flickered on the musty cloth wall like a ghost.

Reiper didn't turn his head, but I could tell by the hard, tense line of his shoulders that he knew I was there. Maybe he'd even been expecting me.

I could feel my heart's wild thrumming and I willed it to slow. I understood what was necessary. My own mother had been given to my father—like a chest full of gold, or a herd of prized steeds—as a way to ally two kingdoms. Though their marriage was not born of love, they found it together. That was the great, astonishing gift of their luck.

I knew that I would not be so fortunate, but I, too, would marry for an alliance. If my worst enemy—the man who killed my beloved father—would have me.

I closed my eyes, steeling my nerve. And then I spoke. "Once you wanted me and I refused you." My voice sounded strangled, as if the words were being wrenched from my throat.

"I was wrong," I went on, a little louder this time. I could see a vein in Reiper's neck, pulsing quick and savage. "I was childish and I was wrong. And now I've come to say that I am yours if you still wish to have me. I will marry you this instant—we can go wake a priest. All I ask is that you stop the battle. Tell Ares that he has greater treasures to plunder, grander kingdoms over which to stake his claim. You know this to be true."

Reiper still didn't turn around. His breathing had changed, growing harsh and ragged. Was it rage—or was it desire?

Either terrified me, but I would not run. My choice had already been made, and so I bowed my head and waited for his reply.

I heard Reiper exhale sharply, and the candle blew out, plunging the tent into darkness. In another instant, he was behind me, and his hand was tight at my throat. I gasped as I felt the prick of the knife in my neck. It was a tiny point of white-hot pain, like the sting of a wasp.

"I seem to remember this position," Reiper whispered. "Holding you like this, just outside your bedroom..."

I could actually hear him smile. A narrow trickle of blood began to slide down my skin, staining the pale silk of my mother's gown.

"It was right after I'd killed your father," he went on. "What a fine night that was, to gut a king and then prick his daughter. Do you remember it as fondly as I do, Sophia?"

I clenched my teeth together, willing myself to stay calm. This was what I had come for: to give myself to him, so that I might spare everyone else.

This is what a queen would do.

"I remember it," I whispered, "though with sorrow rather than pleasure."

Reiper pulled me tighter against him. He wasn't wearing his tooled leather armor, and I felt the heat of his body pressing against the whole length of mine. His free hand grabbed at my gown and pulled it up along my legs, and his fingers were hot and insistent against my skin.

Then he whirled me around and flung me to the cot. I screamed but just as quickly clapped my hand over my mouth. I managed to sit up, but I couldn't stand because he was in my way. He loomed over me, a darker shadow in the dark tent, pulsing with lust and malice.

His calloused fingers tugged at the neckline of my gown. The fabric didn't tear, but I heard the clatter of opals spilling to the ground. "I will have your dowry now," he said.

"You must promise," I gasped. "You must promise to stop the battle." I felt tears streaming hot down my cheeks. I wanted to leave my body, but I had to stay here, I had to do this.

"Or what?" he said mockingly. He pushed me, hard, and I fell back along the cot again, and then he was above me, his weight crushing me. I'd never thought of hate having a smell, but it did. Hate had the smell of a murderer's sweat, the scent of iron thrust into a forge, sharp and metallic, hot and cold at the same time.

"Have I managed to silence that viper tongue of yours?" His hot breath was in my ear, and I tried not to grimace. His knee pressed its way between my legs while his other hand pulled the hem of my skirt again, shoving it up over my thighs.

I gripped the sides of the cot so I wouldn't push him off. This was my duty, I knew.

Reiper pressed his fingers against my cheek. "Do you remember what I said to you that night?"

Of course I did. But I kept my mouth shut, and I turned my face away from him.

"Look at me," he demanded. "Look me in the eyes."

When I stared into their dark emptiness, I felt my soul shriveling up, blackening, like paper tossed into a fire.

"You must promise to stop the battle," I said again.

"I will make no such oath," he hissed, working at his breeches with one hand, the other gripping my neck and face cruelly.

Fear clawed at my heart. *Stupid girl,* I thought, *you should have known this.* For a terrifying moment, despair overwhelmed me.

But I could not resign myself to this fate.

I was queen.

I need submit to no one.

My hands moved as if of their own accord, and suddenly I was reaching into the bodice of my dress, and I was pushing him away. My fingers found the little dagger I'd placed close to my breast and tightened on the handle.

"I will never be yours," I whispered, as I thrust it up and slashed it into his chest.

Reiper sprang back, cursing, a red gash open just beneath his collarbone. He looked at me in shock for a second, and then he lunged. I scrambled backward, but he caught my foot and yanked me toward him. I kicked as I fell, and I felt my boot smash into the side of his face, but he didn't even seem to feel it. He picked me up off the bed and threw me to the ground. Then he started kicking me.

I curled up protectively as the blows rained all over. Somewhere in the back of my mind I was aware of how much it hurt.

But all I could think of was how badly I wanted to survive. I didn't want to give him the satisfaction of killing two of Bandon's rulers.

Blindly I slashed at Reiper's legs with my dagger, and I must have made contact because the blows stopped and he took a few steps backward. I managed to get to my feet and run for the tent opening. I knew he was right behind me; I could almost feel his fingers in my hair.

And so I turned around and threw myself at him, and as I did, my right hand arced up from below, and the blade I held plunged into the hard curve of his neck.

For a moment, we both held utterly still in shock. And then Reiper's lifeblood began streaming down on my hand. There was so much of it, and it flowed out in throbbing spurts. He staggered backward, clutching madly at his gushing wound. His body convulsed and he gasped. Then he fell over onto the ground, and I heard the wet, gurgling sounds of dying. I held the knife, slick with blood, above his chest for a moment. "You like a dull knife," I said. "I prefer a sharp one." I plunged the weapon into his heart, and I then twisted it. "That was for my father." Reiper moaned, and I stabbed him in the stomach, ripping the blade across. "And *that* was for Raphael."

This time he made no sound at all.

CHAPTER 69

At first light, I went to Ares's tent unarmed. As the sun rose pale and cold over the distant hills, I knelt on the rocky ground and waited. The chill seeped into my bones, and my knees began to ache. I didn't move, though: I wanted Ares to know that I came in abjection. Supplication. Not a queen so much as a beggar, in a torn and bloody wedding dress.

A harpy stretched her vast black wings and rose heavily into the bleak blue air. I heard a horse whicker and a soldier curse. Otherwise the camp was quiet; the men still slept. And then, like an evil whisper, I heard a blade drawn from its scabbard.

The hairs rose on the back of my exposed neck. I held my breath and did not move. I knew that Ares stood above me, but I didn't dare look up at him.

"Look me in the eye so you can watch me kill you," Ares said.

This was harder than anything—to keep my eyes on the

ground, to quell the rage I felt. I wanted this fight. But I knew I couldn't have it, not without destroying all that I knew and loved.

"Once, you must have understood compassion," I began.

"I am unfamiliar with the word," Ares said. "And though I do know what patience is, I have little of it at the moment. Not when a head is simply begging to be severed from its small, white neck."

"I live even now because of your mercy," I said, trying not to flinch. "And I beg you to find more of it within you. When I came to you before, on behalf of my own life, you rightly sent me away. Now I come to you as a ruler of many, on behalf of their lives. They have no quarrel with you. What right have I to tell these people to die?"

A laugh bubbled up from his sinewy throat. "Do you not know, Your Highness? That is precisely what rulers are supposed to do! Certainly your father had no trouble marching his men into combat. He always left a good portion of them behind, too, their guts spilling onto the battlefield as they cried for their mothers like lost children."

"But the lion should not bother with the mouse," I said. "You are too powerful to—"

"I am not interested in metaphor and poetry, girl," Ares said roughly. "You're the one who likes books so much. Need I remind you that you lived as my guest? You ate my bread and meat. And with every breath you took, you deceived me. This is not a game. You may not simply begin again. You set us upon a path, and we will follow it to the end."

My desperation grew. Everything hung on this moment. "All that you seek will be yours," I said. "I will open the gatehouse to the castle. You may have our gold, our silver, whatever spoils you seek. I will give it all to you, so you do not have to take it by force." I gestured toward Bandon Castle, squatting dark and gray on the other side of the moat. It had seemed so grand to me once. And now it seemed but a small stronghold, one man's insufficient attempt to keep the night and wilderness and violence at bay.

Ares leaned upon his sword as if it were a walking stick, and then he picked it up and looked at it fondly. "Steel needs blood to keep it strong," he said. "Didn't your father teach you that?"

I said, "That's not what he believed."

I felt Ares's gaze on my skin, as cold as crackling ice. "Oh, really? I think you're wrong. But he's dead now, so no matter."

"I ask not for myself," I said. "I beg for everyone else. I do not think fathers should see axes cleave their sons in two. I do not want a man to watch his neighbor shot through with an arrow. I will not have the head of a child soldier, in insufficient armor, bashed in by a flail. Your men fight for gold and they seek blood. But my people do not wish to fight. All the villagers want is to live." The tears flowed down my cheeks now, and my throat ached with sorrow. "All they ask for is the chance to plant seeds in the spring and to harvest them in summer; to raise animals and children and to sleep at night in peace. To dream something beautiful and to rise in the morning, and to work all day to make that dream come true."

Ares's gaze flicked away from mine and traced the silvery line of the River Lathe.

Follow that river back home, I silently urged. *Turn around and go, laden with every jewel from our coffers, every last piece of gleaming gold.*

I sensed a shift in the air around us — a loosening. I watched, holding my breath, as Ares's hand fell away from the hilt of his sword. And I waited, as Florence had, for his words of mercy. I sensed them on his lips. I bowed my head.

When I could bear the silence no more, I dared glance up at him. I was still on my knees.

And I saw that he was staring at me. I watched in horror as his lip curled and his face contorted itself in dark and infinite hatred.

"I would sooner rip the heart from your chest with my fingers," he said.

I pulled down the bodice of my dress, revealing naked skin that prickled with gooseflesh in the cold. "Do it, then," I dared him, "if it means you'll leave my people alone."

He took a step toward me, livid, deadly.

I braced myself for the pain—it was the only thing I could do. But then Ares started, looking up and behind me, and I watched his expression change from rage into disbelief.

Turning, I staggered to my feet. A hundred yards away, with only open meadow between us, was another army. An army of men—beasts—villagers.

And Raphael was at its head.

CHAPTER 70

There was no time to shout. No time to wonder—or rejoice—that Raphael was alive. In that moment of Ares's surprise, I struck, stabbing at him with a metal tent stake I had yanked from the ground.

Dodging my attack, he stumbled, and for an instant the advantage was mine. I thrust again, trying to sink the spike into the gap beneath his breastplate. But as I pulled back, he kicked the stake from my grip and sent it spinning behind me. I faced him, my teeth bared in fury, with nothing now but my bare hands.

Ares's knights and soldiers streamed past us, rushing forward to meet Raphael's army. Shouts rang out, metal clanged, body thundered against body.

"Before I join the fun," Ares said, his eyes glittering with cruel pleasure, "let's see about that heart of yours."

"Sacrifice does me no good now," I said, backing away from

him. "The battle I sought to avoid has begun. So will you kill me, unarmed, as a coward would? Or will you give me a weapon?"

A faint smile seemed to twitch at the corner of his mouth. Keeping his eyes locked on mine, Ares reached behind him into the tent and produced another blade, which he tossed onto the ground in front of me. The scabbard, encrusted with rubies and onyx, was more ornate than any crown. I began to reach for it and then stopped.

Ares sensed my misgivings. "Go on," he said. "I'm not going to hit you while you're reaching for it."

My hand darted out, and Ares's sword flashed down, missing my arm by a hair's breadth.

"I lied," he said.

I glared at him. "If you want a fair fight, let me pick up my weapon."

"You could have all the weapons in the world, and it still wouldn't be fair," Ares said. "Considering your size, your inexperience, and your sex."

"Are you going to let me get the sword or not?" I asked through clenched teeth.

Ares bowed mockingly. "Of course, Your Highness."

I bent down and took up the sword, pulling it from its scabbard. It was too long for me and far too heavy. But there was nothing to be done about it. I would have to fight with what I had, and with a desperation like I'd never felt before. I tightened my fingers at the hilt. I'd practically need two hands to even lift the blade.

Ares watched my struggle with amusement.

Do not think, Odo had always said to me. *Let your wrist lead you; let it tell your body what to do.* How well he had trained me in flinging knives with the safety of distance, and how little he had taught me of killing up close.

I ran at Ares, slashing maniacally. My blade rang off his armor, and he fell against the tent—he'd not been expecting such a sudden attack. But in falling, he swept a leg underneath mine and knocked me off balance. I stumbled and went down to my knees, catching myself before I sprawled flat. He was already upright, and as I tried to scrabble out of the way, he brought the hilt of his sword down onto my temple.

Blinding white light flared in front of my eyes and pain exploded in my head, tearing through every inch of my body. I rolled over and curled into a tight ball of agony. I tried to get to my hands and knees, but the movement made me dizzy. Chest heaving, blind with pain, I heard Ares laughing above me.

I knew then that I was going to die. *It's all right,* I told myself. *You've died before. You can do it again.*

I heard Ares's blade whistling down. I braced myself for it to fall on my neck. But it didn't strike my body. It rang against another sword.

CHAPTER 71

A dagger dropped to the ground in front of me. Through streaming eyes I looked up and saw Raphael thrust his chin at me—*pick it up!* the gesture said.

"Watch out," I gasped, as Ares swung at him and Raphael leapt back. The blade sliced only air, and Ares cursed under his breath.

Grabbing the knife, I crawled out of the way and, holding on to the front of the tent, I pulled myself to standing. Black spots swam before my eyes and everything around me pulsed and glowed as if ringed by fire. But I took a deep breath and gathered my strength.

Only a few arms' lengths away, Raphael struck at Ares like a madman, his sword swinging so quickly my eyes could barely follow it. His shirt was torn to rags and blood flowed from a cut on his brow, streaming down his face. Ares, who was neither tired nor wounded, barely moved to defend himself; with just flicks of his wrist, he deflected each of Raphael's blows.

I lifted my sword and staggered forward, lurching toward them, so dizzy I had to use my sword to help me stand.

"Raphael, this is my fight," I shouted.

"Actually," Ares called, "it's mine. But it'll be over in just a moment."

Then he began his attack. His flashing blade pushed Raphael backward, past the edge of the camp and into the high dead grass that bordered the river.

I screamed as Ares struck Raphael on the side of the head with the flat of his sword, and Raphael crumpled to the ground. Unsteady still, I ran toward them as fast as I could. Was I to watch him die again? I couldn't bear it. I wouldn't bear it.

But a moment later, Raphael staggered to his feet and stood, half hunched in agony, but still holding his blade.

"Raphael," I shrieked. "Leave him to me."

He shook his head and pain twisted his features. "Run, Sophia," he commanded.

Do not enter the fray too early, he'd said to me in Ares's courtyard. *Run,* he said now.

But I was done listening to him. I was his queen.

I went at Ares like an animal, my scream bloodcurdling and horrible. I struck him from behind with my sword, and when he turned to face me I hit him across the face with a smoldering branch from the night's bonfires. Then I darted away, daring him to chase me.

Ares paused, and his icy eyes bored into mine. Behind him, Raphael, chest heaving, swayed toward him. He could barely even lift his sword.

"You're surrounded, Ares," I said.

Ares threw back his head and laughed. "By a princess and a

peasant," he spat. Blood trickled from the cut on his cheek, and he wiped it away with the back of his hand. "This is the most fun I've had in years."

He advanced upon me and I gripped my sword, bracing myself for his attack. *Don't think. Let your wrists tell you what to do.* But then Ares turned and ran toward Raphael.

Shouting with rage, I chased him, my head blazing with pain.

We were two against one, and despite the strength of our foe I thought we had a chance. But we were like gnats worrying at a hawk. Ares wasn't clumsy like Balor or slow like El Cuchillo. He fought with a cold, quiet brutality, his blade fast and his step light.

Suddenly the air was full of wild, piercing shrieks. I looked up and saw huge black wings unfolding in the sky above Raphael. The harpy swooped over him, then turned and came back, plummeting downward, her outstretched claws raking Raphael's shoulders before she shot upward again.

Ares used that moment to attack. His sword slashed across Raphael's chest, opening a line of red, and Raphael went down to his knees. His head bowed, and he did not lift it up. It looked like he was praying—perhaps begging—for his life. And I knew how Ares felt about mercy.

CHAPTER 72

Ares towered over him, a ghastly smile on his face. The shadow of the harpy passed over me as I ran toward them. I ducked, but her claws caught my hair, yanking a black coil from my head. My scalp burned as I jumped up, swinging my sword in an arc over my head. I felt the blade make contact.

The harpy shrieked as dark, iridescent feathers swirled down through the air. I'd shorn off part of her tail. Rudderless now, she swerved as she descended, nearly crashing into Ares, who sidestepped out of her path. The harpy, scenting blood on Raphael, landed and advanced on him. Struggling to his feet, he looked quickly between her and Ares, not certain who in that moment was the worse threat.

"Blood," the harpy cawed. "Blood, hot blood."

Raphael swung wildly at the creature, who lifted a few feet from the ground and then landed again, still shrieking. Forced to continue his retreat toward the banks of the River Lathe, Raphael breathed in awful, ragged gasps. His face was red with blood, his ripped shirt stained with it. Soon he'd come to the river's edge, and there would be nowhere else to go.

Ares watched thoughtfully. "Only a fool would come between a harpy and her breakfast," he said, almost to himself. "I suppose I shall let her do the killing for me."

I charged. Ares heard me coming, and he turned, lifting his sword to meet mine with a clash that shook me to my bones.

I quickly retreated, hopping from foot to foot—a moving target. "Come on, then," I jeered, "worry about the work of killing me."

Ares's lips parted in a slow, ugly smile. "Why are you suddenly prancing around like a pony? Is that how you queens think one is supposed to fight?"

I didn't answer; I kept up my mad dance, my sword and dagger scissoring in the air.

When I'd first begged Odo to teach me to use a sword—and when he had at first refused—I'd grabbed a broom from the courtyard and brandished it at his face. How crazily I'd slashed, leaping back and forth like a lunatic rabbit, and Odo had laughed until tears came to his eyes. *If that's the way you attack,* he'd said, trying hard to compose himself, *your opponent will chop you in half before you can say Bandon Castle.*

But my ploy had worked. He'd shown me how to hold a weapon, how to keep my stance steady, how to strike hard with a simple, well-timed blow. How to aim for flesh, not armor.

And that day I learned a lesson Odo hadn't even meant to teach me: though warriors praised a show of strength, the appearance of weakness could serve its own purpose.

Ares took a step toward me, and I sliced at the air with my dagger. Then I feinted, making a fake sword thrust at his chest and leaping back again. My legs felt as heavy as lead, but I kept up the hopping, skittering footwork, a weapon in each hand. Despite the cold air, sweat ran down my forehead, stinging my eyes.

"You're going to wear yourself out," Ares said. He sighed. "It's a pity to kill you, really, when no doubt you could be taught a thing or two. You're quite quick for a girl. You'll never make a decent swordsman, of course, but you could be an excellent court fool."

I heard another shriek from the river's edge, and I dared but a quick glance toward Raphael. The first harpy had been joined by her ravening sister, and Raphael now made his stand between them, cutting at their feathered breasts, holding them off but not driving them away. There was a new bloody gash along his brow.

Hold on, Raphael, I thought. *This time I'm going to be the one to save you.*

"Pay attention," Ares said, swiping at me. "Death is coming."

I dodged the strike, but barely, and as I did I turned my ankle. A new flash of pain shot through me, but I ignored it. I slashed at Ares's face and missed. No matter: I wasn't really trying yet. I wanted him to think me weak. To think he could kill me with his eyes closed.

He swung with the flat of his sword, and it slammed into my ribs, staggering me backward. "That hurt, didn't it?" he asked.

It did. *Everything* hurt. I gave him more ground, stumbling backward. This was nothing like fighting Raphael or Odo, and I didn't know how much longer I could last.

Just get him close, I thought, *and then strike.*

Ares circled me slowly, his face half smile, half scowl. His sword came swinging at me, but I parried the blow. My head was ringing, my vision blurred.

Now. I had to attack now.

I lunged forward, my blade slicing through the air. I felt it connect with flesh. But Ares, too, had struck, and his sword sliced deep into my stomach. At first I felt nothing but surprise. I dropped my dagger and pressed my hand over the wound, just as pain began searing through it. Blood soaked through my dress. I fell to my knees and looked up at Ares in shock.

He stood over me, triumphant. And though he could have killed me right then, he didn't. Instead, he watched me gasp, cry, and try to hold the blood inside me, knowing that it wouldn't work. This wasn't mercy—this was sadistic pleasure.

"Don't you remember what I told you about your little friend the pig?" he asked softly. "We do not hide from suffering, girl. We embrace it. We relish it."

My only weapons now were words. "Speaking of suffering, I killed him," I panted. Scalding waves of pain radiated up and down my entire body. I felt like I was burning.

Ares frowned. "Who?"

"Reiper."

"You couldn't have."

Proudly I lifted my head. It felt as heavy as a boulder. "And yet I did."

His face twisted in anger as he stepped toward me. "That is unfortunate," he almost whispered. "But I've done the same for you, haven't I?" He gestured toward the wound in my stomach.

The world spun around me. The pain burned, but the rest of me was cold, and the sticky wetness of my dress repulsed me.

The black spots had almost taken over my vision. I pitched forward and landed on the ground.

Maybe he had killed me, but I had one last hope: I'd fallen over the dagger, lying where I'd dropped it just moments before. Looming above me now, Ares seemed as tall as a mountain.

"It is unfortunate that things had to end this way," he said. But his tone was not of regret, but of relish. "I had hoped to see you wed to one of my men, and now I will watch you slowly die, alone."

My heart was pounding harder than any drum. "Have mercy," I sobbed. "It hurts. Please — kill me now."

Ares hesitated.

"I'm ready to die," I gasped. "I've done it before."

Leering, Ares stepped closer and lifted his sword over my head. But before he got to the top of his swing, I rolled quickly to the side, crying out as my wound twisted, and I flung my knife hand out. I made a mad, desperate slash, and my blade severed the tendon at the back of Ares's heel.

Bellowing in pain and rage, Ares fell, cursing, to the ground, and I scrabbled forward on hands and knees to meet him where he landed, and with the last ounce of strength I had in me, I shoved the thin, sharp tip of my knife deep underneath his left arm.

Ares's eyes went wide as blood began pouring out from beneath his armor.

"You were right, Ares," I gasped. "Death *is* coming, but not for me. How does it feel to be struck down by a mere girl? You can't fix a mortal wound — what was it you said about embracing suffering?"

Ares was trying to take off his chest plate to better reach his wound. "A lucky strike," he grunted. "Better than I would have expected from the likes of you. But I'll recover—"

"You won't," I said firmly. "Odo taught me." My eyesight had become a tunnel, and I could hear blood rushing through my veins, spilling out of my own wound. "But don't worry, it won't take you too long to die. I'll keep you company while you go."

Ares's skin had gone very white. The color seemed to have drained even from his eyes. "This should have been you," he whispered. "Soaking the ground with your lifeblood. I don't understand..."

I felt my own strength fading. "You don't have to understand. You just have to believe." I lay down in the dirt not far from his prone body. "My mother told me that," I whispered.

He turned to face me, his breaths coming quick and shallow.

I looked in his eyes, once ice-blue and now glazing to gray. "You once told me that Bandon Castle needed a ruler on its throne," I gasped. The burning was starting to consume me. "What you didn't realize was that it already had one."

One last spurt of blood. One last exhale. His gaze, now fixed on nothing.

"*Me.*"

I closed my eyes.

CHAPTER 73

First, I was aware only of darkness. After that came the pain—an insistent, pulsing ache deep in my stomach, burning like I'd swallowed coals. Moaning, I struggled to open my eyes. When I did, it seemed as if the darkness had barely abated. I was lying in a bed, in a small room, with a flickering fire and the smell of smoke from damp, green wood.

Again, I thought. It seemed I was always waking somewhere, weak and confused. And where was I this time?

"Hello?" I whispered.

I heard the sound of feet swishing through rushes, the rustle of fabric, and a sharp intake of breath.

"Sophia," someone whispered.

I saw only a shadowy human outline. "Who are you? Where am I?"

"Oh, my dear, one moment—" The shadow moved away, I

heard more rustling, and then bright light struck me in the face like a blade.

I gasped, blinking in the sudden brilliance, and then I saw my own Jeanette, beaming down at me in a room now lit with golden morning light. She placed the tapestry that had been covering the window onto a low wooden bench and hurried to my side.

"Where am I?" I asked again. "What happened?"

"You are in Sacheverell's chambers. There was a battle, Your Highness," Jeanette said softly. "Do you remember? Here, take a draught of this."

She held a cup to my lips, and I tried to raise my head enough to take a sip. It was warm and extremely bitter. I coughed, a white-hot burst of pain shot through me, and I cried out, clutching my stomach. "What is *that*?"

"I'm sorry, Your Highness, but it will help. It's mulberry juice, betony, and henbane."

Henbane—this was what they'd given my father on his death-bed. "Am I dying?" I asked.

"No, you are *healing*," Jeanette said. "The henbane eases the pain."

I spoke through clenched teeth. "It's not working."

"You must give it a moment," Jeanette said, smiling in sympathy.

I closed my eyes against the pain. But the moment I did, awful images rushed in: my hands wet with Reiper's blood, the tip of Ares's sword slicing into my stomach. I saw the harpies, too—shrieking, hungry, and closing in on Raphael. Quickly I opened my eyes again.

"Am I truly alive?" I whispered.

"That you are," Jeanette said firmly.

"And is Ares truly dead?"

"Yes, my Queen," Jeanette said. "You yourself killed him, don't you remember?"

"I don't think I was awake for the last part," I admitted.

"You are a hero," she said. "And to think I used to worry you for not playing the harp! You wield a sword as well as your father did, it seems." She gave a little hiccupping cough and began to cry. "Oh, but you gave us such a terrible fright."

"Prop me up," I said, but I gasped in anguish as she did so.

"I will call for Sacheverell," she said. "He is right—"

"I don't need him," I said. "I'm fine."

But Sacheverell had heard us somehow, and suddenly there he was, his ghastly gray face triumphant. He bent, put his long-fingered hand on my forehead, and smiled proudly. "The fever is gone, Your Highness, and the wound cauterized," he said. "You need only rest now."

A familiar red beard appeared over Sacheverell's shoulder, and then Odo was pushing him out of the way, followed by Elodie and Adelie, who rushed into the tiny chamber.

"Out," Jeanette yelped. "She is hardly fit for such company!"

But I had thought I would never see any of these beloved faces again, and I could not bear to have them sent away now. "Let them stay," I said, smiling. "Please."

Jeanette sighed and acquiesced, but she hurried to shut the door so that no one else could enter.

I turned to my father's most loyal knight. "What happened, Odo? How am I saved?"

I did not ask about the fate of Raphael. It seemed impossible that he could have cheated death again. But until I was actually given the news, it did not have to be real. "Are we victorious?" I asked.

Odo smiled through his beard. "So you would like me to tell you of your great feats, is that it? Well, you have certainly earned your praise. You slew Reiper in the dead of night and Ares the following day." Then he shook his head in seeming wonder. "I cannot have taught you that well, so how you managed it—how you bested such warriors—well, *you* will have to tell *me* someday."

I felt myself flush at his words. "But what of the armies?" I asked.

"When news of Ares's death spread to his troops, they scattered," he said.

"Like sheep," Adelie crowed.

"They lit the fields on fire," Elodie said. "The trees burned like torches."

Jeanette whirled around. "Hush, girls," she hissed.

"Ares's men were mercenaries," Odo went on, "and suddenly the man who'd promised to pay them was dead. So Elodie is right. They lit what they could on fire, and they vanished in the smoke." A flicker of a smile twitched in the corner of his mouth. "And, seeing that Ares's throne suddenly stood empty, no doubt there was a rush to find out who was strong enough to claim it." His smile grew fuller. "May they all kill one another off in trying," he added.

"And how am I saved?"

"It is a miracle that you are alive," Odo said. "Your father's hound, Dogo, found you, and then he led Sacheverell to you." He shot a grateful look at the old doctor. "There are few but he who could have saved you," he said, and Sacheverell bowed to us both.

I took a long, careful breath. My wound still throbbed, but less so now. I couldn't believe that it was over. That we had survived, almost all of us.

But what of Raphael?

The door began to swing open, and Jeanette jumped up to shut it again. I saw her place her hands on the wood, and then I saw her face go white with shock.

CHAPTER 74

W ho—," I began, just as Jeanette sank to her knees with a sharp cry.

At first I thought she'd been struck. Did an enemy somehow remain in the castle? I tried to get up, but I fell gasping back against the pillow. It took me a moment to gather myself, and when I opened my eyes again, I saw—

My *mother,* standing over my sickbed. Alive. Smiling. Right here, in real life.

Odo dropped to his knees, and Jeanette nearly fainted. And Elodie and Adelie looked at her in wonder: they didn't know who she was. I heard the sound of weeping.

But suddenly I felt afraid. Maybe Sacheverell and Jeanette had lied to me, and I really was dying. Maybe my mother was a ghost, and she had come to take me back to her cottage in the endless forest. To life after life. To the Beyond.

"Are we going, Mother?" I said, reaching out to her. "It'll be all right if I get to stay with you."

The sun, shining through the window behind her, seemed to gild her dark head like a crown. "We're not going anywhere, Sophia," she said firmly, grasping my hand in hers. With the other, she gestured to the meager room, to all my attendants who still knelt in the rushes. "This is where we belong."

I reached out to touch her dress. I could feel its soft fabric, and even now, Odo was bringing over a stool so my mother could sit. How could this be true?

"You are really, really here?"

Ringed with golden light, she nodded. "My child," she said, "I am."

I felt like I couldn't bear the happiness. For my whole lonely life, this was my most precious, secret wish. My wildest, most impossible hope. I shook my head dumbly. "I don't understand."

She sat down by my bed and took my hand again. "I don't either," she said. "The boundaries of the material world and the spiritual world are a mystery to me still." Her warm fingers threaded their way through mine. "Maybe each bleeds into the other in ways we cannot understand. But what we can't explain, we still can trust: *I am here with you now.*"

I wiped the tears away as best I could. Everything I ever knew was different now, and immeasurably better.

But still I felt a pang of anguish. My father wasn't here. Nor was Raphael.

"Mother, I hoped you'd take care of them," I whispered.

"Who?" she asked.

"My father—"

"Wherever Leonidus is, you can be sure that he is taking very good care of himself," she said, smiling. "And someday, Sophia, we will all be together again. I believe that with all my heart."

"And Raphael," I insisted, still uncomforted. "You didn't know him, but you would have loved him."

My mother opened her mouth to reply, but Jeanette, who had recovered from her shock, came clucking over to the bed. "Sophia, Sophia," she said. "You must rest."

"There is time for that later. Please, help me up," I said.

And though Jeanette shook her head in dismay and the coals in my stomach flared hotter, I stood. "I want to look outside," I said.

With my mother's arms around me, holding me upright, I inched toward the window. A cool, crisp breeze met my face. Below me lay our fields, barren from winter and now blackened from fire and blood. Our enemies were gone, leaving behind broken weapons, cracked shields, and the charred skeletons of trees rising up from furrows of mud. The River Lathe curved away toward the horizon, a silvery, glittering ribbon. This, now, was my kingdom.

"It's a fair land," I said quietly. "Though it needs a bit of care and labor."

"You will rule it well," my mother said.

I turned to her in surprise. "But now that you're here, shouldn't you rightfully be queen?"

She shook her head. "Most crowns are inherited, Sophia. But yours, I know, was earned."

A crown is heavier than it looks, my father had warned me, and no doubt he was right. But I knew that I'd be strong enough to bear its weight.

As we stood above our kingdom, the sun streamed in the window, and the wind seemed to carry the promise of spring. The land was at peace, and soon the trumpet-shaped gentians — the flower of Bandon — would raise their blue faces to the sky.

So now you scatter the seeds in the furrow, Your Highness, and then you cover them up with the dirt, so they stay warm and safe." Fina looked up at me, her cheeks rosy and her eyes shining with pride. "Mama said the garden is my responsibility this year, now that I am eight."

My spirited horse, Lumi, shook her mane, and Fina patted her satiny neck with a small, dirt-streaked hand. "It looks to me as if you're doing a wonderful job," I said, and Fina nodded mutely, suddenly overcome with shyness.

I leaned down from the saddle so we were almost at eye level with one another. "Would you like to come back to the castle with me? Would your parents say it's all right? I'll bet the cooks have baked a treat to celebrate the new season. And I know my mother would like to see you."

Fina's eyes widened. Without saying a word, she turned and dashed into the cottage, and then a moment later, she emerged, her hair hastily brushed and her hands slightly less grubby. Her father came behind her and lifted her onto Lumi's back.

"I'll have her home by supper," I told him, and he bowed so deeply his nose nearly touched the ground. Though I'd changed many things in the village these last several months—there were brand-new cottages, larger gardens, and a communal herd of fat sheep and sly-eyed goats—I'd been unable to discourage the villagers' habits of genuflection and deference.

Fina wrapped her little arms around my waist, I clucked my tongue at Lumi, and together we set off up the hill to Bandon Castle. We trotted steadily at first, past the square with its fresh green grass, past the well, past the cottages of Signe the weaver and Kirl the butcher, and all the others who lived at the village's outskirts.

When we came to the little cemetery ringed with stones, we slowed, and I felt Fina's hold on me tighten. Rosa was buried there, as well as the hundred others who had died of the Seep. There was even a stone for Raphael, though no body lay beneath it. As we passed, I pressed my fingers to my lips, and I blew my kiss into the wind.

Then I loosened the reins and bent low over Lumi's neck, and the horse, who was always eager to run, turned her gait to a gallop. Behind me, Fina squealed with delight as the wind whistled in our ears and whipped through our hair. *This* was the way to travel—I'd never ride in a carriage again if I could help it.

As we came to the castle drawbridge, Lumi slowed to a trot, and then I pulled her all the way to a stop. There was a figure standing in the center of it, as still as a statue and backlit by the sun so I couldn't see his face.

Who was it? Ares, come back for revenge? Or—worse—Reiper? Though I killed them myself, I knew now that the curtain between life and death was as thin as a spider's web. My hand slid to the dagger that I always kept with me.

Then the man—a boy—slowly raised his hand in greeting.

My heart began to flutter in my chest. "Who is that, Fina?" I whispered.

The girl didn't answer, and I leaned forward in the saddle. I blinked. Squinted.

Surely I was seeing things. Surely it could not be—

Then the figure mimed throwing something at me...just like he'd done on the day we first met.

And then I knew.

I slid off Lumi and started running.

"Raphael," I cried, "Raphael!"

I collided with him, nearly knocking us both off our feet, and then I took his warm hands in mine and pressed them to my pounding heart. I knew not to doubt it this time. Somehow, by some incomprehensible miracle, he'd come back to me, and the world was more mysterious and wonderful than I could ever hope to understand.

"Hello again, Your Highness," Raphael said, smiling.

"Where have you been?" I asked, giddy with joy.

"I'll tell you all about it," he said. "But not now. First—"

And then he pulled me close to his chest, and I breathed in his scent of skin and sweat and pine. I felt I could stay like that forever.

Life after life had truly begun.

And it had been worth dying for.

Listen to "Love Never Dies"—
a Sophia-inspired single by Grammy-winning,
platinum-selling artist Lisa Loeb

JamesPatterson.com/Sophia

JAMES PATTERSON received the Literarian Award for Outstanding Service to the American Literary Community from the National Book Foundation. He holds the Guinness World Record for the most #1 *New York Times* bestsellers, and his books have sold more than 400 million copies worldwide. A tireless champion of the power of books and reading, Patterson created a children's book imprint, JIMMY Patterson, whose mission is simple: "We want every kid who finishes a JIMMY Book to say, 'PLEASE GIVE ME ANOTHER BOOK.'" He has donated more than one million books to students and soldiers and funds over four hundred Teacher Education Scholarships at twenty-four colleges and universities. He has also donated millions of dollars to independent bookstores and school libraries. Patterson invests proceeds from the sales of JIMMY Patterson Books in pro-reading initiatives.

EMILY RAYMOND worked with James Patterson on *First Love, The Lost,* and *Humans, Bow Down,* and is the ghostwriter of six young adult novels, one of which was a #1 *New York Times* bestseller. She lives with her family in Portland, Oregon.

JIMMY PATTERSON BOOKS FOR YOUNG ADULT READERS

James Patterson Presents

Stalking Jack the Ripper by Kerri Maniscalco

Hunting Prince Dracula by Kerri Maniscalco

Escaping from Houdini by Kerri Maniscalco

Capturing the Devil by Kerri Maniscalco

Becoming the Dark Prince by Kerri Maniscalco

Kingdom of the Wicked by Kerri Maniscalco

Gunslinger Girl by Lyndsay Ely

Twelve Steps to Normal by Farrah Penn

Campfire by Shawn Sarles

When We Were Lost by Kevin Wignall

Swipe Right for Murder by Derek Milman

Once & Future by Amy Rose Capetta and Cori McCarthy

Sword in the Stars by Amy Rose Capetta and Cori McCarthy

Girls of Paper and Fire by Natasha Ngan

Girls of Storm and Shadow by Natasha Ngan

Daughter of Sparta by Claire Andrews

You're Next by Kylie Schachte

It Ends in Fire by Andrew Shvarts

The Maximum Ride Series by James Patterson

The Angel Experiment

School's Out—Forever

Saving the World and Other Extreme Sports

The Final Warning

For exclusives, trailers, and other information, visit jimmypatterson.org.

For a complete list of books by
JAMES PATTERSON

VISIT
JamesPatterson.com

 Follow James Patterson on Facebook
@JamesPatterson

 Follow James Patterson on Twitter
@JP_Books

 Follow James Patterson on Instagram
@jamespattersonbooks